Targeted

Don & Stephanie Prichard

Other books by
Don & Stephanie Prichard

Stranded: A Novel

Forgotten: A Novel

Also available along with *Targeted* in *STRANDED the Trilogy*

Dedicated to all our patient readers
who waited and waited and waited for this third novel.

How long, O LORD?
Will You forget me forever?
How long will You hide Your face from me?
How long must I take counsel in my soul
And have sorrow in my heart all the day?
How long shall my enemy be exalted over me?

Consider and answer me, O LORD my God;
Light up my eyes,
Lest I sleep the sleep of death,
Lest my enemy say,
"I have prevailed over him,"
Lest my foes rejoice because I am shaken.

But I have trusted in Your steadfast love;
My heart shall rejoice in Your salvation.
I will sing to the LORD,
Because He has dealt bountifully with me.
—Psalm 13:1-6

PART 1

Chapter 1

July 1985

The last thing Jake Chalmers expected was an armed invasion of a croquet game with his fifteen-year-old ward, Crystal Oakleigh.

The morning was comfortably warm for July in Chicago, the grass underfoot a perfect height for batting wooden balls through wire arches. Honeysuckle draped on Judge Evedene Eriksson's house wafted a heady scent of sugar over the backyard. All that was lacking was Eve's presence to add a touch of romance to a perfect day.

Out front on South Hyde Park Boulevard, traffic growled, city buses slammed brakes, a black sedan pulled up to the front gate. Jake barely gave it a glance. Whacked his ball through an arch, trotted after it for his next shot.

A second sedan scattered gravel in the back alley. Halted at the rear gate. At the slam of car doors, Jake's nerves spiked to full alert.

Suits. Two per sedan, exiting to peer through the wrought iron bars of the fence.

At him.

With weapons drawn.

His heartbeat accelerated. Every hair on his body stood erect. He grabbed Crystal's arm. "Stay calm. They're law enforcement."

"Who?" Crystal twisted to peer around the yard. A squirrel in the backyard's largest oak tree whipped its tail and scolded the would-be intruders.

"Chalmers," shouted a man at the front gate. "US Marshals. On your knees, hands on your head. You—girl—unlock this gate."

Jake released Crystal's arm. "It's okay. Let them in and wait there." He raised his hands to clasp the back of his head and lowered his six-foot-two frame to his knees. He was wearing shorts, and the stubble of recently mown grass bit his legs.

Crystal admitted the men, and they raced to Jake, pistols targeting his head as if he were a coiled snake. They cuffed his hands behind his back and hauled him to his feet. Jake flared his nostrils, breathed slowly, put the burden on them to speak first.

"Jacob Chalmers, you're under arrest for violating a restraining order protecting Evedene Eriksson."

Jake blinked. His recall dredged the restraining order from murky waters at the far back of his mind. "From three years ago?" Incredulity raised his voice, cracked it with a half-laugh of disbelief.

"Stalking a federal judge is no laughing matter, scumbag." The marshal shoved Jake forward, hard enough to make him stumble.

Jake caught his balance and glared at the marshal. "I am a guest of Judge Eriksson. Have been for three weeks. Does she know you're doing this?"

"Hey, let him go," Crystal shrieked. She ran up and planted herself, hands on hips, face red, in front of the marshal. "You can't do this!"

The memory of Crystal at age twelve, hefting a Japanese katana sword high in both hands as if to chop off Goliath's head, flashed into Jake's mind. A skinny, half-pint Amazon standing guard between Jake and the python she was sure was coming after them. The year stranded on a jungle island in the Philippines had made an indelible mark on both of them. On Eve too—if only her memory hadn't erased it.

"Crystal"—his voice caught on the sweetness of the memory, on the preciousness of an existence none of the castaways had known to treasure— "I have to go with them. They're the law, and we need to obey." He cranked out what he hoped was a reassuring smile. "Best to go call Eve, tell her what's happened."

The corners of Crystal's mouth twitched down as she stepped aside. She scowled at the marshal in charge. "You'll wish you'd come down with the plague rather than face Judge Evedene Eriksson."

The marshal snickered and pushed Jake toward the front gate. "You have the right to remain silent. Anything you say—"

Jake smiled. The poor guy had no idea how preferable the plague was.

***

Eve hung up the phone. Steam all but boiled from her forehead. Muscles taut, she stared out her office window until the blue sky and fluff of clouds nestled over Chicago's skyline settled her brain into the tranquility of rational thinking. Her shoulders softened, her stomach muscles relaxed. Crystal's news was upsetting, but not beyond redeeming.

In minutes, Jake would arrive at the Metropolitan Correctional Center, only blocks away from her office in the Dirksen Federal Building. The same jail where Jake had been deported three and a half years ago to face trial for murder in the Philippines. An unjust deportation she could have stopped if she'd only known then what she knew now.

Guilt pinged like the small, steel ball in a pinball game, battering her heart, creating pockets of acid in her stomach.

Never again. A few questions researched and she'd have him out before evening.

Two phone calls later, she punched in the number of the correctional center. "This is Judge Eriksson at the DOJ. Has a prisoner named Jacob Chalmers arrived, escorted by a US Marshal?"

"I'll check, ma'am." A minute later, the answer came through. "Judge Eriksson? Deputy US Marshal Jackson just now finished admitting the prisoner."

"Thank you. Can you catch the marshal before he leaves? I'd like him to come *immediately* to my office." Her voice honed sharp edges on the *immediately.*

"Yes, ma'am. I'll see he gets the message."

Forty minutes passed before Deputy US Marshal Jackson put in an appearance. Twenty-five minutes more than Eve deemed necessary. He entered the office and halted before her desk, a grin evidencing expectation of praise for a deed well done.

She didn't ask him to sit. Instead, jaws clenched, the corners of her mouth drawn down, hands folded on her desk, she stared at him until the cocky grin dropped to the floor. "Marshal Jackson"—she modulated her voice in a stilted monotone—"you are responsible for today's arrest of Jacob Chalmers?"

"Yes, ma'am."

"For a restraining order protecting me?"

"Yes, ma'am." The grin reappeared.

Her voice shifted to arctic temperatures. "Did your prisoner tell you he was my guest?"

The tip of Jackson's tongue slicked the grin away. "Yes, ma'am."

"And you chose not to call me?"

"No, ma'am. My job was to arrest him."

"If you had called me, you would have learned the protective order had expired."

Jackson blinked. "I ... was following orders, ma'am."

"Evidently without reading them."

Jackson answered with a curt nod.

Eve leaned across the desk toward him. "Did you and your men bare weapons to arrest the prisoner?"

"Yes, ma'am."

"Did you see the child next to him?"

Jackson lifted his chin. "My orders had Chalmers tagged as a hostile."

"Did his response evidence that?"

Jackson's mouth tightened. He darted a glance at the floor.

"Did he display a weapon? Look like he'd run? Say something threatening? Show any kind of resistance?"

"No, ma'am." The two words bit the air.

She sat back.

"Did you serve in the military, Deputy Jackson?"

"Yes, ma'am. Marine Corps."

"Perhaps you'd be interested to know that Jacob Chalmers is a twenty-three-year veteran of the Marine Corps, a colonel, as a matter of fact, still serving in the reserves. A veteran of Viet Nam, awarded the Purple Heart and the Navy Cross. A far cry from a *scumbag*, wouldn't you say?"

Jackson's Adam's apple bobbed in a tight swallow.

She let him boil in oil for a full minute before she continued. "Tell me, why was a US Marshal enforcing a state-issued order instead of Chicago law enforcement?"

"Orders from the Department of Justice, ma'am."

"The DOJ?" Her voice rose in surprise. "Who gave those orders?"

"The US Attorney, ma'am."

"Bradley Henshaw?" For a second, her brain shut down.

"Yes, ma'am."

She rose, shoulders rigid. "If there is ever another encounter with Jacob Chalmers, I want to be informed. At once. He is …"—she almost slipped and said *my fiancé*—"of particular concern to me."

"Yes, ma'am." Catching his dismissal, Jackson exited with a pale face.

Eve slumped back into her chair. So. Her former boss had ordered Jake's arrest. All these years gone by, and he still had it in for Jake.

Weary from chastising the marshal, a tough-judge task she excelled at but hated, she punched the DA's office number into her phone. Last thing she wanted was a second showdown. But Brad Henshaw had started it, and she needed to finish it.

Chapter 2

The receptionist confirmed the DA was in. With his office only a few floors below hers, Eve chose to take the stairs to work off some of the perplexity scratching like cat claws at her emotions.

On the one hand, Brad Henshaw was her mentor of ten years as an assistant US attorney. And now, with her recent promotion to magistrate, he was both friend and ally in her role as Drug Czar combatting illegal drugs in Chicago.

On the other hand, Brad was the prosecutor who had unjustly deported Jake to the Philippines. For three years Jake had waited in a hell-hole of a prison to face a trial that never happened. A prison she had helped release him from only three weeks ago.

Her anger mounted with each step. She and Jake had thought they were free at last from that past. Thought they could leave this pot-hole-ridden road behind and build a shiny bridge to the future. Could focus on falling in love again.

She stormed into the District Attorney's Office, unresolved whether to throw lightning bolts at Brad or not.

Stella, office manager and mother hen to all the women in the office, welcomed Eve with a big hug. They had burned through six replacement coffee pots in their ten years of working together. "Hi, Judge. How's life at the top?"

Eve chuckled and stooped her five-foot-ten body to accommodate Stella's five-foot-two, well-rounded one. "Thanks for looking up the data on the restraining order," Eve whispered.

Instead of releasing Eve, Stella held onto her. "It was in Brad's personal correspondence file." Her voice was so low Eve had to strain to catch her words. "I don't know if I should tell you this, but there's a sealed envelope in the file that says to open only in the event of his death." Stella pulled back and raised a face tight with worry to Eve's.

Eve's mouth went dry. "Should I ask him about it?"

"No, no. I'm the only one who has access to that file—he'd know I told you. It's just … I can't stop fretting about it. He put it in there four years ago when you went missing in Guam. I thought it had something to do with your disappearance—maybe a threat to his life. But when you were found a year later in a coma, he didn't remove the envelope."

Eve frowned. Why would she be connected to Brad's sealed envelope? "You two are close. Can't you ask him about it?"

"I did, and he said not to worry and to open it only in the event of his death. Said a copy is in his safety deposit box, but he didn't want to have to wait on the courts to disclose it."

"Then his request needs to be honored."

"I know, I know. I just … now that you're a judge and no longer here in the office"—Stella puffed out a sigh—"I wanted the comfort of sharing the burden with someone I can trust." Her face crumpled and she blinked back tears.

Eve squeezed her friend's shoulder. "Thank you, Stella. It's okay, it's our secret."

Stella sniffed in a quick breath and exhaled a rumpled smile. "I just got Brad a cup of coffee. He's in his office."

Well, if nothing else, Stella's interception had calmed the storm roiling in Eve's heart. She tapped on Brad's open door. "Got a minute?"

Was that a flicker of guilt that punched across Brad's face? The lightning bolts flashed back into her grip. She didn't give him a chance to duck. "Did you order the arrest of Jacob Chalmers at my house this morning?" Electricity all but crackled around Brad's head.

"Eve, hello. I heard you were back in town." He rose gracefully, taking advantage of his height to tower above her, even halfway across the room. "With a friend," he added darkly.

She folded her arms across her chest and waited.

"Yes, I ordered Chalmers' arrest."

"With an expired restraining order …"

He pursed his lips, frowned. "Considering the urgency of the situation, I opted for expediency."

Eve picked up his telephone receiver and thrust it at him. "I'll wait while you call and cancel the arrest. Then you and I can discuss what to do about your illegal expediency."

Brad raised his eyebrows. "You skipped over the key word, *urgency*." He gestured at the chair on the other side of his desk. "Sit, please."

A decade of respect and cooperation made resistance impossible. She huffed, slammed down the receiver, and dropped into the chair.

Brad resumed his seat. Folded his hands on his desk. Unfolded them. Tapped the fingers of his right hand on the wood. Eve sat up straight. This was serious. Her heartbeat quickened.

"A wiretap on Danny Romero's phone picked up a call from the Philippines this morning. From Emilio, Danny's illegitimate son incarcerated at Salonga Prison."

Eve fired a scowl at him. "Yes, north of Manila, where Jake ended up after your wrongful deportation of him."

Brad's shoulders stiffened. "An assumption I suggest you reassess, Eve."

They glared at each other over their three-year battle about Jake's connection to drug lord Danny Romero. Romero's instruction left on Jake's phone recorder three years ago to "Kill her," though circumstantial, was enough to convince Brad that Jake was a threat to Eve. On her part, she believed the recording was a plant and that Jake was innocent of any involvement with the Romero crime family.

"Eve, this morning's phone call was about a contract on your life."

The blood drained from Eve's face. Her energy, her confidence, her empowerment as a judicial authority drained with it. Breath, muscles, heartbeat came to a standstill.

Brad spoke softly. "That's why I ordered the marshals to pick up Chalmers."

At the explanation, she inhaled life back into her lungs. "No." She shook her head vehemently. "Jake is not an assassin. Let him go." She picked up the telephone receiver and thrust it at Brad a second time, her hand shaking. "Call. I'm walking over there now to get him."

They rose at the same time, eyes locked on each other. Eve tried to erase the fear numbing her face, replace it with defiance, but her lower lip betrayed her with tiny tremors.

Gently, Brad relieved her of the phone. "I will call if you promise not to take him back into your house."

She hesitated. Then nodded. Words—arguments—the strength to defy someone wanting to protect her—were out of reach. Surely Jake would understand. Understand she had to make a trade to acquire that Get Out of Jail Free card. She swallowed hard against the cannon ball of terror that shot to her throat. If he wasn't free, how could he deal with Emilio?

She strode from Brad's office, past Stella at her desk, and all but ran to the elevator. The long walk to the correctional center would do her good. Would trample her fear into powder. Would release the powder into Chicago's relentless wind.

And then … maybe … without her knees quaking … she could face the question of why Emilio Romero was targeting her.

Chapter 3

One look at Eve, and Jake's gut crunched like an accordion. She stood in the correctional center lobby, face pale, lines tightening the corners of her eyes and mouth, gaze fixed, unseeing. Three weeks ago, she had secured his freedom from Salonga Prison in the Philippines, and her smile had radiated sunshine. Now, freeing him a second time from wrongful imprisonment, she looked as if she'd walked in from the Apocalypse. Something was dreadfully wrong.

He hastened forward and wrapped his arms around her. She clung to him, head buried against his neck, the smell of summer heat rising from her hair and skin. "Eve! What happened?" Her shoulders twitched in a shudder, and alarm shot like pistol fire across his nerves.

She stepped back, her breath catching in a raspy gasp. Law enforcement personnel and cuffed prisoners crisscrossed the lobby. "Let's get out of here," she croaked. "Get coffee." She grabbed his hand and didn't let go until they were seated in the farthest booth of a nearby café.

He waited until she was calm enough to speak. Until her hands didn't shake when she brought the coffee cup to her lips. Until her eyes sought his. "The Romeros," she whispered. "They've got a contract out on me."

One thump of his heart, and he knew why. Because of him. He hadn't fulfilled his promise to Emilio.

Her lower lip jerked. "That's why Brad Henshaw sent the marshals to arrest you."

"The DA who deported me to the Philippines?" Jake all but spat out the title. "He still thinks I'm a hired gun for Danny Romero?"

"He wants you off my property." Eve dropped her gaze to the table.

Jake grimaced. "And you're going to cooperate." A statement, not a question. Not with her eyes avoiding his.

"I think you should go back to Indy and steer clear of this whole mess. Give Brad no ground for suspicion."

"So Brad Henshaw has the say in this, not me?" Anger undergirded his words like a tightrope.

"What can you do, Jake?" Her gaze bounced back to his, begging cooperation. "I'll be okay. I'll have the protection of a marshal assigned to me around the clock. You can set up a reunion with your kids and I can come down, just like we planned."

"What if I told you I have the solution?"

"What, whisk me away to a secluded island?" She actually smiled at him. Her amnesia had washed away all memory of being stranded on a jungle island in the Philippines with him and Crystal and Crystal's elderly aunt. But Crystal had told her—probably way too often—that Jake and Eve had fallen in love and planned to marry.

Marriage. It was the elephant in the room, wasn't it? The expectation of a permanent relationship had a dampening effect on the romance that needed to precede it.

He grinned at her tease. "I like the idea of an island, but I was thinking more of quashing Romero's contract."

"You can't get involved, Jake. You need to be far, far away from the Romeros, from having anything to do with them. Give Brad an inch and he'll string you up. Please, no more arrests. Promise me."

He bit back the hurt that she had so little faith in him. That another man usurped him. "I can't promise what I can't control, and I certainly have no control over Brad Henshaw. But I will leave your house, if that's what you want." He fought the bitterness that wanted to clamp his mouth shut and stomp his feet out the door. He couldn't let resentment get to his heart.

"Thank you, Jake." She reached for his hand, and he opened it to clasp hers. "We'll be back together in no time, I promise. Call Brett and Dana, set up a time for us to get together, and I'll be on your front doorstep in the blink of an eye." She lowered her voice to a whisper. "I'm falling in love with you, Jake. I don't want to be apart anymore than we have to."

Happiness swelled his chest, and he swept her hand to his lips. He loved this woman, contrary though she could be, and whether she wanted to hear it or not, he was the only one who could free her from Romero's death threat. Perhaps Brad Henshaw had done him a favor by booting him from Eve's house. He could proceed now without having to reveal his plan.

***

An hour later, with dusk casting a gunmetal twilight over the neighborhood, Jake stared out a taxi window at the huge building enclosed in a brick and pre-cast concrete wall a block long and at least twenty feet high. "You sure this is the Romero *residence*?" His insides melted into mush. Once inside that fortress, a person could disappear for life. Man, he wouldn't be surprised if the place had its own cemetery.

"Yep. An' you gotta decide if you're gettin' out, cuz I ain't sittin' here another minute."

"Sure, sure. Here you go." Jake handed the driver his fee and exited the taxi. It roared off, tires squealing like an animal in terror, bristling every hair on Jake's body.

He should have let someone know he was coming here. Mailed Eve a letter about his plan, just in case. He swallowed. The discovery of his disappearance could take awhile. The last Eve knew, he was headed home to Indianapolis.

He strode to the entrance and immediately felt the icy stare of eyes prickle his spine. Eyes no doubt hovering behind weapons targeting his head. He raised his chin in defiance, straightened to full height, held his shoulders wide. Face grim, he approached the gate.

Beyond the steel bars lay an expanse of manicured lawn and shrubs fronting a massive building that was more a medieval castle than a mansion. Its composition was of the same material as the wall, only darker. As an architect, Jake couldn't help admiring the artful blend of blacks, charcoals, and grays. Sinister, disturbing … yet with an alluring beauty.

A stronghold of evil. The warning sliced through Jake's gut as if it were a spear thrust by an archangel. His breath bolted from his lungs and his belly flamed into embers. *God, help me!* What was he doing here? He grabbed the steel bars to stabilize knees suddenly gone weak.

A face cut off his view. The barrel of a pistol gouged his cheek. No words were spoken, but the message was clear. *Leave, or wish you had.*

He cleared his throat. "I am an emissary from Emilio Romero to his father."

A pause. Then the static of a walkie-talkie and subdued voices.

The gate opened. Jake stepped through. It shut behind him with a barely audible click.

A shiver raced up his spine to his scalp. Whatever happened now sealed his fate—and that of Judge Evedene Eriksson.

***

His entry into the Romero stronghold was worse than when he'd been dumped into the foul pit of Salonga Prison. The Romero goon cuffed Jake's hands behind his back and marched him to the equivalent of a medieval dungeon, where he was questioned and searched—not with a pat-down but stripped and every body cavity examined. By the time Jake's clothes were returned to him, every nerve quivered with the rage of humiliation. His mission from Emilio took on a new reality. No longer was the undertaking one of simple mercy, but of utter salvation.

A handsome man with black, slicked-back hair and sullen eyes entered the room where Jake sat cuffed. He studied Jake with an intensity that probed beyond Jake's stated business at the Romero residence. An intensity that inferred something in common between them. Something dark, something resented on both their parts.

Jake's heart grabbed him by the throat. *You know what it is!* He swallowed to moisten a tongue suddenly gone dry.

"So, Jacob Chalmers, is it?" The man's voice was as suavely slick as his hair. "On assignment from my big brother, I hear."

Jake caught his breath.

Riccardo Romero.

Murderer of Emilio's wife. Abuser of Emilio's son. Romancer of Eve's heart.

Jake's hands curled into fists, his lips into a snarl. Before he could leap at his opponent, the goon stepped between them and landed a fist on Jake's left cheek. His head rocketed sideways. Blood and spittle flew from his mouth.

The goon rammed a pistol into Jake's ribs. "Wanna crack at the other cheek, boss?"

Ric sneered. "I'll do more than a cheek. For now, get him to my father."

The goon shoved Jake through the doorway and down a hallway with more twists and turns than Jake could keep track of. *Ric—aka Rock Giannopoulus.* He had wondered if their paths would cross. Not just because the man was Emilio's half-brother—the youngest of Danny Romero's three "legitimate" sons, who hated Emilio and had raped and killed Emilio's wife and now brutalized his young son. But because Ric and Jake loved the same woman.

Eve.

Jake ran his tongue over his split lip. Would Ric's love help save Eve's life … or would jealousy cement the contract to kill her?

Chapter 4

The three men rode an elevator up to Danny Romero's office. Jake's escort mashed him into a corner of the lift, pistol grinding against Jake's spine, evidently to thwart any plan on Jake's part to resist them. As if Jake hadn't come here voluntarily. As soon as Eve mentioned the contract on her life, he knew Emilio was behind it. A clear message to Jake—get going on freeing my son or lose your girlfriend.

He had been remiss. In the delight of spending time with Eve, he'd let the three weeks slip by since Emilio's confrontation with him at Salonga Prison. There'd been no threat against Eve's life then. Only Emilio's plea for Jake to rescue his son once Jake was released.

He wished he'd never made the promise. But the commitment was to God, an affirmation that he'd forgiven Emilio and no longer held anything against the man. The forgiveness was true; he wouldn't renege on it. And now that he saw what the young son was up against, there was no way he'd leave without him.

Surprisingly, the photograph Emilio had given him of the battered boy was still in Jake's trouser pocket. Romero's goon hadn't confiscated it. Emilio claimed his father didn't know about the abuse, nor about the threat to kill little Dan once Danny Romero was in prison.

The elevator dinged, the doors slid open, and they exited into a lobby with a lone secretary's desk next to a window. A curvy blonde perched on a crimson office chair smiled at Ric and used a long, red fingernail to punch a button on her desk phone. "They're here," she cooed. A second later, her heavily mascaraed eyelashes fluttered at Ric. "He's ready for you." A click sounded on the steel door to Danny Romero's office. For sure no one was going to storm that room.

Eve had told him Danny Romero was in his late fifties. The man sitting behind the polished walnut desk looked twice that. Though he was resting against the thickly padded back of a leather office chair, his shoulders were shoved up and forward, evidencing a rounded spine. Black hair, obviously dyed, layered a pink scalp and magnified every dark line in his face. Danny's hawk-like Roman nose, square jaw, and cleft chin had stamped Emilio's genes. Not so, Ric's. No doubt the resemblance didn't help Emilio's popularity with the rest of the family.

"Jacob Chalmers." The old man snarled the name as if he were plunging a knife into Jake's chest. "You cripple my son, then rat on him so he's on death's row."

And you planted the false evidence that sent me to Salonga Prison in the first place. Jake bit back the words, kept his voice and facial features calm, one step above bored, as if he'd had nothing better to do this evening than call upon the Romeros. "Emilio asked me to take a message to you."

"Last message I got was to kill you."

Jake raised his eyebrows. "He's changed his mind."

"I haven't."

"Message is no good once Emilio faces the firing squad." Jake crunched his shoulders to his ears, hitched his brow and one side of his mouth upward in an *oh-well* gesture.

"I'll take care of both, Pops—the message and the body bag." Ric's footsteps rapped the wooden floor, moving briskly from behind Jake to his father's desk.

Jake didn't hide his alarm. He focused wide eyes on Danny. "Emilio definitely wouldn't want his request to fall into his brothers' hands. It's for your ears only."

"That's ridiculous," Ric spat.

Danny's eyes narrowed at Jake's warning, shifted from Jake to Ric. "The guard stays, you go."

Ric didn't argue, but his clamped jaw did not bode well for Jake.

Once the office door clicked shut, Jake spoke. He could only hope the guard was loyal to Danny and wouldn't pass the information to Ric. "In my pants pocket is a photograph for you from Emilio." His cuffed hands prevented his retrieving it, so he waited for Danny to order the guard to fetch it. Jake's years of dealing with the Salonga Prison warden had taught him that telling those in authority what to do was the same as kicking their precious pecking order in the shins.

Danny quirked his head at the guard, who then extracted the photo with a swift dart of his hand into Jake's pocket. *The correct pocket.* So, had the man left the photograph in Jake's clothing on purpose? Perhaps in sympathy with the boy, guessing the purpose of Jake's visit to the Romeros? He looked closer at the guard's face, but the man avoided Jake's eyes.

Danny inhaled a raspy gasp at the photo. "Where'd you get this?" Anger burst the question into flying shrapnel.

"Emilio's brothers sent it to him."

"You saying they did this to my grandson?" The old man flapped the photo at Jake as if it were a whip.

"Emilio says it." Jake clenched his jaw against the emotion the photograph evoked. A five-year-old boy crouching in a corner, clad only in briefs, with bruises—some yellow with age, some freshly black and blue—covering his body wherever clothing would hide their discovery. Terror screamed from the boy's eyes and wet his crumpled face with dirty streaks down his cheeks. "He says his brothers will finish the job the day you go to prison."

A tremor wobbled Danny's head. Spread down his neck and the hunched-over shoulders to his arms. Twitched into a quake in his hands. "I'll … send him away. Hide him." A spasm of coughing shook his chest, and he pulled a handkerchief from his back pocket to hold over his mouth.

Emphysema. Eve had told Jake that Romero could die of the disease before the courts ever got him to prison. In spite of himself, Jake felt a twinge of pity for the old man. His oldest son facing execution … his grandson's life threatened … his own days terminating in a six-by-ten concrete cell.

Danny finished coughing, wiped his mouth, and glowered at Jake. "What was Emilio's message?" he barked. "He'd have said more."

"He did. He wants you to legally transfer Dan's care to me so I can raise him."

Danny's mouth fell open, then segued into a sharp laugh. "You cripple my son and end his life before a firing squad, and I'm to believe he wants you to raise his son?"

Jake bobbed his eyebrows in a quick twitch. "Surprised me too."

"And it would surprise Emilio even more, I'm sure," Danny snarled. "You're lying. What are you up to, Chalmers? Why do you want the boy?"

I don't. But for sure I want him out of here. "Call Emilio. He's the one with the answers."

"The prison refuses contact between us." Bitterness sharpened a metal edge to Danny's words.

"I can get through. I know the people in charge." Jake swallowed. Emilio and his father needed to touch base and get on the same page. For the boy's sake. For Eve's. For Jake's on-the-scene survival.

"Well, aren't you the big shot!"

Jake said nothing. He'd just kicked the pecking order in the shins, hadn't he?

Ego … or last words with his son? Danny's struggle with the choice waged battle across his face. "Bring Dan to me," he finally said.

The pistol muzzle dug deeper into Jake's back as the guard barked the demand into his shoulder-mike.

"Dan or Emilio proves you wrong, and I'll enjoy killing you myself. Piece by piece." The old man sat back and contemplated Jake as if already mapping out the pieces.

Fear crept up Jake's backbone, seized him by the throat, clamped a bony hand across his nose so that he had to open his mouth to suck in oxygen. What if that had been Emilio's plan all along? Send Jake straight into the Romero stronghold, give Emilio's father the pleasure of revenge, give Emilio the last laugh?

No question about it, Jake was Enemy Number One for Emilio. Never mind that Emilio had murdered nineteen cruise ship passengers four years ago, including Jake's wife. Never mind that Emilio had initiated the attack on Jake at Salonga Prison that ended in Emilio's shoulder dislocation. What mattered to Emilio was that Jake had damaged his shoulder, and that Jake had turned him in to the authorities for the cruise ship murders.

Why had he believed Emilio was sincere about rescuing his son and raising him? Jake swallowed. Because of the photo. Rage slammed the back of Jake's throat, threw flames of heat onto his face. Emilio had conned him with that photograph.

And now Eve's life would be added to the carnage.

A sharp pain twisted through his bowels, and he barely suppressed a groan. Results of the cavity search. He fought back the urge to seek relief in his britches.

"Dan's here," the intercom chirped. The door clicked, and a guard entered, hand on a young boy's shoulder. The youngster ran to his grandfather and buried his head in Danny's lap. Danny stroked the boy's curls.

At the display of affection, a measure of peace seeped into Jake, nurtured seeds of hope that maybe, maybe, Emilio's intention hadn't been to dupe him after all.

Danny raised his grandson's head and kissed his face. "Dan-boy, I want you to take off your shirt for me, okay?"

The boy drew back, eyes wide with panic. His lower lip quivered and his chest quaked under swift breaths through his nose.

"Here now, what are you afraid of?" Danny drew him into his arms. Distress plowed deeper furrows across the old man's wrinkled face. "Has someone been hurting you?" Gently, he pulled the long-sleeved shirt over the boy's head and dropped it to the floor.

The boy ducked his face to his chest, fisted slender fingers at his belly. Every spot of skin hidden by the shirt was black and blue or splotched in older bruises of yellow and green.

No one spoke.

Danny slid the boy's pant legs above his knobby knees. The same discoloration covered every inch of skin.

Danny raised his eyes to Jake's. Both men's mouths contorted, both blinked back tears. "Let's get this shirt back on you now, Dan-boy. There you go." The task completed, Danny hauled his quaking grandson onto his lap. He opened a desk drawer and withdrew a pack of gum, slid out two pieces, and handed one to the boy. In perfect synchronization, they removed the wrappers, licked the sugar off the foil, then popped the gum into their mouths. The ritual ended with shared smiles.

Cuddling the boy to his chest, Danny leaned forward and punched the intercom button. "Get me Salonga Prison."

Jake tightened his lips. This was the real test. Either Emilio wanted his son free, or he wanted Jake dead.

Chapter 5

The prison operator's voice came across faint and garbled. Jake stepped closer to Danny Romero's desk, ignoring the guard's pistol barrel sliding up the side of Jake's throat. If he couldn't get through to Emilio, Jake's life was forfeit anyway.

"Enzo, is that you? It's Jake Chalmers." He held his breath. A pause, and then an answer in Tagalog burst from Romero's speakerphone. "Yep, all the way from the USA," Jake responded, forcing what cheer he could into his voice. Although he could speak Tagalog, he stuck to English so Romero wouldn't think Jake was pulling something. Like most Filipinos, Enzo could manage English, but he wouldn't bother if he thought he was talking only to Jake.

Jake chatted for a minute before making his request to speak to Emilio. "It will take awhile to get Emilio to a phone," he whispered to Danny. No sense mentioning Emilio was in solitary confinement.

At least Danny used the delay to send his grandson out of the office. Did the boy know about his father? Jake's guard had been angling the pistol so the youngster wouldn't see it. How much shelter was the boy getting from the reality of his crime family's life? For sure it would spill over into the challenge of Jake raising him … assuming he got the chance.

"So you got my message." Emilio's voice sneered across the miles.

Jake flared hot. "Call off the contract on Eve, you—" He cut himself short, leveled his rage with a breath that burned deep into his lungs. "I'm with your father now. He wants reassurance."

Jake even more so.

Danny leaned into the desk. "'Milio?" His voice quivered.

"Papa?"

Jake fidgeted as the silence between the two men lengthened.

"Papa," Emilio blurted, "give Dan to Jake. It's what I want."

Jake's heart flipped a double somersault. A tsunami of relief quaked his body from head to toe.

"He's your enemy," Danny hissed.

"Mine, yes." Emilio's voice reverberated with hate. "But not my son's."

"I will send Dan-boy away, hide him from your brothers."

"They're taking the phone away here. Do what I want, Papa. Make it legal." A grunt of pain ended the call.

"Wait!" Jake yelled. "Tell your father to call off the contract." He bent over the burring phone, then glared daggers at the old man. "That's the deal, Danny. Call off the contract on Eve, or I won't take the boy."

"Pah! Because of you, my son faces a firing squad. Because of Judge Eriksson, I face lethal injection. You both deserve to die. What do I care if you take my grandson?" Danny jerked his head at the guard. "Get him out of here."

"Emilio cares." Jake said the words solemnly, without rancor.

"Stop," Danny snapped. "Take him to a cell in my quarters. Allow no one near him."

Jake inhaled a quick breath. Did the command bode hope of release … or the horror of torture?

The guard propelled him through the door, marched him to the elevator, and from there to a corridor on the right. Several turns later, the sound of voices spilled into the hallway. The guard purposely blocked Jake's view as they passed the room hosting the chatter, but halted when a woman called him to stop.

"Who do you have there?" The voice was not one to be argued with.

The guard shoved Jake to the doorway. Inside, seven adults, formally dressed, sat at a dining room table set with fine china, silverware, and crystal. Two servants stood on either side of the room.

Jake immediately spotted Ric. He sat on one side of the table with two men Jake figured from their resemblance to Ric were his brothers. On the other side sat three young—very young—women. At the end of the table closest to the door, his back turned three-quarters away from Jake, little Dan sat stuffed into a high chair. No food or drink was on his tray. He was sucking his thumb, his eyes downcast.

At the other end sat a regal older woman Jake guessed to be Danny's wife. Her features were sharp, as if her skin had been pulled back tightly to her hairline. Bleached hair styled into the fashion of the day doubled the size of her head. She might have come across as pretty for her age, or at least elegant, but for her eyes. In spite of the carefully applied mascara and eye shadow, the soul that peered from her eyes was that of a viper.

Jake couldn't pull his gaze from her.

"Jacob Chalmers." Ric broke the spell. "My replacement in Eve's affections."

Jake clenched his teeth, swallowed back the dragon fire that leaped to his tongue. Eve hadn't told him much about her romance with Ric. Only that he had posed as Rock Giannopoulus, a successful businessman who lulled her into a courtship and proposal of marriage. Would Eve have married Ric if she hadn't discovered he was Danny Romero's son? "Call off the contract on her," Jake growled.

"That's why you're here?" Ric didn't hide his surprise. The woman's face flickered the same response.

Too late, Jake realized Emilio's request had been picked up on the DOJ's wiretap but not passed on by Danny to his family. He winced. Of course not. Who in the Romero family would take orders from Danny's bastard son?

The woman smiled, her lips thinning like stretched rubber bands. "We'll look into it, Jacob Chalmers." She nodded, and the guard pulled Jake away. They hustled down the hallway at a fast clip, as if any moment they would be pursued.

Jake's cell was a bare improvement from the dungeon where he'd been stripped and searched. A thin mattress on the floor and a shallow drain for a toilet. Nothing much to make an assault with, if that was the worry. The odor of filthy bodies, vomit, and sewage brought back vivid memories of Salonga Prison.

Eventually the stench settled into a new normal, and Jake fell asleep. There was no window to monitor the passage of time, and his watch had been confiscated. He slept fitfully. When he awoke, he settled himself into the opportunity before him. A full fast with no water, no food, flat on his face, crying out to God.

**

"Get up!" The guard snapped.

Jake rose with purposed dignity from where he had been lying prone on the floor. Okay … looked like God's answer to his prayer was at hand. He was ready, spirit mellow like oil poured on water, calm, completely at rest.

The guard stepped to the side, and Danny Romero shuffled into the cell. In one hand he held a satchel, in the other hand Dan-boy. They stopped in front of Jake. Danny put the satchel on the floor, didn't look at Jake or the boy. "I've been telling you your daddy would come for you …"

Jake got to his haunches as Danny let go of the boy's hand, took his shoulders, and turned him to face Jake. "He's here now," Danny said. The words were hoarse, his voice barely audible. "It's time to go with him." And just like that, Danny walked away.

Jake blinked. Wha-a-a-t?

Chocolate eyes stared at Jake. With a tremulous smile, the child stepped forward, arms outstretched. Air jolted into Jake's lungs and out again. He scooped the boy into his arms, stood, and clasped Dan-boy to his chest, pressed the mop of curls against the crook of his neck and shoulder. He melted as the little guy nestled in. Words came unbidden out of Jake's mouth. Words that, as soon as he whispered them, he recognized as totally true. "I love you, Dan-boy."

"Go. Quickly," the guard spat. Jake grabbed the satchel and hastened after him. He didn't know what day it was, nor what time of day it was, but he sure hoped it wasn't when the rest of the Romero household was up and stirring.

Chapter 6

Eve summoned Crystal over the intercom to come to breakfast, but pushed her own portion aside. The night had been rough. Although a marshal was posted outside her house, it wasn't the same as having Jake down the hall in his bedroom. She'd made an emotional decision based on fear, turning him out like she had. Had he flown to Indy or taken the train? In the upset of his departure, she hadn't asked.

She wanted him back.

Her promise to Brad was to not let Jake stay at her house. Hello, woman— that didn't mean Jake couldn't stay in a nearby hotel! She picked up the phone and punched in his number.

"Eve!" Crystal, still in her lazy-day-Saturday-morning pajamas, dashed into the kitchen. "Jake's here! He's getting out of a taxi."

Joy soared like a gala of balloons in Eve's chest. She ran out the door, barefoot, glad she had dressed and wasn't in her nightgown and robe. Crystal pulled a jacket from the hall closet and scampered to join her.

Already the marshal was at the gate. Eve slipped through and ran to Jake, stopped when he leaned into the taxi's back seat and emerged holding a young boy. "Who's this?"

Jake crooked a grin at her. "Uh, little Dan." The boy wrapped his arms around Jake's neck and hid his face. "Dan-boy, this is Eve and Crystal, my friends."

"Hi, Danny-boy," Crystal chirped.

Both Jake and Eve cringed. "Dan-boy," Jake said. "Not … anything else."

"Oh. Yeah. Sorry, like, I didn't think about You-Know-Who." Crystal patted the youngster's leg. "You guys hungry? Mom was just making breakfast. I bet Dan-boy would go for some pancakes, huh, Mom?"

Eve smiled as the little guy peeked one eye at Crystal. "Coming right up."

They tromped into the kitchen with the gaiety of a circus parade. Eve's spirits soared. "I was just about to call you. I take it you didn't go to Indy after all."

"No, I booked a hotel, had an errand to run first."

She wanted to ask what errand, and exactly who is this boy, but did she have that freedom after sending him packing last night? For now she'd best settle for stirring up a batch of pancakes.

Dan-boy kept his chokehold on Jake until Jake settled into a kitchen chair and shifted the boy to his lap. Even then, he twisted to hide his face from Eve and Crystal in Jake's shirt.

Within minutes, Eve set a mountain of pancakes on the table. If food was the way to a man's heart, then pancakes were the way to a kid's heart. She smiled expectantly.

"Hey, look at this, buddy—Eve's made us smiley-faced pancakes," Jake exclaimed.

Dan didn't look.

Jake poured syrup on the cakes and helped himself to several bites before offering a forkful to Dan.

Dan buried his face deeper in Jake's shirt.

Jake's mouth settled into a firm line. Eve held her breath as he all but forced the fork into Dan's mouth. Anger flitted across Dan's face but quickly shifted to pleasure. After the first swallow, he opened his mouth for more. Three more bites and he wriggled around to face the table and use his own fork.

Crystal, elbows on the table, palms on either side of her face, studied Dan. "Are you going to tell us about him, Jake? He looks familiar somehow."

***

Jake squirmed at Crystal's request. Oh boy. While Dan wasn't the spitting image of his father, the boy's curly hair and dark eyes with those long eyelashes were enough to bring Emilio to mind. "Uh"—Jake licked the syrup off his lips—maybe he could break the news to them gently. A bit at a time. "He's my, uh, son." The boy smiled up at him.

The impact was hardly gentle. Eve's and Crystal's mouths dropped open in resounding gasps. Widened eyes glazed momentarily in the equivalent of a blow to the head.

"I promised God at Salonga I would raise him."

Eve blinked. "You had him in prison?"

"Whoa! No! Dan is five years old. I was at Salonga three years—"

"Before the cruise?" Crystal's voice blared at the same high pitch as Eve's.

"Stop!" Jake took in a deep breath. Leaving information to people's imaginations always ended in a worse scenario than the one trying to be avoided. "He's Romero's grandson."

"D—Danny Romero?" Eve stared at Jake.

"I went to the Romero residence last night—"

Eve dropped onto a chair. Hard. Her face was ashen.

"—to rescue Dan." Jake frowned. "And you, Eve."

"Huh?" Crystal looked from Jake to Eve and back. "But Eve was here. Rescue Dan from what?"

"Here, let's clean up this syrup, buddy." Jake pushed Dan's sleeve to his elbow and looked pointedly from the discolored skin to Eve and Crystal. "Because, Crystal, the Romeros were threatening Eve, and Dan was next in line."

Crystal jumped up and grabbed Eve's hand. "Are they safe now?"

"Yes. That's the deal I made." The statement niggled Jake's stomach. Danny Romero's affection for his grandson gave at least some credence to his sparing Eve's life. But was there anything to stop Ric and his brothers and mother?

"You can't trust a Romero," Eve squeaked. Her face was still white as porcelain, her body shivering as if caught in a blizzard.

Jake ached to take her into his arms. He shoved back his chair. "I want the marshal to stay with you, just to make sure."

Eve's face pinked as he stood. "How could you do this?"

"I told you I knew how to stop—"

"No, Jake! How could you make that *promise?*" She rose. "You inserted a Romero into our … our relationship, without considering me."

His heart sank. She was talking about their prospective marriage. Was she saying young Dan put it in jeopardy? "He's just a little kid, Eve. A needy one. We can do this."

Her eyes glazed, and she shook her head. "I'll never be rid of the Romero family, will I?" Her voice sank in a mire of despair.

"Eve …" Jake pulled her close with his right arm, but the embrace wasn't returned. Dan, held in Jake's left arm, gave her a shove.

She jumped away as if burnt. "So. What are you going to do now?"

You, not *we*. Jake winced. "I'll stay in the hotel, and the four of us—"

"No." The word cracked the air like a whip. "Brad will have a fit once he hears what you did. He'll think for sure you're in cahoots with the Romeros."

Jake shrugged. "I'm not worried about what he thinks."

"Maybe you should when you consider he got you deported to the Philippines."

Every muscle in Jake's body went rigid. "Just say it, Eve." His voice hardened. "You want me to kowtow to him, let him make our decisions."

Eve inhaled sharply. "No, Jake, that's not it at all!" She seized his hand. "I should have stopped him from deporting you three years ago, but I didn't. I don't want to give him that kind of power again."

"You should stand up to him. Don't let him bully you."

"Please, Jake. Don't you see? Last night you increased his basis for suspicion by going to the Romeros … staying overnight … coming out alive, and …"—she glanced at Dan—"with a son in tow. One of their own."

Jake brought her hand to his lips and kissed it. "You're still alive too, you know." He gave her a flirtatious wink. "And I have an explanation for anything he wants to ask."

"Please, Jake. Humor me and put space between you and Brad."

"Do I get a vote?" Crystal patted Dan on the back. "I say they should stay."

Before she could remove her hand, Dan twisted around and slapped it. Hard. A fierce scowl pinched his face.

"Whoa there, buddy!" Jake corralled the boy in both arms. Eve's and Crystal's faces mirrored astonishment at the cute little guy's not-so-cute reaction.

Jake's left cheek twitched. Guess that swayed the decision, didn't it? "I don't like ceding to Brad"—it was hard not to glare at Eve—"but it looks like Dan-boy could profit from some major bonding time before he and I widen our social circle. We'll leave for Indy on the next train." He secured Dan in his left arm and gave Eve and Crystal a swift hug apiece with his right arm.

"I have no doubt you'll be safe, Eve, but keep those US Marshals close by, just in case."

He grimaced. Chances were, he was the one needing to look over his shoulder.

***

The train ride turned out to be a good idea. They sat next to a window, Dan on Jake's lap, absorbing the paternal contact. Jake pointed out sites and murmured words with no demand for responses. So far, the boy had not spoken one word. Most likely he had set up a safety zone to operate in: keep his body covered and his mouth shut.

When at last the boy's head lolled in slumber against Jake's shoulder, Jake hushed. He was exhausted, but there'd be no napping for him, not with the Romeros a constant threat. With one eye, he kept watch over activity in the train car. With the other eye, he looked inward at the morning's escape—

Once Danny Romero had departed Jake's cell, the guard guided Jake and Dan through a maze of passages to a back entrance to the street. Sunrise bathed the horizon in hues of pink, a witness to the length of Jake's stay in the Romero stronghold. "Can you call a taxi for me?" Every nerve urged a quick getaway.

"No. Get outta here." The door slammed in his face.

Dan's legs didn't last the length of the block. "We'll do this piggy-back, okay?" Jake stooped with his back to Dan, and the boy crawled on. "Atta boy." So much easier than carrying dead weight against his chest. He clutched Dan's spindly arms to his neck and walked as fast as he could for forty-five minutes before finally finding a taxi.

At the hotel, he had to get a new room key, retrieve a credit card from the wallet he'd purposely left behind, and pay the taxi driver before he and Dan could settle in. Dan was shaking by then, so Jake turned on the TV to cartoons and cuddled the boy on his lap for a good hour. Dan never laughed at the shenanigans on the television, never smiled. But he did stop shaking.

The satchel, he discovered, contained clothing and legal papers. Jake's heart skipped a beat. This really was going to happen.

"Okay, Dan-boy, you and I stink, so we're going to take a shower and put on clean clothes." The boy tensed when Jake removed his clothing, and Jake had to lift him stiff as a store mannequin into the shower. Jake used a soapy washrag on Dan, careful not to touch him with his hand. He clenched his teeth at the bruises covering Dan's body.

The satchel bore no shorts or short-sleeved shirts. Understandably. Jake donned trousers to match the boy's attire, but wore a short-sleeved tee.

"We're going to visit"—he decided it best not to say *family* yet—"friends, okay?" But what started well hadn't ended well. Was it jealously, or Crystal's touch on Dan's bruises that had caused the boy to react?

Suddenly Jake felt woefully unprepared for the task ahead of him without Eve and Crystal as his allies. Task? Raising young Dan was like entering a battle zone with a target in neon lights on his uniform. *If-only*s assailed Jake like lobbed grenades. *If only* Dan weren't a Romero. *If only* Eve weren't handicapped by her history with the Romeros. *If only* she could love the little guy anyway. *If only* Dan hadn't been so horribly abused. *If only* …

Jake's breath caught in his chest. *If only he hadn't made that promise to raise the boy.*

No.

Heat scoured his throat, drove his breath barreling from his lungs.

*If-only*s were deceptions. They denied Who was in charge. They made His goodness behind every circumstance a lie.

Dan stirred at a jolt in the train's movement. His little hand slipped up to Jake's cheek, then curved back behind Jake's neck. A sleepy sigh sweetened with syrup puffed from his lips.

"I love you, Dan-boy," Jake whispered. The two went hand-in-hand, didn't they? The love and the son. Both a gift from God.

Eve would come around. He felt certain they were meant to be a family. The only surprise was that he was starting with the nucleus of a young boy instead of his long-awaited bride.

Maybe it was time to shorten the wait and present Eve with a ring.

Chapter 7

Ric trudged glumly to the cavernous living room where his parents often called the five of them to meet. The huge room could easily accommodate large family gatherings, but that required Romero marriages and Romero offspring. Neither Ric nor his brothers had the slightest interest in being burdened with demanding wives and squalling brats, especially with the luscious supply of young things available from their father's trafficking.

Until Eve Eriksson changed Ric's mind.

His father's assignment a year ago for Ric to pose as Rock Giannopoulus and insert himself into Eve's life had been eagerly accepted. For twelve years she had been a hound from hell chasing his father, and Ric relished the challenge of devising a fool-proof plan to kill her. What he hadn't figured on was falling in love. His marriage proposal to Eve had been genuine. He would gladly have forsaken his father's kingdom for a life as Rock Giannopoulus and wife.

As if Eve would have cooperated once she discovered he was a Romero.

That dream had soured, anyway, and he'd dismissed it.

Until meeting Jake Chalmers yesterday. And learning his father had freed Chalmers this morning. With Emilio's son in hand. The lining of Ric's stomach burned like charred tires.

His father wasn't in the living room. Ric's brothers sat slouched side-by-side on the couch like Tweedle-Dee and Tweedle-Dum. An arm's length away, his mother was enthroned as usual on her Queen Anne wingback. Ric halted uncertainly in front of the Brentwood accent chair he always used.

"Sit," his mother commanded. "Your father isn't coming."

That was a first. Ric clenched his jaw. Was his father grieving the departure of Emilio's brat? Smoke from the scorched tires in Ric's gut burned his nostrils. "He let Chalmers go!"

His mother closed her eyes, held them shut, opened them slowly. Her way of blotting out what she didn't want to hear. "Your father's trial has been moved up. Your brothers managed to install a mike in Eriksson's office. Tomorrow, her residence gets its annual security checkup, and they will place surveillance equipment there for us as well."

Ric's nerve endings sparked. He'd have access to Eve in her home? Pinpricks of excitement flared in his brain. A second later, dread of his mother's intentions snuffed them out. "Why Eriksson? She's neither prosecutor nor judge in the trial."

"But she did get your father arrested, didn't she, dear boy? Or is her memory loss contagious and you've forgotten you spent six months in prison because of her testimony against you?" The contempt in her voice scratched a line across his throat like the tip of a dagger.

"You're planning revenge?" He gulped, hoped his voice hadn't evidenced his dismay—although what difference did it make since he couldn't have Eve anyway?

"Think, dear boy." His mother's disdain pushed the dagger deeper. "She may give testimony against your father. If so, we want to know what it is. As for vengeance, it will depend on whether your father wins or loses. If, as usual, he goes free, Eriksson's anguish at losing yet once again will be a sweet reprisal."

And if his father lost? A no-brainer—Eve would be terminated. Without warning, anger bashed open the cage door he and his brothers cowed behind. "Why did Pops let Chalmers go?"

He could almost hear his mother's spine stiffen, hear the vertebrae click as they stacked to lift her head like a rattlesnake ready to strike. Fangs, fueled with poison delivered in the sweetest of voices, struck hard. "You boys know how much your father *adores* Emilio. And how he absolutely *fawns* over his namesake, little Dan." She paused, as if to let the poison seep into every cell.

"Emilio wants Jacob Chalmers to raise little Dan, so of course your father consented. He loves Emilio so much, it didn't matter that Chalmers is responsible for killing off your Pop's beloved son. Nor that it cost him the loss of his precious little namesake."

She pushed up from her chair, nostrils flared, narrowed eyes glaring down on each son in turn. "And that, dear boys, is why your father let Chalmers go. And why your Pops isn't here. He is in mourning."

She exited on wooden legs, lips equally wooden over tight jaws. His brothers stared bug-eyed at Ric, as if he had slapped their mother across the face. Pumped by his defiance, Ric grinned, leaned toward them, and whispered, "Be sure you put cameras in the judge's private quarters."

***

"Judge Eriksson?" The voice of Eve's secretary wobbled in uncertainty over the intercom. "US Marshals are here for, uh, their one o'clock appointment."

Eve sat up straight. US Marshals instead of Brad Henshaw, who had made the appointment? "Thank you, Elisa. Please send them in."

Two men in suits sauntered into her office and without invitation plopped into chairs across the desk from Eve. The older one, dark hair salted with gray, a modest paunch restrained in a tightly buttoned white shirt, introduced the two of them. "Good afternoon, Judge. I'm Senior Inspector Maurice Mills with the US Marshals, and"—he inclined his head at the second man—"this is Inspector Dale St. John."

Neither man offered to shake hands. Clearly this was not a friendly visit. Eve settled back into her chair, shoulders loose, arms slack, mirroring the casualness of their postures. "How can I help you, Inspectors?"

Senior Inspector Mills leaned forward. "Judge, mind if I come straight to the point?"

"Please do."

"You've had a Mr. Jacob Chalmers as a guest in your home. How well do you know him?"

"Rather well."

When she didn't elaborate, Mills' mouth tightened. "Mr. Chalmers' conduct has raised several concerns in our inspection team. Because of this, we looked into his history. He appears to have been a model citizen up until his wife's death four years ago—successful architect and construction contractor, Viet Nam war hero, twin children serving their country in the military. Three years ago, after his wife's death, there was an abrupt change. A wiretap on Danny Romero's phone indicated Chalmers was on Romero's payroll. Chalmers got deported to the Philippines on a murder charge, but was released after three years for lack of evidence. A few weeks ago, he arrived in Chicago and was arrested for violating a restraining order. A charge that involves you."

"I'm aware of all that."

"Are you aware that two days ago Chalmers went to Danny Romero's home, placed a phone call to Emilio Romero at Salonga Prison in the Philippines, and left the next morning with Danny Romero's grandson?"

"Yes." The inspectors knew full well that Jake and the boy had gone to her house afterwards, and that she wasn't in the dark.

The left corner of Mills' mouth ticked in irritation at her one-syllable reply.

The other inspector, broad-shouldered, eyes grim behind glasses, clapped open palms onto his knees. "Not meaning to overstep here, Judge, but are you in love with Mr. Chalmers?"

Eve's lower jaw dropped. "That is an audacious question, Inspector! Quite out of line." She rose, as if to cast the men from her office. "I can vouch for Jake Chalmers' character and the fact that his minimal contact with the Romeros is not, and never has been, criminal."

Inspector St. John raised his hands in a gesture of surrender, but a smirk belied any intent of apology. Eve glared at him. He'd meant to provoke her—and had succeeded.

"Pardon my boldness, Judge. Please, sit. I ask only because Chalmers' connection with the Romeros endangers a successful outcome for the Danny Romero trial. Whatever Mr. Chalmers is to you, he's a loose cannon for us. We simply can't have someone close to you running around with the person we're prosecuting."

The senior inspector chimed in, his voice louder, gruffer. "If Chalmers contacts the Romeros again, in any way, for any reason, he will be arrested for conspiracy. The future of your career will be affected as well, Judge. Even if Chalmers gets off, your judicial reputation will be tainted by his association with you and the Romeros."

Eve's chest tightened. Her success in finally being able to arrest Danny Romero and her consequent promotion to Chicago Drug Czar had boosted her career two rungs up the judicial ladder. Two hard-won rungs.

She sat down and wove her fingers together on her desk, tight, to hide their trembling. "You've made your point, Inspectors. I understand what you're saying about Chalmers, and that you want to warn me and protect me. I appreciate it. I can assure you there's no need to investigate Chalmers. But if you feel it necessary, I won't oppose you. I'll even authorize a wiretap on his phone if you think that will net you any results."

The salt-and-pepper-haired inspector sat back, crossed his right leg over his left, relaxed his hands on his lap. The younger inspector lifted his chin and nodded.

Eve slipped her hands into her lap and straightened shoulders she hadn't realized had slumped until now. Pausing only to confirm her heart, she looked each inspector in the eye. "But if you should arrest him, know this: I will defend him, and your evidence, compared to my evidence, will fall short. My career won't be the only one in jeopardy."

After the inspectors huffed out of her office, Eve slumped back into her chair. With Danny Romero's grandson under Jake's wing, how likely was it that Jake would have no further contact with the Romero family?

She blew out an exasperated huff. Uh-huh, little to none. She chewed her lower lip. Because of the kid, Jake had already jeopardized her hopes of a happy marriage. Would he care about jeopardizing her career? Or would he presume to take that in hand too?

Chapter 8

"Have you ever camped out, Dan-boy?" The prospect lit fireworks in the lad's eyes. Jake dug the family equipment out of the attic and took Dan to K-Mart to select his very own sleeping bag. Hands down, the Teenage Mutant Ninja Turtles won. In addition to getting serious bonding time on the campout, Jake hoped the Turtles would train the boy in independent sleep habits.

He chuckled, remembering their first night in Indy when he had put Dan to bed in Brett's room. In the middle of the night, Jake woke to find the boy snuggled under the sheets with him. Not a problem for now, but definitely one after he married Eve. He snorted, imagining Eve's expression at waking to discover Dan-boy fast asleep at her side.

As it turned out, the Turtles didn't help. For six nights in a row, despite eighty-degree weather, Dan plastered himself against Jake.

Grumbling under his breath, Jake rolled up the sleeping bags and stored them and the tent in the car for the trip home. Should he call Danny Romero and ask what Dan's sleeping situation had been? A bedroom with his own bed? A thin mattress on the floor in a cell similar to Jake's? Or worse? Jake's stomach knotted at the possibilities, and he pushed them away. Never mind. For now, it was clear a frightened boy needed comfort and security.

"Let's finish up these marshmallows before we douse the fire," he said. Dan ran to fetch the smoky branches they had used every starlit night before bedtime. Had that been Dan's favorite part of the campout? Jake teased the flames by holding his marshmallow-laden stick just out of reach. He laughed as Dan mimicked him. Six days of heavy-duty bonding. Had it filled Dan-boy's emotional cup at all? He still hadn't said a word.

"So, what did you like best about camping?" Jake asked the question absentmindedly. Boating, fishing, hiking, picnics at the waterfalls—they'd done them all, more than once. McCormick's Creek State Park was a goldmine for keeping a boy busy and happy.

"The baby rabbit."

Jake almost dropped his marshmallows. Dan had talked! Could talk! Wanted to talk! Jake's breath shot out like a missile, veered back to explode in his lungs in a kaleidoscope of joy.

The baby rabbit. He belted an exuberant guffaw. Every day they'd made at least three trips to the nature center to see the tiny kit rescued from a camper's dog, and the mother cat that had given birth to her own kittens and taken him in. "What did you like about him?"

"His fam'ly."

Jake nodded slowly, though his heart was hammering at their communication. "They were nice to him, weren't they? They ate together, and cuddled together, and mama cat loved them and fed them and bathed them and protected them, didn't she?" *All right, Chalmers, no need to beat it to death.* He glanced at Dan. The boy was looking into the fire, a hint of a smile on his lips. And, it struck Jake, he wasn't sucking his thumb.

"Like you and me, Daddy." Chocolate eyes gazed up at Jake, a smile widening to reveal perfect, little, white teeth.

Daddy. Jake's eyes watered. "So I'm a momma cat and you're a baby rabbit?"

Dan giggled. "Nooooooooo! We're fam'ly!"

Jake's throat tightened. A spasm twitched his lower lip, jumped to twitch his chin. He cleared his throat. "Ohhhh, gotcha! Daddy and son!" He tousled Dan's curls.

And hopefully, before too long, they'd be a family with a mom and a sister.

He could hardly wait to tell Eve.

***

On impulse, Eve called Jake's number from Ace's Gym instead of waiting until she got home. Best to check out plans with Jake ahead of time than get

Crystal's hopes stirred up. The girl's seven-day sulk since Jake's departure was just beginning to ease up, and she didn't want to send her into another tailspin. Jake had called every day, and Crystal's self-pity that she wasn't camping with him and Dan-boy had spared Eve no mercy.

The burr of the dial tone ended abruptly. "Chalmers."

"Jake." Her spirit lifted, just knowing he was there for her. He wasn't merely romancing her as Rock—Ric—had done. The past three weeks with Jake had revealed the depth of his character, and that to be loved by him was to be loved with a deep and abiding devotion that would never fall short.

"Eve!" Jake's voice carried the lilt of an ear-to-ear grin. "Everything okay?"

"Yes. No … I mean, Crystal and I are fine, but I need your help."

"Okay."

The corner of Eve's mouth twitched. As a communicator, Jake was sometimes a plodding Dobbin, at other times a raring racehorse. She'd have thought her request would generate more than a placid *Okay*. "I think I know who Romero's mole is in the DOJ."

"Oh yeah?" Definite enthusiasm in his voice now. "Who?"

"Brad Henshaw."

"The DA?"

Eve pictured the jump of Jake's eyebrows, the drop of his jaw. Exactly how she'd felt. "Yes. I'd like you to help me expose him."

"Wouldn't that be a US Marshal's job?"

"Not without evidence. I can't just accuse him out of the blue."

"So forget keeping my distance from him—now I'm to go at him with guns blazing?"

She bit back a smile. "Well, you could go at him as a Romero thug."

That generated several seconds of silence. Jake's reply was sober. "Truth to tell, that sounds like a bad idea. A very bad idea."

Was it? She pursed her lips. "We'd take advantage of his *thinking* you're a Romero thug—let his own thoughts intimidate him."

"I can't risk arrest, Eve. I've got Dan to think about now."

She inhaled razor sharp air through her nostrils. The sting sliced down her throat to her heart.

"Tell you what," he said. "Dan and I will drive up to Chicago tomorrow and meet you at a hotel to discuss alternatives."

"Okay, sure." That was all she could choke out. She hung up. Her stomach hurt as if Jake had punched her hard in the abdomen. The blow rode up to her heart for a second wallop. Climbed to set her eyes blinking back tears.

She picked up her workout bag, pushed through the mugginess of sweat-glazed bodies and out the gym door into the blaze of sun-grilled concrete and metal-sizzling traffic.

Get a grip. He's coming.

Her eyes watered. Yes, but what consolation was that when she'd been usurped from first place in Jake's heart?

Chapter 9

There's nothing to worry about. Eve swallowed convulsively. After all, she was inside the Dirksen Federal Building, Crystal and Dan-boy were safe upstairs in her office, and Jake was here by her side. And if worse came to worse, Brad would never hurt her.

"He's here alone, I'm sure." She bit her lower lip. Silly to whisper with no one else in the hallway. She inserted her key into the door of the District Attorney's Office. It still worked. No one had changed the lock since her move upstairs.

The sharp click of the latch reverberated in her ears. Hands shaking, she turned the handle, pushed the door open, stepped inside. The smell of stale coffee and faded perfume assaulted her nose. The cleaning crew hadn't come yet.

"Where's his office?" Jake's voice boomed behind her, catapulting her heart into her throat.

"Who's there?" Footsteps thundered down the office hallway, rolling Eve's heartbeat into its own thudding peals.

"Just me, Brad—Eve. And, uh, Jake."

Brad charged into the front office. She gulped. Was it her imagination, or was Brad a head taller than the last time she'd seen him?

"You let yourself into the office?" Brad's glare bounced from her to Jake and back.

"I'm returning my office key, and thought since it was Saturday I'd see if you were in." Heat burned her cheeks at this surely obvious stretch of the truth. "Got time for a question?"

Brad folded his arms over his chest, clearly unhappy with their invasion.

She'd never seen Brad in anything other than a suit and tie. Her eyes slid over the length of his bony arms in a short-sleeved shirt, the long, skinny legs, hairy over pale skin between his shorts and Reeboks. Huge Reeboks. Her eyebrows jumped involuntarily. She startled at the realization that she had given the man a frank once-over. Her cheeks rekindled their flush and spread flames across her face.

The inspection reddened Brad's face too. Unquestionably, the poor man hadn't planned on getting caught in weekend casual wear. He led the way to his office and slipped into the over-sized chair behind his desk. Eve was careful not to look at Jake as they settled into seats across from Brad. This was her gig, that needed to be clear to Brad. Jake's advice had been to confront Brad head on, and now, as hard as her heart was beating, she was grateful for the simplicity of the plan.

She'd rehearsed for this face-off as if it were an important courtroom trial. She knew Brad—knew what he'd respond to, knew what he'd see through. There'd be no manipulating him. He liked facts presented linearly with no rabbit trails. Irrefutable logic from beginning to end. An incontrovertible conclusion.

I can do this. She inhaled deeply. Set her shoulders. "Four years ago, I disappeared in Guam after I boarded the cruise ship, the *Gateway.* Did you at that time put a sealed envelope, designated to be opened only in the event of your death, into your personal file here at the office?"

Brad folded his hands and leaned over the desktop toward her. "Yes. You were here when I did it."

She snuffed in a startled breath. "I have no memory of that."

He stared at her before sitting back. "It doesn't matter. I could probably dispose of the envelope now anyway."

"Mind if I see its contents?"

His eyebrows rose. "Why?"

"Because I'm concerned they're linked to my disappearance."

"Of course they are."

"You … you're admitting your connection with the Romeros?" She couldn't help the horror in her voice. Brad had betrayed her? Had ordered her death aboard the *Gateway*?

The center of Brad's brow furrowed into stacked Vs. "Yes—through the connection of our undercover agent, your former boyfriend, Scott Ryker."

Eve's heartbeat doubled. "I have no memory of him either." Her mind muddled at the unexpected direction Brad was taking her.

Jake stood abruptly. "So you are confessing, then, to being the Romero mole in the DA office?"

"What are you talking about?" Brad sat up ramrod straight. "You think *I* am the office mole?"

"You acknowledged your connection just now," Jake said.

"Connection, yes. But working for them, no. You're the one working for them, Chalmers! Did he put this idea in your head, Eve?"

"He didn't. It's my suspicion, Brad, because of the alignment of the dates. The appearance of your envelope at the same time as my disappearance can't be coincidental."

"Of course it isn't." Brad's voice rose in exasperation. "The possibility of the Romeros harming you was the reason I set up the envelope."

Jake frowned, glanced at Eve, and lowered himself back into his chair. "It sounds like we're talking at cross purposes here. An easy solution would be to simply examine the contents of the envelope."

"The easy solution would be to burn it. Here and now." Brad jerked open a desk drawer.

"Don't, Brad." Eve glared at him. "If I have to, I'll get a court order for the envelope."

Disappointment, then what looked like sadness, settled on Brad's face. "All right, Eve. I have no problem opening it for you, but Chalmers will have to step out of the room."

***

There was no way he was going to leave Eve alone with the district attorney. Jake darted a peek at Eve. The clamp of her jaws set him at ease.

"Jake's not leaving," she said.

"Even though the information is highly personal?" Brad's tone clearly intimated she'd regret it.

"Doesn't matter. Jake's my fiancé. There's nothing I need to hide from him."

Fiancé? Jake's heart leaped. Well, kick the elephant out of the room, he was sure going to move on that!

Brad huffed, shook his head. "Eve, trust me ..."

"You heard her, Brad. I'm staying. Please proceed."

Eve nodded. "Let's don't make this any harder than it already is."

"All right." Brad heaved a sigh. "In the spring of '81, Scott received a ... let's say, *compromising* ... photo of the two of you from the Romeros—"

"Compromising? In what way?" Eve frowned.

Brad ignored the question. "They wanted to blackmail Scott into leaking information from you to them about Danny Romero's trial. If Scott didn't cooperate, they'd send the photo to the press and claim you shouldn't be the prosecutor because you were divulging information to a Romero spy. Your reputation would be ruined as a federal prosecutor, and Scott's as a federal agent."

"Compromising in what way?" Eve insisted.

Brad grimaced. "Of the two of you in bed. Scott was separated from his wife, but not divorced."

Silence swallowed the room.

Numbness crept over Jake, a slow deadness from the inside out.

Brad continued, his voice scratching on Jake's soul like fingernails on chalkboard. "Scott came to me, and we managed to get the negative and destroy it. In retaliation, the Romeros saw to it he stumbled and fell onto the track in front of the El." Brad paused, cleared his throat. "You and I were concerned one or both of us would be next. If so, the envelope contained information to help pin down the Romeros' involvement. Barring that, your reputation was safe."

Your reputation was safe. Jake blinked. A reputation he didn't know had a basis for threats. But how could he, when he didn't know Eve's history? When she didn't know her history? Her memory loss had erased almost everything but the last three years of her life. It wasn't as if she had hidden the relationship with Scott from him …

Still, the air in Jake's lungs refused to move, his heart to beat.

Finally, Brad broke the silence. "I'm sorry, Eve. I … I'll get the envelope." He scooted his chair to a filing cabinet behind him, retrieved an envelope, and scooted back to offer it across his desk to Eve.

"You read it, please." She whispered, her voice hoarse.

Brad grunted, slit the envelope open, and removed a single, folded sheet of paper. He leaned back in his chair to scan it. Abruptly, eyes wide, he jerked upright. "This isn't my note!"

Jake's numbness broke. But before he could act, Eve shot from her chair and snatched the paper from Brad's hand.

Chapter 10

"Let me see it." Eve hopped back a good foot out of Brad's reach. Her eyes gulped the paper's content in one glance. Two sentences and Brad's signature. She gasped. "What have you done?"

"I didn't write that." Brad's voice was calm now, his mouth settled in a resolute, pinched line. "Someone set me up."

"I'm sorry, Brad"—Eve tried to blink away the revulsion paralyzing her brain—"I've got to take this into custody."

Jake grasped her elbow, and she realized her legs were quaking. The warmth of his hand radiated strength, removed the daze from her head. Even as she related the note's contents to Jake, she began questioning its reality. "It's a confession that he was forced to leak information to the Romeros and conspired in Scott's murder to shut him up."

Except for further tightening his lips, Brad didn't move.

"It's got to be a plant," Jake said. "I suspect your office mole switched it out so it could be released during the trial to get Romero off."

"A plant?" Her mind chewed dully on the possibility. "Why do you think that?"

"He opened the envelope willingly in front of us, with full confidence about its content. If he'd known what was actually in there, he wouldn't have offered you the chance to open it first."

It made sense. She dropped back into her chair, unable to drag her eyes from her lap to meet Brad's eyes. He hadn't betrayed her—she had betrayed him. She'd twisted his arm to reveal embarrassing information he wanted to protect her from in front of Jake. And she'd readily accepted the envelope's bogus confession claiming he was a traitor and a murderer. Added to that was her suspicion that he had plotted her disappearance four years ago. Her stomach roiled as if she had swallowed a rotting animal carcass. All those years of trust between her and Brad, and *poof!*—she'd vaporized it with hardly a second thought.

Brad spoke, driving her eyes to his. "You said you don't remember being here when I wrote the note—the real one. So how did you know it was here?"

"Stella." She sucked in her lips as the implication hit home. Stella had told her no one else in the office knew about the envelope except herself and Brad.

"Then there's your suspect," Jake said softly.

Was she going to hurt yet another relationship? Eve shook her head. "Uh-uh. Not Stella."

Brad's eyes hammered nails into Jake. "Eve has a key to the office. You could have slipped in here anytime and made the switch, Chalmers."

"Brad, stop it!" Eve jumped up, slammed her palms on Brad's desk, and leaned toward him with a voice the equivalent of bared fangs. "He is not a Romero thug! Stella could have told any number of people besides me!"

Brad deflected her anger with his own to Jake. "The only way I'll come close to accepting that possibility is for you to vanish from Eve's life until the Romero trial is over. Don't you see how your contact with her and with the Romeros puts her in their ballpark, playing their game? You're handing them a win and jeopardizing her reputation and career, possibly her life."

Eve flinched as Jake's shoulders drooped. "He's not going anywhere, Brad. You are not shipping him out again."

***

Jake's chest ached as if he'd received a one-two punch to the ribs. First punch, the revelation about Scott. Second punch, Brad's assertion that Jake was now the one endangering Eve. Either one hurt. Together they knocked him off his feet.

"C'mon, Jake." Eve's growl—at him or at Brad?—brought him to his feet. Dully, he trailed her out of Brad's office. Each step away from the office helped. Helped jog his soul back to life. Helped jog it into sensibility. By the time they arrived upstairs at Eve's office, he had strapped up his wounds and was no longer seeing cross-eyed. He was on top of it.

Eve removed her office key from her pocket and unlocked the door, but before turning the handle she squared herself face to face with Jake. She touched his cheek, the tip of her forefinger light on his skin, as if she were a pin and he a fragile balloon. "Jake. I have no memory of Scott ... of our relationship."

He slipped his hand over her mouth. "Hush. It's not an issue. Reality is you and me, right here, right now." He slid his hand down to cup her chin, touched his lips to hers. Gently. As if she were the one falling apart.

He'd get over it. The ache would fade. Like Dan-boy's bruises.

***

Dan and Crystal were camped at Eve's desk, coloring. They barely looked up as Jake and Eve entered the office. Jake expected Dan to run to him, to hug Jake's legs, to shout *Daddy!* Looked forward to that boy-sized dose of unconditional love. Needed it, as a matter of fact. When Dan kept coloring, Jake swallowed the sting.

Eve slipped Brad's envelope into a file drawer, locked it, and slipped the key back into her pocket. "I'll take the evidence to the lab on Monday. They'll check it for fingerprints and compare handwriting samples of people in the office."

"You don't think the mole is Stella?"

"No."

"You should prepare yourself, just in case."

"I prepared myself for it to be Brad, and he turned out to be my protector. I'm embarrassed to have accused him. I'm not going to do the same with Stella."

"You know handing over the envelope means investigating Scott's death. Maybe an investigation of Brad too, since he didn't report helping Scott obtain and destroy the negative." He paused. "Your name will come up. Can the Romeros use it against you at the trial?"

Dan and Crystal looked up at the mention of the Romero name. An uneasy feeling pinched Jake's stomach. The boy had never paid attention to the name before.

Eve followed his glance at the children. A plastic smile accompanied plastic cheer in her voice. "Well now, those … challenges … can be delayed until after the trial, can't they? I'm not involved, anyway, except as a consultant to Brad behind the scenes."

Then why did Brad want him to vanish if there was no threat? Jake huffed, weary of it all. Tired of being a punching bag. He checked his watch. "Sorry, I've got to go. C'mon, Dan-boy." He held out his hand, hungry to have the boy clasp it. "Thanks for watching him, Crystal."

"You don't mean you're going back to Indianapolis, do you?" Disappointment wobbled at the edge of Eve's voice.

Jake halted. If he felt like a punching bag, Eve must feel like she'd stepped into a minefield. The meeting with Brad had set off unexpected explosions. Eve's suspicion of Brad blown sky high … her friend Stella now suspected as the mole … the intimacy between Eve and Ryker revealed. Any one of those situations was upsetting. All three at once had to be devastating. He should stay and comfort her.

But—he swallowed a prickly lump at the back of his throat—he needed recovery time himself. His hurt over Eve's relationship with Ryker was logically unwarranted—it was before Jake knew her, before she was even a Christian—but it was bleeding nevertheless. And what about Brad's accusation? Would Jake's presence give the Romeros ammunition to harm Eve? His visit to their stronghold put muscle into the reality of the threat.

"I'm sorry, Eve. I'd stay, but I have an appointment this afternoon I can't miss."

"You're making a seven-hour round trip to come here for half an hour?"

"That's how important you are to me." Blood boiled to his face at the words. *Important enough to come … but not important enough to stay?* Shame at his selfishness burned his face. His legs stiffened. His feet lost feeling. He couldn't move, couldn't budge, couldn't will himself to do an about-face and stay.

Dan-boy slid into his vision, lips and brows gnarled in a pout. "Are we going?"

Jake's paralysis broke. "Yes." He was halfway through the door before he thought to turn and say, "I'll call you."

***

Minutes later, when Eve and the girl departed, Danny's wife switched off the hidden mike in Eve's office. *So, that's what happened to the negative of Eriksson and Ryker!* Shaking, cane seesawing in her hand, she lurched across the surveillance room to a more comfortable chair. The anger of four years clambered out of its grave and took on new flesh. She breathed heavily. US Attorney Bradley Henshaw would not escape her revenge.

She inhaled through her nose, exhaled through her mouth, until her heartbeat calmed and the tightness in her face and lungs dissipated. Teeth clenched, she laid out a plan.

First and foremost, get rid of the office mole. Then—she had to gasp at her brilliance—why, dispose of Danny too! The old fool had as good as announced his incompetency to rule the Romero family when he let Jacob Chalmers walk out of the compound. And with Emilio's brat, at that! A blatant confirmation as to which of his offspring Danny favored. She would *not* let her sons' kingdom fall prey to their father's sentimentality.

She stood, her cane now quaking with glee. The mole's demise had to be immediate, but the destruction of Henshaw and Danny ... ahhh, those she could prolong. Stretch out the torture, relish it, sun herself in the radiance of their slow agony.

Back in her room, she placed a phone call to her right-hand man. The only man she trusted. The only man whose dark appetite matched hers. "Blue, love, it's Roza. I have three assignments you will positively glut on. The first I must watch while you execute it. Tonight."

Chapter 11

Jake was ten miles out of Chicago before he tuned in to the little boy scrunched into a ball in the far corner of the front seat, sucking his thumb. "Hey, buddy, you okay?"

The ball folded tighter into itself, squeezed its eyes shut.

"You and Crystal have fun? Looked like a mighty good coloring job going on there."

The ball's jaws tugged harder at the thumb.

"I had a bad time with the man Eve and I went to see. He made me very sad."

The ball's eyes opened, the sucking stopped.

"I think I need a snuggle. Can you do that for me?"

The ball unraveled into a tousled-hair boy that scooted across the seat and tucked into Jake's side. Warmth seeped from the young body into Jake's, swept a path of comfort to his heart. "Atta boy."

"Are you gonna dop me?" The boy's voice teetered between accusation and fear.

"I don't know. What's a *dop?*"

"Crystal said you and Eve are gonna dop us so we can be a fam'ly."

"Ah, gotcha! Yep, I'm going to adopt you right away, and when Eve and I marry we'll adopt Crystal." He slipped his right arm around Dan and pulled him tighter against his ribs. "That's where we're headed now, buddy, to an appointment with the lawyer who's helping us."

"Crystal says you aren't my real daddy."

Oh boy! Crystal had a way of throwing boomerangs that came back to clobber Jake on the head. "You have a daddy named Emilio, and now you have a daddy named Jake—me."

Silence. Then, "Like the baby rabbit?" Dan's voice tipped up in the exuberance of a light bulb moment.

"Exactly. Daddy Emilio can't take care of you, so he asked me to be your daddy."

"Like the momma cat."

Jake guffawed. "Yep, we're a family like the momma cat and the baby rabbit."

"Crystal says my name is Dan Romero. She says Eve doesn't like that name and I should change it when I'm dopped."

Jake's left cheek ticked. What other boomerangs had Crystal thrown? "When I marry Eve, her name will become the same as mine, Chalmers, and when we adopt Crystal, her name will become Chalmers. That's our family name. You will be at the front of the line and get to become a Chalmers first. You'll be my son Dan Chalmers, instead of Dan Romero. Do you like that?"

"Romero is a mean name."

"Because they were mean to you?"

The boy's head bobbed against Jake's side. He snuffled and buried wet eyes in Jake's shirt.

Jake inhaled a stinging breath. *Thank you, God, for letting me rescue this boy. For making him my son. For loving him through me.*

"Where is daddy 'Milio?"

'Milio. Had Dan heard it from his grandfather? "He's in prison."

"Why?"

"He did something bad, so he's being punished."

"What'd he do?"

Jake crunched his bottom lip. Hopefully, Crystal had not thrown a boomerang on this question. "He hurt people."

Dan was quiet so long Jake figured he'd fallen asleep. Then, "Can I see him?"

Jake's stomach looped into a knot. Could he say no when Emilio was due to be executed any day now? Would Dan resent the lost opportunity when he was older? Jake cleared his throat. "Uh, to say goodbye?"

"Uh-huh. Cuz I'm in the Chalmers fam'ly now."

Jake stamped a hefty kiss on the top of Dan's head. Would have swung him around in a circle laughing if he weren't driving. "When we get home tonight, we'll make plans to fly where he lives to see him."

So, Brad Henshaw wanted him out of the way for the Romero trial, did he? All right, the trip to the Philippines would accomplish that. It would be good to see Puno again, and Detective Lee, perhaps find out how the warden was faring in his new job.

And Eve? She'd like the news that young Dan didn't want to be a Romero, that she didn't have to expect that name to be part of the Chalmers family.

He blew out a hurricane-sized breath of relief. And when he returned from his travels, he'd get down on one knee and officially make Eve his fiancée.

***

Although the sun still brightened Chicago's evening sky at eight o'clock, the backyard squirrels had retired for the night hours ago, the birds for the most part had gone to roost, and the rabbit burrowing behind Eve's three-car garage had completed its fifteen-minute evening meditation and withdrawn. Only the heat lingered, hosting tenacious lightning bugs seeking mates.

As was Eve.

C'mon, Jake. He had to be home by now. And she wasn't going to call him. Not after the way he had departed her office.

When at last the phone rang, every chest muscle tightened. Her lungs barely released her hello.

"Eve." The grin was back in Jake's voice. Not a hint of the hesitation that had strangled his parting words this morning. "Sorry to be calling so late. Getting Dan to bed is like wrestling a jack-in-the-box on steroids." He chuckled at his humor.

She glowed, melting into a soppy daub of whipped cream on hot chocolate. "Did you make your appointment in time?"

"Yes. A lawyer friend who's handling my adoption of Dan."

So he was going ahead with it. The soppy lump crystallized into ice shards.

"On the ride home, Dan asked about being *dopped*." Jake chuckled again. "Apparently Crystal shared the news about his adoption while the two were coloring. Also the advice to chuck the last name of Romero. Dan told me it's a mean name and he doesn't want to keep it."

Eve ducked her head and swallowed. Dan's bruises evidenced he had a first-hand understanding of *mean*. "That … that helps, eliminating the name." But it wasn't the name that bothered her. It was the bloodline. No good could come from Romero genes.

"Dan also asked if he could say goodbye to Emilio. I think it's important to not withhold that from him"—Jake's words sped to the end of his sentence—"so I'm booking a flight to the Philippines."

She clutched the phone, speechless.

Jake's voice took on an edge of bitterness. "That should make Henshaw happy. And remove any accusation of manipulation by the Romeros—you know, because of my relationship with both of you." He hesitated at her silence. "You'll be free to work without distraction … get the trial off the table … move on to our finally becoming a family." The warmth of a smile radiated across the telephone line, wrapping her in a tight hug.

"I don't like your going so far away, Jake. But I promise, it'll go fast." She beamed her own smile, hesitant as it was, across the miles. "I've already put in for a three-month leave when the trial is over."

"Atta girl! Just don't let those US Marshals out of your sight. The Romeros are wily."

Yes. She bit her lip. Exactly why she didn't want a Romero in her nest.

***

Ric Romero's cheek twitched in irritation. Eve must be talking to Chalmers. Stupid brothers—they had added surveillance cameras and mikes to Eve's house, but no mikes to the telephones. "Too easy to detect," they'd whined. So now all he gained from inside the Romero surveillance room was Eve's side of a phone conversation. Unless she repeated the content to Crystal, Ric had to guess at it.

What appointment were they talking about? What name was being eliminated? And what faraway place was Chalmers going to? It sounded as if he would be gone during the trial. Now *that* piece of information might come in handy.

Eve's three months' leave after the trial, though ... the intent of that was clear. A honeymoon. He snarled. After watching Eve prepare for bed every night, he resented the idea of Chalmers getting to have her. The love Ric had tried to push away was back, burning his every thought, making his hands shake. There was no way he was going to let Chalmers come out the victor.

Chapter 12

"Blue, you were magnificent." Roza Romero slithered her finger up the inside of his bare arm to the damp maleness of his armpit. In spite of the early hour, sirens and the throat-clogging stench of smoke had drawn curious Chicagoans out of bed to congregate across the street from the burning apartment building. Hoses from three fire trucks blasted water at flames feathering two windows on the fourth floor.

"Grabbing her in bed, seeing her eyes jump wide open in the flashlight, was"—tremors quivered tiny gasps in Roza's voice—"... rousing."

Blue put his mouth to Roza's ear. "I barely got my hand across her mouth to stop her scream. Did you see how she struggled?"

"Oh yes. Yes. Even after you gagged and tied her to the chair, she didn't stop. It was luscious."

"And then when I brought her son out—"

Roza moaned. "So sleepy, so unaware."

"But not his sweet mama. I wanted to hold onto her, she was ... she was like a tornado—"

Blue's breath was curling-toes hot in Roza's ear, and she closed her eyes in ecstasy.

"Twisting and writhing in that chair. But I couldn't squeeze the boy's neck and touch her too, so I just watched." Blue hushed as a cop walked by.

"Their panic was ... delicious," Roza whispered. "And you, Blue—your hands ... so strong, so masterful."

A gasp huffed from his chest. "And then when I cut her thigh—"

"And she knew it was her turn …"

"Her eyes, saucer-big at all that blood—"

"Until she looked at her son … and didn't care anymore."

Blue giggled. "Until I poured gasoline on her—"

"And you stood there with a match … a whole book of them." Roza hunched her shoulders to her ears. She and Blue, they were a perfect pair. Synchronizing thoughts and words like the swings of a pendulum. "Lighting them one after another."

"Until—."

"The last one lit her up." Euphoria shuddered through every cell in Roza's body, magnified by Blue's ecstatic convulsions next to her.

The cop approached the crowd and bellowed, "Everyone go home!" He stalked toward Roza and Blue standing at the edge. Before he could glimpse their faces, they turned and walked away. Separating from her companion, Roza flagged a taxi and snugged inside.

She had promised Blue a glut for his first assignment. Her darling had exceeded her expectations. She closed her eyes and tugged shuddering breaths through her nostrils.

One assignment down, two more glorious ones to go.

***

Eve responded reluctantly to Brad's recorded message to call when she and Crystal got home from church. She dropped her purse on the kitchen counter, pulled tuna sandwiches and leftover tomato soup out of the refrigerator, and waited for Crystal to run off to change clothes. The conversation with Brad would be awkward after yesterday's confrontation in his office. She steeled herself.

Brad's voice was gruff. Trouble-gruff. Her heart skipped a beat. His tone foretold pain. Always, without fail it seemed, pain for her. "Eve. Have you heard about the fire?"

"No." She switched on the tiny TV in the kitchen to a news channel.

"Early this morning." Brad's voice lowered, his words shoving at her. "Stella's apartment."

Eve froze. A fire alone wouldn't affect Brad this way.

"Stella is dead. Murdered. And her son." Brad's voice choked to a halt.

A wrecking ball slammed into Eve's stomach. Her breath exploded in a wail.

Minutes—what seemed like hours—later, heart pounding against the back of her throat, she squeaked out a question: "What happened?" But Brad didn't need to tell her. She knew. Knew without a doubt the Romeros had killed Stella. Stella and her disabled ten-year-old son. They must have used him to force her to operate as the office mole. Bribed her by supplying the boy's expensive meds and therapy and daycare, threatened her with withdrawing them.

Until they needed to silence her.

Eve didn't stop shaking until she went to bed, and then she tossed and turned for hours. Two things she knew for sure by the time she fell asleep. In spite of Stella's betrayal, Eve didn't doubt her friend's love for her DA office-mates.

And secondly, never, ever, could Eve accept a Romero into her family.

***

Few mourners showed up at the mortuary for Stella and her son's funeral. The absence of all but a few DA office staff stung Eve worse than Stella's betrayal. Only Brad, shoulders slumped, hands buried deep in trouser pockets, eyes glazed with grief, evidenced she had a companion-in-sorrow. When he saw her, he opened his arms wide and she walked into them, her resolve to not cry completely undone. "Her son … the Romeros used him to—"

"I know, I know," Brad whispered. "I should have seen it, should have helped her."

"We've got to do something," she hiccupped. "I …you still want my help with the trial?" Or was he done with her after she'd accused him of being the office mole?

"Of course I want your help." He squeezed her shoulder. "We'll start tomorrow. But not in your office or mine. Not your place or mine, either.

Somewhere free of the possibility of Romero surveillance." Anger hovered over his last words like tornado clouds.

She nodded in quick agreement, grateful he hadn't written her off. "Someplace out of our routine. Change the location every time we meet."

The left corner of Brad's mouth curved up. "And we'll wear disguises, just to make sure no one spots us."

Eve laughed. For sober Bradley Henshaw to show humor was a message that all was well between them. All was forgiven. For the first time since Jake had taken off for the Philippines, a ray of sunshine—a narrow ray, but still golden—touched her heart. If she could keep hold of it, wrap herself in the light, maybe it would show her a solution to the problem of Jake's commitment to raising the Romero boy.

Chapter 13

August

Jake stood immobile at the front of Salonga Prison, feet glued to the concrete apron, eyes glued to the front gate's steel bars, hand glued to the sweaty clasp of a young boy. Gone were the fragrant pots of tropical trees, ferns, and colorful flowers that had decorated the apron six weeks ago for his daughter's wedding—the wedding that had brought him and Eve back together.

And now, here he was, his life diverted in an entirely unexpected direction, not with his bride in his arms but a with a vicious criminal's son in his care. A criminal due to be executed in three days. His son brought to say goodbye.

"You ready?" With a start, he realized the question was addressed as much to himself as to young Dan. Dan-boy, his grandfather called him. What did Emilio call his son? *Daniel Bennett Romero*, the name on the boy's birth certificate, would soon be changed to *Daniel Bennett Chalmers*. He would become Jake's son, and *Romero* would be swept away as surely as the flowers had been from the prison's entryway.

Was he ready to take on a five-year-old son? A son whose formative years were marked with black-and-blue bruises? A son who most likely would act out once he got his feet under him?

Jake's stomach tightened into a knot. *A son who might cost Jake his bride?*

Dan tugged on Jake's hand. The son was ready.

***

Two guards brought Emilio into the Visitors Room and fastened him into a steel belt bolted to the chair across the table from Jake and Dan. One guard secured Emilio's feet to the floor while the other locked the prisoner's chained hands into a bolt that allowed Emilio a small range of motion. A ragged beard covered the lower half of Emilio's face; the other half hosted strands of oily curls that hung limp over eyes as chocolate as Dan's. Shorts, shirt, and skin were crusted with dirt and sweat.

For a split second, Jake's heart squeezed with pity. This was the handsome captain who four years ago had welcomed passengers aboard the small cruise ship *Gateway*. Tall, trim, wearing a crisp white uniform and blue jacket with gold braid and brass buttons, his cap perched on freshly cut, curly hair— Emilio had been a striking figure.

The split second segued into a visual of nineteen passengers flung skyward from two boats in a sequence of violent explosions. Explosions plotted by a remorseless man. No, the only pity Emilio deserved was payback, nineteen times over, for what he had dealt out.

"I didn't ask you to bring him here." Emilio's eyes didn't move from the reciprocated stare of his son.

"He asked to see you."

"Spoiling him already? I should have let my father send him back to his grandparents."

Jake's mind jumped to the middle name on Dan's birth certificate. "The Bennetts? How long did he live with them?" And where? Why did Danny Romero take Dan away from them?

Emilio darted a glance at Jake, planted it back on Dan. "What do you want, boy?"

Dan got out of his chair and stood at stiff attention, his voice barely above a whisper. "To say goodbye cuz … cuz I don't want to be in the Romero fam'ly. I'm a Chalmers now."

Emilio's head jerked to face Jake square on. "I said 'raise him,' not adopt him."

"And have no legal recourse against your brothers if they came after him?"

Emilio's face tightened above clenched jaws. "Come here, boy. I want to tell you something."

Nerves on high alert, Jake stood, but he let Dan edge closer to Emilio. This was the last time the two would see each other. Emilio's eyes slid over the boy's arms and legs, exposed by shorts and a sleeveless tee, free of bruises.

Emilio spoke quietly, his tone short of plaintive. "Son, that's all I've got to leave you with—my name."

Dan hung his head, eyes to the floor.

"Don't let them take that away from you. They can't make you. Don't let them."

Dan snuffled, slipped his thumb into his mouth.

Emilio's face flushed crimson. "What are you doing sucking your thumb?" Straining against the steel belt, he whipped the back of his left hand across Dan's face. The boy crashed to the floor.

Jake leaped to rescue Dan, the guards leaped to control Emilio.

"You're five years old, not a baby!"

Hands quivering to bash fist-sized indentations into Emilio's skull, Jake set Dan on his feet. "Get him out of here," he roared.

Before the guards could act, Dan broke away from Jake and marched up to Emilio. Blood seeped from four scratches on his cheek where Emilio's fingernails had sliced him, but his eyes bore no tears. He pushed his face next to Emilio's, jutted out his chin, and plunged his thumb into his mouth. "You're not my dad," he said, thumb clamped between his teeth, "and I'm not a baby."

Jake pulled Dan out of harm's way. It was all he could do not to crow, "Atta boy!"

***

"Puno!" Jake let go of Dan's hand and strode across the Visitors Room to his friend. They did the manly thing of pounding each other on the back and grunting greetings from mouths stretched in full-capacity grins. Jake's release from prison six weeks ago seemed like six years, so much had happened. In Jake's life, anyway. Not so much in the monotony of prison life for Puno. They had exchanged letters every week and were well acquainted with the events in each other's life.

When the ruckus of the greeting settled, Dan dashed across the room and slammed to a halt against Jake's right leg. He stared wide-eyed and unblinking at Puno.

"So this is young son Dan." Puno's Filipino accent made the name sound like *Yun Sun Dan.* The old man inclined his head in greeting, and wisps of snow-white hair caught the overhead light and floated like an aura around his head. A goatee, equally white, flowed from his chin to his midsection.

"Dan-boy, this is Puno, our friend. Would you like to shake hands with him?" Jake gave the boy a nudge. They had been working on Dan's non-existent social skills.

To Jake's surprise, Dan didn't hesitate. The boy took two steps forward and gazed up at the wrinkled face barely a foot above his. Then he grinned, raised his hand to Puno's chin, and trailed his fingers down the goatee to its tip. "Is he fam'ly?" His fingers closed in a grip and he yanked Puno's beard with a gleeful laugh.

Puno yelped, and Jake grabbed Dan's hand away. "Whoa there, son! What were you …? Did you think it was a fake beard?"

Dan raised astonished eyes to Jake's. "Like Santa's," he mumbled. The corners of his mouth tugged down and his thumb flew to his mouth but stopped before parted lips could capture it. He lowered his hand to his side and his face toward the floor. "Like Gran'pa at Christmas."

Jake's heart somersaulted to his throat. Surely not Dan's grandfather Danny Romero! He swallowed. "Grandpa Bennett, you mean? Your other grandpa?" His heart pounded tremors to his lungs so hard he could hardly breathe. If Dan remembered the Bennetts, then maybe his stay with the Romeros had been months rather than years.

Dan hunched his shoulders forward and buried his chin in his chest. "I don't got a Gran'pa Bennett," he said petulantly.

Jake sighed. Dan was embarrassed, and evidently ditching the comfort of a thumb. There'd be no getting information out of him now. But maybe later. And if not, there was the hope that someone with a fake beard had brought laughter into Dan's life, that bruises didn't define the sum total of the boy's childhood.

"Yun Sun Dan good at surprises," Puno said. "I too have surprise for you."

Chapter 14

Eve waved Brad over to her table. It was the second time they had met for lunch at the newly opened Cuppa Chocolatte Café to confer about the Romero trial. The café's location on South Dearborn was a swift walk from their offices in the Dirksen Federal Building, which, with her and Brad's busy schedules, won big points for being handy. The menu was limited, but the service fast, and who didn't love free hot chocolate if you remembered to bring the coupon?

Eve raked in the notes spread across the small, circular table, huddled them along with her pen to the side, and hung her purse on the back of her chair. "Can you believe it? I asked for a quiet table and they gave me this nook. I can actually hear myself without shouting."

"I'd prefer a cot and a fifteen-minute nap." Brad turned his chair at an angle, sat, and stretched out his long legs. "But I'll take this leg room as a definite plus any day." They placed their orders and made small talk until their hot chocolates arrived. "We've had a breakthrough," he announced with his first sip. "A snitch."

"A snitch on the Romeros?" Eve laughed. Brad had to be joking.

"Staggered into the police station, badly beaten, and claimed he wanted revenge on Danny Romero."

"No." Eve shook her head. "Don't believe it. It's a set-up. No one witnesses against the Romeros and lives to take the stand."

"He says he's not a witness but knows how to get them."

Eve snorted. "Ha! In exchange for what?"

"No price named so far. Just sweet revenge."

"And you believe him?"

Brad leaned back, slid his bottom to the edge of his chair, and extended his legs farther into the dead space next to him. Eve giggled. Brad hadn't been kidding about needing a nap. "No belief," he said, "just desperate hope."

"Who is he?"

"Appears to be a bona fide bum. Nasty fellow. No arrest record we could find, nothing from his fingerprints. Refuses to give a history, and won't reveal his connection to the Romeros. No identity on him, no name. Only that he's always been known as 'Blue.'"

Eve shrugged. "May as well test the cheese in the trap, see what he comes up with for witnesses." She buried a second snort with a swallow of hot chocolate. No one would betray the Romeros. So what was this Blue up to?

***

Jake stared wordlessly at Puno. From outside the Visitor Room, footsteps slapped the cement hallway. They stopped and a voice murmured to Puno's guard standing outside the door. The acrid smell of cheap cigarettes wafted into the room.

"Sit, so heart beats and brain computes." The skin at the edge of Puno's eyes crinkled in amusement. He gestured at the Visitor Room's scarred table and chairs. "I suppress surprise for your arrival."

Jake sat and pulled a sulky Dan onto his lap. Puno rarely dropped bombshells, so the news had to be good.

"Tomorrow, I leave Salonga Prison. I am free man."

Fireworks exploded in Jake's head. His jaw dropped, and he gaped bug-eyed at Puno, disbelief grappling with the reality that his friend wasn't kidding. "Free?"

"New warden pull strings."

"I can't believe it, Puno—that's great! The other political prisoners too?"

Puno shook his head. "Sadly, warden's string not that long."

Still, Puno out of prison … Jake couldn't wrap his brain around it. "What will you do?" Rumors of impeaching President Marcos were circulating in the

US press. Would Puno help lead the movement? It was doubtful he could be reinstated in his former job as a university professor.

"You come tomorrow with car and suitcase for pleasant trip. One picture worth a thousand words."

All kinds of possibilities swept through Jake's mind, but none of them stuck. One thing for sure, until they arrived at that picture-worth-a-thousand-words spot, Puno would not cede one clue.

***

There was no escaping the hubbub of traffic noise and sidewalk chatter. It draped Manila's downtown like curtains of gauze at open windows. Amir easily ignored it, the din's unceasing continuity rendering it as bland as the smooth plaster walls of his office. The clamor of the phone was another thing altogether. Never was anyone to interrupt him when he was teaching his son! *Unless*, he remembered, unless the call was urgent. He snatched the receiver off its cradle. "This had better be important!"

A man's voice, iron-hard but with appropriate deference, offered an apology and hurried to deliver its message. "You wanted to know when Jacob Chalmers returned to the Philippines. He arrived this morning."

"Where is he?"

"Visiting Salonga Prison."

"Find out where he is staying. Immediately." Amir hung up.

Across the desk from him, Salmid's brown eyes widened. "A job, father? Muhamoud is home in Mindanao ..."

Amir bit back his irritation. Always the boy wanted to shine brighter than his older brother, but what Salmid needed was to acquiesce to his proper place in the family, show respect for his elder brother's ascendancy. Muhamoud would rule the family when Amir died. Loyalty and submission would be required of Salmid. Always. The best he could do for Salmid was to equip him with accounting skills his brother would esteem. Skills young Salmid at seventeen had yet to value over the excitement of warfare.

"It would be good practice for me, would it not, father?"

Amir spoke gruffly. The boy was dear to him, tempting him to foolish decisions. "No. This job requires expertise beyond what you and your brother have."

Salmid bowed his head in acceptance, yet the stiffness of his shoulders belied surrender. "Then teach me why, please, father, that I may be wise as you."

Amir doubled his gruffness. "The target is formidable. I sent two of my best warriors to kill him, and he defeated both."

Salmid's head shot up. "He has humiliated us, father. He must not succeed again."

"Foolishness! It was a failed job arrangement, nothing more." Amir's tone moved to a growl. "You must learn to distinguish between mere business and family honor."

The phone rang again, and Amir swept it to his ear. "He's staying at the Manila Hotel," a voice reported. Amir glanced at Salmid. "I will see you next week, son." When the boy, obviously disappointed at being cut short, pulled the office door shut behind him, Amir gave instructions to the caller. This time, he would not give Chalmers the honor of a warrior, but only the swift fate of a sniper's bullet.

***

Salmid slipped his pinkie against the doorjamb to prevent the door from shutting all the way. His breath fluttered against the back of his throat, held captive until his father should continue his phone conversation. Or had he noticed Salmid's subterfuge, and at any moment the door would fly open?

His mind leaped to an excuse. He'd say he had forgotten something … had dropped his pencil and was returning to get it. He stopped as the gravelly voice of his father—the voice he used to underscore his authority with other men—seeped through the crack in the door. Salmid exhaled the flutter through his nose and put his ear to the door's slivered opening.

"Yes, at the hotel. Position yourself to strike under the canopy. It is massive and will make the angle awkward."

That was all Salmid needed to hear. He strode down the hall before his father could exit the office and spy him. The target's hotel was easy to identify.

The massive canopy meant it had to be the Manila Hotel in Rizal Park, popular with tourists from all over the world.

He had to get there early, make his move before the assassin. There was much to do in preparation. Who was the target, what did he look like, and how could Salmid best kill him to win his father's approval?

Chapter 15

Yazeed had come through! Salmid couldn't help but feel smug at how easily he had obtained the information about Jacob Chalmers from his cousin. The two exchanged favors all the time, and Yazeed, though the older of the two, looked up to Salmid because of the fire burning in Salmid's belly for *jihad*. He too, Yazeed said, dreamed of serving Allah in Afghanistan against the Russian invaders. He agreed to slip Salmid not only the victim's name but also the means to kill him.

Again, Salmid's breath fluttered against the back of his throat like a pesky Diamondback moth. He entered the Manila Hotel, made a show of peering at his wristwatch in case the desk clerk was watching, and selected a couch close to the entryway. The lobby took his breath away. Glittering black and white floor tile, laid in a pattern of huge diamonds, hosted island upon island of lush red carpets furnished with tables, chairs, and lamps under bright chandeliers. For a moment, he considered how such opulence could be his as an accountant for his brother. The deserts of Afghanistan meant a dry throat and a hard bed.

But his brother was dull as cassava root. Under his rule, there would be the same monotony Yazeed suffered working in the office under his father's thumb. Desk work—pah! At least managing the contact list of assassins supplied Yazeed with exciting stories to tell. But shuffling numbers around in ledgers? No, better to be a member of Osama Bin Laden's Afghan Arab fighters and take up arms with the Mujahideen.

A concierge brought him a newspaper and offered coffee. It was a test, Salmid was sure. He lowered his eyes to half-mast and raised his chin, mimicking his father's haughtiness on similar occasions. "Please." To timidly refuse, and especially to offer an explanation for his presence, would be an invitation to an escort out the door. He swallowed, grateful he had heeded Yazeed's advice to wear shoes and trousers with a pressed shirt. No one off the street dressed like that.

Neither, he saw, did the rich tourists exiting the shiny gold elevators in shorts and tees to saunter to the dining area for breakfast. Would Jacob Chalmers stop for breakfast too? Or order it sent to his room? Or sleep in after his long flight yesterday? Salmid squirmed on the hard leather of the couch. How long would he have to wait? Yazeed had shrugged when asked what Chalmers' plans for the day were.

And more and more, Salmid needed badly to pee.

***

Jake called the front desk for a taxi, snapped his suitcase shut, and ushered Dan-boy down the hall to the elevator. He remembered the eagerness with which he had awaited Detective Lee the day of his own release from prison six weeks ago. After two decades in Salonga, Puno would be tapping his sandaled foot, counting off the seconds until Jake arrived.

But first he needed to go to the airport to pick up a rental car. It wouldn't take long, and he'd grab something for Dan and him to eat. The boy needed a bit more taming before Jake exposed him to the fine art of eating in a restaurant where your cloth napkin was shaken out and placed in your lap.

At the front desk, not knowing if he'd be gone for a night or a week, he canceled his room. Suitcase in one hand, Dan in the other, he crossed the lobby to the front door. Already a taxi was waiting outside.

A smiling youth wearing trousers and a dress shirt held the heavy glass door open for Jake and several others exiting the hotel. Dan echoed Jake's thank-you and glanced up at Jake for approval. At the same time, the taxi driver opened the car door to the back seat for them. Before Jake could pull Dan out of the way, the door slammed against Dan and knocked him to the ground. The boy's wail echoed off the hotel canopy like a World War II air raid siren. Everybody froze.

"He's fine," Jake shouted, and everyone bumbled back to life, jostling shoulders as they resumed their destinations. Mumbling an apology, the taxi driver hastened to his seat behind the wheel, leaving Jake to dust off Dan and restore peace to the little guy's soul. "Let's go, fella, climb in." Jake bent to shove his suitcase into the car along with the boy.

The sharp crack of a fired rifle split the air, followed by the almost simultaneous splat of a bullet hitting flesh behind Jake. He flattened to a crouch. Twisted to glimpse behind him. Jumped into the car. "Drive," he yelled, jerking the door shut.

Outside on the sidewalk lay the youth who had held the hotel door open. A crimson bullet hole marked a tunnel through his forehead. Jake's breath barreled from his lungs in horror.

It took a minute for an object that had rolled onto the sidewalk between the youth and Jake to register in Jake's mind. A hypodermic needle. Plunger extended.

Jake's breath stilled. If he hadn't ducked, the bullet would have bored through *his* skull. And if the bullet had missed, the hypodermic needle wouldn't have.

Double jeopardy.

Thwarted.

The words of Psalm 139:5 flooded to mind. *You have hedged me in, behind and before.*

With a cry, he pulled Dan-boy to him and kissed the scraped boo-boo on his bony, little knee.

***

"Get ready," Roza hissed at the waiter. "I'll distract her." She slipped through the kitchen door into the Cuppa Chocolatte dining area and trudged to Eve's table like a tired middle-aged matron. She wore no makeup and her hair was the perfect touch of frowzy. If only Blue could watch her performance as she had watched his with Stella. But they had to work separately now.

"Good afternoon." She smiled as Eve looked up. "My name is Laina, and I'll be taking your order." She fished a pen and an order pad out of her pink-

and-white-striped apron pocket. "Can I begin with a cup of free cocoa?"

"Oh my, yes, your hot chocolate is delicious. My mother made cocoa for me every morning when I was a child. In fact"—Eve's eyes darted to the nametag pinned on Roza's uniform—"her name was Lana too, although spelled without an *i*."

"Yes, the *i* is unusual." Roza grinned. "I always have to spell my name." In back of Eve, the waiter approached with a cup on a small tray, and Roza's heartbeat quickened. "Has your mother been in the café with you?"

"She died when I was five."

"Ah, then the cocoa is even more special to you." The waiter tripped, and Roza gasped as the cup tipped off the tray and landed with a loud splat of liquid and crash of ceramic on the tile floor. Eve turned, wide-eyed.

"Sorry, ma'am." The waiter squatted to clean up the mess, while another waiter dashed over with a replacement cup of cocoa and set it on the table in front of Eve.

"My apologies," Roza said. "That must have startled you"—she fluttered her hand over her heart—"it certainly did me! I promise you we'll do better with your lunch order. May I show you what's new on today's menu?" She drew Eve's attention to the plastic-encased carte du jour and explained the offerings.

Unh, her bad leg was getting wobbly. A sour taste pinched her tongue, and she had to stop to swallow. It would help if she could lean on the table, shift her weight onto her good leg. When had she become so dependent on her cane?

She didn't dare glance at the squatting waiter to see if he was done. What if Henshaw arrived and caught the waiter with his hand in Eve's purse? That would be the end of using the Cuppa Chocolatte Café to take down Eriksson and Henshaw.

Eve sipped contentedly at her cocoa, in no apparent hurry to place her order. The rich, chocolate aroma cloyed Roza's sinuses. She was probably allergic to the nasty stuff, but the drink's sentiment for Eve had made it ideal for drawing her to the café. And, if Roza could help it, for keeping her coming back for more.

"What sounds good to you?" she asked. Loud enough for the waiter to take it as a signal.

"You know, I'm waiting for a friend." Eve glanced languidly at her wristwatch. "He should be here any minute, and then we can place our orders together."

The waiter's head bobbed up behind Eve's chair, and he rose to his feet and sauntered away. Roza suppressed a sigh of relief and stepped back from the table. She could put her weight on both legs now. She felt stronger, able to make it to the kitchen without limping. "Very well, I'll keep an eye out for him and see to it he gets his cocoa without a floor show." She smiled at her joke, knowing Blue would have laughed.

When she entered the kitchen, the waiter handed her a flattened lump of clay. "It took you long enough," she snarled. But the impression of Eve's house key in the clay was flawless. And, really, her performance had been too.

And Blue? She must call him and see how he was doing as a bum. And tell him she had Judge Eriksson's house key.

Chapter 16

"Not hi-im," Dan-boy grumped. "I don't like him."

"That makes me sad, because Puno likes you." Jake stopped the rental car at the prison apron, put it in park, and reached back to chuck Dan under the chin. The little guy had squeezed himself into a tight wad of arms and legs in a corner of the car's back seat. "I hope you'll change your mind and become good friends on this trip. But no matter how you feel, you must show respect to Puno. That means you talk nicely and be kind."

"I tol' you I thought his beard was pretend!" Fire burned in the chocolate eyes sandwiched between lowered brows and pouting lips.

Jake's right cheek twitched. How long before the kid's thumb-sucking withdrawal pains subsided into freedom? "Puno has been hit and kicked and beaten up all over his body, and you know what he told me he does?"

"Mmmph."

"He says, 'I wrap my hurts in God's love and let Him make me smile.'"

"That's stupid."

"Okay, buddy, but if Puno smiles at you when he gets in the car, you know he isn't mad at you."

"I don't care."

"Sure you do. That's why you're angry, because you want him to like you and you're afraid he doesn't."

Dan folded his arms across his chest and set his face in a glare toward the front seat's door.

Puno appeared at the open window. The late morning sun backlit his wisps of white hair like an angel's aura. Never had Jake seen so many teeth grinning from between his friend's parted lips.

"Behold a free man!" Puno announced. He opened the door and slid in, wedging a canvas bag of his possessions between his feet. "What could make me happier than to spend first day with best friend Jake and young best friend Yun Sun Dan?"

Jake peered into the rearview mirror at Dan. The scowl hadn't melted.

After Puno gave directions for the drive, Jake updated him on the morning's events. "I called Detective Lee when I got to the airport and told him what happened," he finished. "He said I didn't have to come in to the station, that I could catch up with him when I get back."

"You and Yun Sun Dan are safe where we are going."

Wherever that was.

Jake drove north on Route 8, then west on Route 3 to Olongapo, where they stopped on the harbor and ate steaming bowls of rice and vegetables topped with shrimp. Dan picked at his and avoided eye contact with Puno.

"Now north," Puno said at the car, "to Iba." In no time at all, the South China Sea lay on their left, its shoreline ragged with coves and inlets. They drove with the windows open to catch the roar of waves and the smell of brine. "That's what our island was like," Jake said to Dan. "You can look down there and pretend you were with Crystal and Eve and me." Sadness rolled over him like the white caps skating the ocean's surface. Why did they have to be apart again?

Dan popped to his knees and peered out the window. "I wanna go to your island, Dad. Can we, huh?"

Jake grinned at Dan's excitement. "Someday, son. Maybe when Crystal and Eve are with us."

Dan scooted across the seat to the other window and pointed. "Well, can we climb *them?*"

"Ah, Zambales Mountains." Puno said. "A long dragon's tail of volcanoes." He nodded solemnly as widened chocolate eyes turned to him. "In Iba are three waterfalls waiting for us to climb."

"Three?" Dan leaned on the back of the front seat. "We can climb all three?"

"All three," Puno affirmed.

Dan's hand stretched over the seat toward Puno's face. Jake held his breath as four fingers and a thumb plopped onto Puno's chin. "I'm sorry I pulled your beard." A pat gentle as a feather tapped the white hairs. "I promise I won't do it again."

"My beard thanks you." Puno waved the scraggly tip at Dan, and the boy giggled.

"So Iba is our destination?" Not exactly what Jake had expected.

"Destination for Dan and me," Puno answered. "Destination for you and me farther on."

***

The climb to three waterfalls followed by a dip in the ocean at Iba's wide expanse of beach left Dan sprawled on the car's back seat with sweet dreams and a sealed friendship. The corner of Jake's mouth twitched up at Puno's equally tired sprawl on the front seat as they drove north. "Quite an ambitious day for someone fresh out of prison."

The twinkle in Puno's eyes matched that of the stars beginning to poke through the soft veil of evening sky. "Beard and boy reconciled—worth it, though foolish for old bones and forgotten muscles."

"We could stop for the night and go on tomorrow."

"Picture worth a thousand words not far. Long-waited reward, Jake, next only to heaven."

A reward? Excitement stirred Jake's stomach, sent goose bumps to forest his arms. Puno had never asked anything for himself. Always his efforts, his prayers, his goals had been for others. And now he was talking about a long-awaited reward?

Jake's breath stopped short. He didn't mean going back home *to die*, did he? "Puno, are you okay? Your health …?"

Puno chuckled. "I'm not dying, Jake." He pointed ahead. "Turn inland up there, drive to the top of the hill, and stop."

Relief leveled Jake's goose bumps. He turned off the paved highway and bumped over sun-baked ruts hard as cement. In a matter of weeks, the monsoon season would arrive and the cement would become mud that sucked tires into slick graves. He needed to be sure to return the rental car before then.

The jarring woke Dan. He sat up and laughed as the car tossed him like a beanbag.

At the crest of the hill, Puno whispered *"Stop"* so softly Jake barely heard him. He pulled the car off the road and parked. The three of them stepped outside to the cacophony of insect chirps and the faint stirring of a breeze off the ocean.

Below them lay a flatland of pale green rice fields dotted with clusters of trees. Houses built on stilts poked up from some of the fields, while farther out against the backdrop of the Zambales Mountains a small village crowded the bank of a large stream. "Picture worth a thousand words," Puno murmured. "My home."

Warmth flooded Jake's heart. Puno's home. How good to get to see it, to see Puno's family welcome him back into their arms when the passing years had all but declared he would die at Salonga Prison. How good to know he would leave Puno with loved ones when he returned to the US to his own loved ones.

The warmth disintegrated, and with a pang he realized he wasn't ready to return.

Not yet. Not when the photograph of Eve and Ryker's intimacy, though destroyed, nonetheless burned images in Jake's mind. Not when Eve, almost without thinking, so easily granted Bradley Henshaw preeminence over Jake in her mind.

Not yet. Sadness curled icy fingers over his heart.

"New life here," Puno said in a loud voice. "New life for lost souls. What do you think, Jake? Does our work at Salonga Prison stop there? Or shall we build a center here, train men for missions in all of Asia?"

Jake blinked. *We* build? "You own land down there?"

"Yes. Only one wish on bucket list: convert earthly inheritance for one man to spiritual inheritance for many."

Puno's intent clicked in Jake's mind. "The money Betty left you as an inheritance—you want to use it to build a seminary here?" He didn't have to think twice about it. "Oh yeah, wouldn't she love that! And for sure I will help you, Puno. With Eve as busy as she is with the Romero trial, there's no need to hurry back."

No need to hurry. Time was his ally. Time … and a worthy distraction … would release the icy fingers squeezing his heart.

Chapter 17

Dan-boy hung his head out the car window and sniffed at the smell of dirt and green things growing. The road winding across the rice fields was barely wider than a path, and there were no streetlights like in town, only twinkling stars and a yellow slice of moon to show the twists and turns. Dad said they should've parked the car and walked, but it was too late cuz that had to be decided at the top of the hill, not on the way down. Anyways, it wasn't really that dark out, and climbing those waterfalls had been enough walking.

At the village, people crowded around the car and peered in the windows, all friendly-like. But when Puno got out and spoke to them, no one hugged him and told him they loved him and were glad to see him. "It's possible no one recognizes Puno," his dad said. He said it'd been a long time since Puno had gone away as Marcos' prisoner, and a day at Salonga aged a man like a thousand days at any other prison.

Salonga. That was the prison where his ex-daddy was gonna die cuz he killed all those people. Dan had to swallow away the pinch in his throat so he wouldn't think about it.

Finally, an old woman with at least a thousand wrinkles in her face hobbled close to Puno, so close she almost touched noses with him. "Puno? Is that you?"

"Perla?" Puno cried out and gathered her into his arms just like Dad had with him at Grandpa Romero's. Then Puno brought her to the car and they said hello and Puno said, "My mother's cousin. Only relative still alive from parents' generation." Dan guessed "generation" was another word for *fam'ly*.

Next thing, with Perla in the car, head poked out the window to see and give directions, they drove around the village and in between crowded homes to one that Puno laughed and said was only three minutes away had they walked. Dan had never seen such houses. All of them were made of sticks Puno said were bamboo. Some had metal roofs, and some had roofs made of big leaves Puno said were palm fronds.

"Did you forget where you live?" Dan asked.

Puno chuckled. "Family location always new. Typhoons raze houses, villagers raise new ones. Like playing Chinese checkers."

Dan laughed. He didn't know what typhoons and razing were, but he and Crystal had played Chinese checkers, and jumping bamboo houses around had to be grand fun.

They emerged from the car, and neighbors who had been clustered around cooking fires shifted to Perla's house. The odor of charred wood clung to their clothes. Dan pressed against Jake's leg and hid his face from so many eyes. He peeked out only when Perla introduced her family gathered around the cook fire. Her oldest son Zenon, his wife Isla, and five of their children. The youngest stuck out his tongue at Dan.

"*Mabuhay*, welcome." The daddy gave a quick hug to Puno, shook hands with Jake, and ignored Dan. Dan glared at him. He would've shook hands—that was what Dad wanted him to do, to be friendly and greet people. Anyways, Zenon wasn't friendly. He could tell cuz right away the corners of Zenon's mouth tipped down.

Perla shooed the onlookers to a distance, and Dan squished tight next to his dad on a seat at the cook fire while Puno and the family took their seats. Zenon's wife and two of the bigger girls brought out tea and rice cakes from the house, and Puno got his canvas bag from the car and took out a white paper sack of gumdrops to give to his hostess. "Gift for family important tradition," Puno had explained at their stop in Iba.

Dan did a hard blink when Zenon refused a share of the gumdrops. Wasn't that bad to not at least take some? What was wrong with him? Dan couldn't help staring. Why was Zenon crunching his brow so it sank down like the corners of his mouth? And why, every time Puno spoke, did Zenon's back stiffen as if Puno had punched him?

Zenon didn't like Puno, did he? Dan's stomach twisted into a knot. Well then, he didn't like Zenon! And not Zenon's stupid son, either, who kept making faces at Dan.

Puno stood and put down his empty teacup. "Moonlight sufficient for walk. I wish to see my land before I sleep."

Everyone stood, and Perla looked from Zenon to his wife. Neither moved. "Take my arm, Puno, and I will remind you of the way. Shorter to walk than to drive car."

The distance wasn't far, but Perla made it a slow journey of hobbling to get there. Dan and his dad followed behind them, and then Zenon's family and what seemed like half the village strung out in a parade. When Perla stopped and pointed at the land ahead of them, Puno waved at Zenon to come nearer. "Your mother says my fields have prospered under your care."

The screech of Zenon's voice exploded across the rice fields, and Dan's hair jumped like Chinese checkers. He grabbed his dad's hand. "*Your* fields?" Zenon shrieked. "Did my mother say she told me they were *mine*? That you had forfeited them in prison?"

Dan trembled from his tummy up to his chest as Zenon closed in on Puno with an angry face only too familiar to Dan. "Will you tend them now, old man? Will you sire children to plant the rice and to harvest the trees of their fruit? Will you laugh at my offspring as they stand by with empty hands?"

Zenon's fingers flew at Puno's head and halted claw-like an inch above his face. "You do not belong here, nor does anything here belong to you!"

With a bellow, Dan dropped Jake's hand and dashed at Zenon's son. Puno was his friend and no one should yell mean things at him! No one's dad should either! He plowed stiffened arms into the youngest son's chest. The boy fell back but kept his feet. With a shout, the son leaped forward and shoved Dan. Dan plopped fanny-first onto the ground, huffing a loud *Oof.* In a blink, he was up and swinging balled fists. A string of bad words used on him by his uncles roared from his mouth.

"Whoa there, son." His dad snatched him off his feet. He caged Dan's thrashing limbs in his arms and capped the hateful words with his hand over

Dan's mouth. "Stop now. Puno is okay." Zenon's son ran to his father.

Dan burst into tears. His dad removed his hand, and Dan buried his face on his dad's shoulder. The hand slid to his back and patted him with a slow, soothing rhythm that eased the rage from Dan's chest.

Puno spoke in a loud voice that carried his words across the fields like a ringing bell. "You are wrong, Zenon, to claim these fields as yours. They are my inheritance." He walked over to Jake and pointed north. "I ask advice of noble friend. Is rise of land good for mission compound?"

Jake's head moved against Dan's cheek in a nod. "It's perfect."

Puno returned to Zenon, and Dan squirmed to be set down. Again Puno's voice rang across the fields. "Indeed, I am old man, but I will sire spiritual children in compound I build. Rest of inheritance I bequeath to Zenon. In exchange, he and offspring will feed mine with fruit of their labors."

A murmur rose from the crowd that had followed them. His dad's big hand squeezed Dan's shoulder, and he understood something good had happened. Puno had shared more than a paper bag of gumdrops. He had shared what was his with his fam'ly.

Zenon hung his head and mumbled words to Puno that Dan couldn't hear. But this time when Zenon hugged Puno, it was with eyes that teared and a mouth that tipped up.

Dan glanced at the youngest son. Should he say he was sorry for shoving him and give him a hug?

The son looked at Dan and stuck out his tongue.

Dan returned the gesture. Uh-uh. What that boy needed was beating up.

PART 2

Chapter 18

Two Months Later

Eve shed her jacket and hung it with her purse across the back of her chair. The Cuppa Chocolatte Café was proving a hit with downtown Chicagoans, and she was having to come in earlier and earlier to secure a table for her and Brad. But she didn't mind. It allowed her to indulge in more than one cup of hot chocolate—a sweet comfort at the end of an increasingly chilly walk as September slipped into October. Even more so, it gave her time to chat with Laina. The waitress was becoming like a mother to her—a replacement for Stella, she supposed. But best of all, Laina was someone she could talk to about Jake.

Within seconds Laina approached her table, accompanied by a waiter bearing a mug of cocoa on a small tray. He set it in front of Eve, and she wrapped her cold fingers around it. The aroma rose to her nostrils, and she closed her eyes in anticipation of the sweetness on her tongue, the warmth on the back of her throat, the incredible peace that would spread outward from her stomach as she finally was able to let go of the morning's burdens.

"You look tired, sweetheart. Are you okay?" Laina plopped heavily into the chair across from her. She had given up hiding her limp from Eve as their friendship progressed.

Eve opened her eyes and sighed. "I got a letter from Jake yesterday."

Laina nodded. She was a good listener. Patient. Respectful about letting Eve draw the lines at what she was willing to share. The sensitivity gave Eve confidence to open the door to her heart wider than she might have otherwise.

"He says the mission compound is completed. It's bare bones, kept simple because that's how the church planters will be expected to live wherever they go."

Laina shook her head. "I live simple, but I suspect they live way simpler than I'd ever want."

Exactly. "Jake said he'd like us to consider it. Become resident faculty." She swallowed, her throat creaking as moisture suddenly deserted her tongue.

Laina blinked widened eyes. "So he's got a 'calling'—is that the right word?" She paused in a visible attempt to hide a negative reaction. "What about you, dearie?"

"I'm a federal judge," Eve blurted. *The Drug Czar of Chicago—wasn't that what God had called her to?* "We've got to live here, not ..." She choked. Not *simple.* "... not there."

As if rallying strength for the two of them, Laina sat up straight. "You've got plenty of time to consider this, honey. You and Jake, both." Her mouth pulled into a reassuring smile. "Now, tell me how that boy he took on is doing."

She always asked about Dan. Eve couldn't help a full-face, chin-to-brow tic of irritation. "Getting worse. Getting into fights." *Getting Jake's full attention while she languished back here.* "The scourge of the village."

Laina seldom commented on the boy. She probably thought Jake was brave and kind to want to adopt him. The dear woman didn't know who the Romeros were, that Dan was bad seed. That Eve could not, would not, accept him into her family.

"I'm sorry to hear that." Laina braced both hands on the table and pushed to her feet. "Now, I want you to sit back and let those worries go, enjoy your hot chocolate, and I'll be back for your and Brad's lunch orders." She smiled, but her eyes communicated a heart full of sympathy for Eve's plight.

Eve planted her elbows on the table and leaned in to massage her temples. The trial must be wearing her down. When she and Brad first met to strategize, she'd left the café with brain cells ramped up and energy to burn. She'd increased her workouts at Ace's Gym from four days a week to six. She'd taken work home and labored long into the wee hours of the night. She'd sung in unaccustomed gaiety on the way to work and again on the drive home.

But the headaches and fatigue weren't because of the excitement of the trial, were they? She took a swallow of her cocoa, savored the touch of bitterness on her tongue from the dark chocolate. No, the euphoria, the power surges, the on-the-bull's-eye alertness—it was all to bury the emptiness of Jake's absence. And now the months were beginning to stretch thin. The café, Laina, Brad, coming home to Crystal—without them, her days bore no comfort.

She looked up as Brad arrived, face sagged with tiredness, but unusual excitement enlivening laughter lines around his eyes and mouth. He chugged down his hot chocolate, ordered another, sat back, stretched out his legs, and grinned at Eve.

She couldn't help but giggle at this sober man turned comic. "Okay, drama man, enough of the suspense. Out with it!"

"Danny Romero is in jail."

She responded with a dropped jaw.

"Blue tipped us off that Danny was skipping town. We caught him in his private plane just before it took off with flight plans for South America."

Eve blew out a breath. "Hoo. Three witnesses from Blue and now this. Your bum is proving to be a pot of gold at the end of the rainbow." She handed Brad the lunch menu. "I still don't trust him. A Romero trial just doesn't proceed without bumps in the road and potholes the size of moon craters. Has Blue named his price yet?"

"Still insists his motive is revenge."

"And his three witnesses continue to prove reliable?"

"Good enough to prompt Danny to flee. Things keep up like this, the trial will be over in a matter of weeks." He winked—actually *winked!*—at her. "You'd better be thinking about moving your wedding date up and bringing your man home."

Eve's jaw dropped a second time. "Who are you? What have you done with my friend Brad Henshaw who insists my fiancé is a Romero thug?"

Brad threw back his head and laughed, exposing a mouthful of gold crowns. "I confess to uncharacteristic giddiness and good will as a result of today's arrest and the prospect of a long, *long*-awaited judgment pronounced on Danny Romero."

Brad's merriness was contagious. Jake's silly request to join him in the Philippines poofed into pea-sized nonsense next to the momentous prospect of *guilty* declared on Danny Romero. She raised her mug and clanked it against Brad's. "Here's to prison bars and wedding bands, the sooner the better."

Laina, appearing fully energized herself, gimped toward them, as big a smile as Eve had yet seen on her face, her companion of a waiter bearing two more cups of hot chocolate. "We'd better decide on lunch," she whispered to Brad, "or Laina will put us into a chocolate coma."

***

Ric Romero halted his car once he was inside the Romero compound and the gate had clicked shut. He rolled down his window and growled a question at the guard: "Anyone else here?" Specifically his mother, although he didn't ask. The radio announcement that his father had been arrested was not alarming. Happened all the time, and well-paid lawyers saw to it that he seldom suffered a night in jail. But that his father had been fleeing the country definitely set off alarm bells. Had his mother advised that? Was the trial actually that threatening?

"Mrs. Romero is here. Mr. Blue just arrived."

Mister Blue. Ric scowled, shut the window, and sped to the garage. He exited straight to the surveillance room. Unknown even to his supposedly techno-savvy brothers, he had installed cameras and mikes in every space in the compound—from closets to bathrooms to the guardhouse. Nothing would get beyond him that affected the Romeros. Or at least him.

He found his mother and Blue at a workbench in the storage shed. Side by side. Bent over a task. Hands gloved. He angled the two cameras until one caught the granules being pounded into powder. Nearby lay a bag of Mole-Kill. DANGER: CYANIDE was printed in inch-high letters. Quick as he could, he typed in the video "record" command.

Mother, what are you up to?

Chapter 19

Eve ground her teeth at all the hoops to jump through for a long-distance phone call to the Philippines. With Jake out of reach at that ridiculously primitive mission compound, Detective Lee was her only hope of contacting Jake. *If* she could ever get through to the detective.

The long telephone cord in the kitchen allowed her to pace. Thankfully, Crystal was at youth group—at least one bit of relief tonight to not have to hide information from the inquisitive teen. Eve's symptoms—the headaches, the fatigue, the increasing number of panic attacks—were getting harder to conceal.

She brushed her fingertip against the scar above her right eyebrow, left by Jojo's bullet three years ago aboard the yacht. She winced. Stupid to risk releasing fear again by touching it! But like an alcoholic falling off the wagon, she was compelled to continue once she started.

Sure enough, her body went rigid. Panic shot up as if she were a human canon and encapsulated her gut in a fifty-pound steel ball. Sweat broke from every pore in her body. Her vision blurred and she sank to the floor to keep from falling. *God, help me! I can't wait any longer.*

"Detective Lee."

The voice, familiar even over the distance, melted the cannon ball. "Lee," she gasped. "It's me, Eve. Eve Eriksson." She laughed—did she sound insane?—and corrected her name to the one he knew better. "Eva Gray."

"How are you, Eva?" His calmness soothed her. Called to mind his flirtatious wink from when he stood at guard at the wedding of Jake's daughter.

The question, a silly social convention, nevertheless broke her. She erupted into hiccupping sobs. "Not well. I … I need Jake to come home."

Lee's alarm crashed through her deluge of tears. "Hey, easy there, Eva, you're okay. I'll hunt him down for you. What do you want me to tell him?"

"I don't know. I have a doctor's appointment—" Fear resurrected the cannon ball so that all she could do was pant heaving breaths. She lowered herself to lie flat on the floor and clasp the phone receiver to her ear. *What was wrong with her? Please, God!*

"Where are you? Should you call someone for help?"

"No, I'm … I'm okay … just scared is all. I'm home." She closed her eyes and drew in a shuddering breath. "I need Jake …"

"I'll find him. Tell me what to say. Why a doctor? What symptoms? He will shoot me if I have no information."

She blurted a tiny laugh. Yes, Jake would want to know everything. "Headaches. My vision blurring. No appetite. Can't think straight." The list, so bluntly outlined, sent a second cannon ball crashing to her stomach. "Lee, I …"—she jerked in a breath—"I think I have a brain tumor. Where Jojo's bullet got me."

For a second, the phone went silent. Then Lee came on again. "Do *not* wait for Jake—do you hear me? Promise me you'll go to the doctor whether Jake is back or not. I will find him, and you know he will race home. Promise me."

Lee's insistence was as good as a hug. "I promise. Just … hurry." They hung up, and she imagined Lee rushing to his squad car, peeling rubber as he took off.

Slowly, her panic evaporated, her breathing normalized, and she got to her feet. The compulsion to touch her scar was gone. She felt fine. She could go to work now, go to the café and meet with Brad and Laina, go home and spend evenings with Crystal. No one would know her secret.

Only Jake, and he was coming home.

***

Ric whipped his face away from the surveillance monitor to his mother. "What'd you do to Eve, Mother!" Eve's panic attack in the kitchen all but disemboweled him. He shook, barely able to keep his hands from snapping his mother's scrawny neck. Even then it was only because she obviously hadn't used the cyanide poison on Eve, who would have fallen dead, foaming at the mouth, in minutes. What the cameras in the storage shed had shown him was a secret he wasn't about to let slip.

"Concerned about your lady love, are you?" His mother's tone of voice cut deep, burning familiar flames of humiliation in his cheeks. She swiveled her chair to face him. "Well now, lover boy. You'd best be concerned that the love of *her* life is returning home. From what we heard, we have no time to spare."

Dread of what she intended constricted his chest. "You can't kill her!" he spat out. "I won't let you."

His defiance took him by surprise. Surprised his mother too. Her face paled and she blinked in rapid-fire succession. With sudden clarity, he grasped that she no longer held him in her power.

His mother raised her chin and glared at him from beneath stiff eyelids. "Tonight our family will meet with Blue. I have plans in place, and you will comply."

Blue again. Was his father no longer in the picture? Perhaps Eve wasn't the only one being threatened …

"I'll be there," he said. Whether or not he'd comply was no longer within her control.

***

Danny Romero fingered the stick of gum slipped into his cell that morning, no doubt by a bribed guard or maybe the medical chump who'd checked on Danny's emphysema. Didn't matter. What mattered was he'd been at the Metropolitan Correctional Center three days and was only now hearing from his wife.

He palmed the gum in his left hand and rubbed his thumb over the paper in a circular pattern—to the right, anger that Roza had waited so long; to the left, relief that she'd finally contacted him. The vacillation was like plucking petals from a daisy—she loves me, she loves me not. Ever since he'd released

Chalmers and Dan-boy from the Romero compound, for sure the petals hadn't ended in "she loves me."

But now? Who would have expected those witnesses to show up at his trial—that they would have dared to brave the Romeros' wrath? His thumb stilled. Yes, that was it. Faced with Danny's prospect of life imprisonment, or worse, Roza had relented. She'd sent the gum—their usual signal that all was well or soon would be. Wherever the feds had hidden the three witnesses, they'd been found out. Blue would take care of them. Good old Blue.

The tightness in his chest loosened. The jail wouldn't let him have an inhaler—a dangerous weapon in his hands, they'd said, as if he'd clobber someone over the head with it—so he had to take every precaution to control his breathing. Stay calm. Not think about how he'd survive on 80% oxygen in prison.

He unwrapped the gum and was pleased to see it was his favorite, Black Jack. The sweet aroma of licorice spiked saliva over his tongue. It was Dan-boy's favorite too. His chest jerked in a spasm of grief at the thought of the boy, so that he had to close his eyes and inhale slowly again. Oh how he mourned the departure of that boy. The only innocent thing in his life.

He separated the gum from the wrapper and held the wrapper in front of his mouth in his left hand, the stick of gum inches away in his right hand. He'd taught the boy this ceremony, special between the two of them. By it, Dan-boy would remember his grandpa with love all his life.

Danny exhaled a deep sigh, flicked his tongue over the crystals of powdered sugar on the wrapper, and popped the gum into his mouth. He got in one burning chew before he went motionless.

The wrapper fluttered like a paper daisy petal to the floor.

Danny, foaming at the mouth, preceded it with a thud.

***

Roza dabbed at her eyes with a daintily laced white handkerchief. Its perfume wafted from where she sat in her Queen Anne wingback to her three sons and Blue seated nearby. Ric resisted the temptation to fan his face as the fumes saturated the living room. No sense irritating her before she shared her plan, once this farce of grieving for his father was over.

The news of Pops' death had put him in a tailspin. He should have guessed his father was the target of the cyanide powder in the storage shed. Should have immediately confronted his mother about its use. Now he'd have to wait, have to maintain his secret to use down the road against her.

"They put your father in jail specifically to kill him," his mother said in a tremulous voice. "They took away his inhaler, withheld medical treatment, and finally just poisoned him." As if pulling herself together, she inhaled theatrically through her nose. "Bradley Henshaw and Eve Eriksson must pay."

The threat against Eve made Ric want to jump on his mother *now*, this very minute. Throttle her. Tell his brothers what she and Blue had done to Pops. But Eve's safety held him back. He needed to discover his mother's plan first, even participate in it, if necessary, in order to foil her.

The insult of Blue's inclusion tonight in their family circle had the blood vessels in Ric's temples throbbing. He had arrived in the living room to find Blue seated in the Brentwood accent chair that Ric had always claimed as his. Before Ric could eject the intruder, his mother pointed Ric to the line-up with his brothers on the couch. He felt his face purple as he caught the message in his mother's seating arrangement.

The visual of Blue's greasy hair, yellow teeth, and filthy fingernails required Ric to stare at the carpet and grit his teeth in order to get through the meeting. The animal shouldn't be allowed in the house, much less in Ric's chair. For sure, Ric would see him dead before he let his mother install Blue as his father's replacement.

"Henshaw will pay with his life. But out of respect for lover-boy here"— his mother's smirk raked coals over Ric's cheeks—"we will let Eve live." She paused in obvious satisfaction as Ric's eyes leaped in surprise to hers. "We will let her live, but in hell. A slow, progressive death that will rob her of health, career, and Jake's love."

Ric's protest died at the last two words.

Chapter 20

Eve snugged the collar of her coat higher onto her neck with one hand, snugged her stocking cap over her ears with the other hand. The wind bit with icy fangs through both garments. She should have taken a taxi in spite of the short distance from the office parking lot to Cuppa. At least she wasn't wearing heels. Still, she was staggering. Because of the wind? Or was another panic attack coming on?

Jake, it's getting worse. Where are you?

She stumbled into the side of a car parked at the front of the café. A black limousine. She jumped back, the hairs at the nape of her neck prickling. *Romeros!* She never encountered the model without her archenemy leaping to mind.

A scan of the dark interior found no one inside. Jaws clenched, senses on high alert, she entered the café and closed the door against the cold but kept a grip on the doorknob. A few early-morning customers were scattered at tables, mostly alone, one couple chatting at a nearby booth. Was it her imagination that the waiters looked surprised at her entry? She'd never come this early before, so maybe that was it. Or had she caught something shifty going on?

The rich smell of chocolate, espresso, and bacon seeped into her thawing nostrils. She was still clutching her collar. She lowered her hand, saw it was trembling. No, shivering—adjusting from the freezing cold outside to the comfort of the café's warmth, that was all.

"Well, good morning!" Laina, awkwardly attempting to tie on a pink and white striped apron, limped toward her from the kitchen. "Taking the morning off?"

Eve's caution dissipated with Laina's greeting. She released her grip on the doorknob, tugged off her stocking cap, and followed her friend to the table where she and Brad usually sat. "I dropped Crystal off at school and decided I couldn't wait till lunch to tell you my news."

"It must be a doozy." Laina waggled her eyebrows, pulled out a chair for Eve, and dropped into the one opposite her. "The way your eyes are dancing, I suspect it's about that boyfriend of yours."

"It is! He called, and he's on his way here from the Philippines."

They paused while a waiter placed a cup of cocoa in front of Eve, and Laina ordered one for herself—to celebrate, she said. "Now tell me all about it, beginning with when he's due in. Today?"

"I wish. He didn't have a reservation, so he's having to travel standby. Today is possible, but tomorrow is more likely." She kicked herself mentally. If she'd gone into the office before coming here, she might have found a message from him. "Crystal and I are playing hooky tomorrow in hopes we'll get to pick him up from the airport."

"Standby—sounds urgent. Is everything okay?"

"I ..." Did she really want to discuss her symptoms, make them a topic of conversation? She cleared her throat. Seemed way too intimate, a line she wasn't ready to cross. "I have a doctor's appointment I want him to go to with me." She'd let it rest at that.

Laina's eyes widened. "You and Jake are going to have a—? Are congratulations in order?"

Eve almost spewed her cocoa over the tabletop. "No! Goodness no!" She laughed. "That's an event for the future, for sure."

"I'm sorry, honey, I don't mean to pry. I tell you what ... I want you to try our new specialty and tell me what you think." Laina signaled a waiter over to their table. "A Cinnamon Cocoa for the judge here," she said. She patted Eve's hand. "I have things to finish up in the kitchen, then I'll bring my cocoa and be back to get your opinion."

Eve shrugged out of her coat, sipped her drink, and studied the other customers. Did one of them belong to the limousine? No reason, really, to suspect the vehicle was Romero-owned. She supposed she could go outside and copy the license plate number for Brad to check out, but she felt too mellow now to stir. In fact, maybe she'd just lounge here till lunch, take the morning off. In case Jake did arrive today, she'd told him to come to the café if she wasn't at home or in the office. It would be fun to have Laina finally meet him.

A waiter brought her the specialty cocoa. The chocolate was darker than usual, sprinkled with a light brown dust, a dollop of whipped cream on top. She sniffed at the spice. Cinnamon, all right. The whipped cream melted into the chocolate, shoving the cinnamon into a thin donut circling the rim of the cup. She took a taste. Not bad. Not bad at all.

By the time she finished the cup, she felt a bit giddy. She chuckled, then had to outright laugh at Laina's guess that she and Jake might be expecting. Wouldn't that take the cake! Well, they were getting up in years—what, she had just turned thirty-eight, and Jake was forty-six—so they did need to get going on starting a family. At one point she had thought it was too late, that she'd gone into early menopause, but two weeks ago Mother Nature had put that concern to rest.

"How do you like it?" Laina, her own Cinnamon Cocoa in hand, plopped down into the other chair at the table.

"I wike it. *Like* it," Eve corrected herself. She giggled. Her tongue felt doubled in size.

"The owners want to start featuring a new specialty every month. I'm suggesting pumpkin-flavored whipped cream for November." Laina stared at Eve. "Are you feeling okay? You've lost all color in your face."

Eve blinked. How did Laina get two heads? "I muh bit woozy …"

"Here, honey, put your head down."

Laina moved Eve's empty cocoa mug aside, and Eve put her arms on the table and rested her head on them. *Whaz happening?* She had the muscle strength of a rag doll.

Laina's voice faded in and out. "You should go home, darling. I wish I could take you, but here's an old friend of yours, he'll see to you."

Eve raised her head, squinted to focus her eyes. A man with dark, slicked-back hair emerged from the kitchen and hurried to her side. She shivered as a whiff of aftershave identified him before she even made out his face. "Rock," she mumbled. Or was it Ric? Her mind convoluted in on itself. "Why'd choo leave me?"

"I'm here now, sweetheart. I'll take care of you. You want that, don't you?"

Did she? She peered at her arms to see who was holding her down. No one? Really? Exhaustion squeezed the pulp out of her. The cannon ball was back, but in her head now, squashing her brain.

"Can't. Stand. Helbme."

***

So Eve was remembering him as Rock Giannopoulus. Ric grinned at his mother. This was better than he'd hoped for. Eve had all but fallen in love with him when he'd posed as Rock six months ago. He'd even asked her to marry him—and she would've if only she hadn't discovered he was a Romero.

She was fading fast, slumping onto the table, speech slurring—people would notice. He grabbed her coat and stuffed her arms into its sleeves, wrapped his right arm around her waist and pulled her upright against him. Her head rolled against his shoulder, and he inhaled the fragrance of her shampoo. He groaned, thought of how every night he watched her from the surveillance room. Now here he was holding her, smelling her, practically tasting the chocolate on her breath.

His mother jammed the stocking cap onto Eve's head. "Go," she hissed. "We can't miss this opportunity. I called Blue and he's on his way."

Eyes stared at him as he hauled his beautiful captive out the door. He should have thought to hide his identity somehow, but who'd have thought Eve would sack out like this? How heavily had his mother drugged her, anyway?

The cold outside slapped him like a full-body ice pack. Behind him, his mother slammed the door, her voice cut short in a cheerful explanation. "Big time on the town last night, folks. She'll be okay—"

He opened the limousine's passenger door and tipped Eve in on her side.

His hands trembled opening the driver's door. He got into the front seat and drove slowly to give Blue time to get to Eve's house. All the man had to do was open the front gate and unlock the house without setting off alarms. No marshals anymore for Blue to take out, and the girl was at school. Lucky for her. He knew what Blue liked to do to kids.

Morning traffic on South Hyde Park Boulevard was lively. Cars and buses hurled down the street, and clusters of pedestrians huddled at street corners for traffic lights to change. A crowded bus stop stood only yards away from Eve's house. Stomach acid surged to his throat as curious eyes followed him— a limousine with a big shot inside slowing down right where they could peer inside.

Blue opened the gate to Eve's yard and rapped on Ric's window. "Side door's unlocked, alarms off," he said. Before Ric could get out, Blue had the passenger door open, eyes fastened on Eve.

Ric leaped out and shoved Blue hard enough he fell to his knees. "Don't you touch her," he snarled. "Get out of here, and don't forget to change the license plate." He gathered a limp Eve into his arms and carried her inside the house. He knew from the surveillance cameras where every room in the house was. He paused to electronically close the front gate after Blue screeched off, then headed for the stairs.

His brothers had hidden the master bedroom's camera next to a hinge on the closet door. Clever. Not the vent or the overhead light where anyone would look. Ric knew exactly where to lay Eve so she'd be out of sight. His mother wouldn't be watching this minute because she still needed to tend to Brad Henshaw, but she'd be all eyes for the recording once she got home. As would his brothers. And—but not if Ric could help it—Blue.

He propped Eve on the bed and removed her coat and stocking cap, took her nightgown from beneath her pillow, and dropped the three garments to the floor. From his own coat he removed a small package and unwrapped it, placed it at the foot of the bed. Then, smiling at the camera, he slid Eve onto the floor behind the bed and ducked out of sight with her.

He'd waited forever for this, and he wasn't about to share it.

Chapter 21

Jake handed the cab driver a hefty tip. "Wait five minutes and let me see if she's here." He hoisted Dan-boy from the back seat into his arms and carried him six shivering steps to the Cuppa Chocolatte's door. Neither of them was prepared for a wind that stalked Chicago's streets with arctic claws. Summer trousers and light-weight jackets packed for the Philippines offered little defense. Man, was he ever ready for a cup of hot chocolate!

And Eve.

Anticipation floated bubbles of happiness to his throat. The news that Eve might be ill had flung aside any doubts about marrying her. Her past with Scott was just that—the past. History done and over with. From this point on, he wouldn't let anything come between them and their future together.

He set Dan down inside the café and scanned the restaurant for Eve. The boy clung to Jake's leg, pressing the cold fabric of Jake's trousers against skin already raised in goose bumps. Customers turned to gaze at Dan, and he hid his face. The boy's mop of curls never failed to win smiles.

Eve was nowhere in sight. Jake's shoulders sagged. But there, in the alcove, wasn't that Bradley Henshaw? Probably here to meet Eve for coffee. Or hot chocolate. Jake suppressed a scowl, took Dan's hand, and trudged reluctantly toward Henshaw's table.

A waitress in a pink-and-white-striped apron, her back to Jake, was talking in a low voice to Henshaw. Dan-boy stopped, hauled in a squeaky breath, and crashed backward into Jake. The boy's terror blared alarm sirens across Jake's nerves.

Henshaw caught sight of them and rose from his chair. "Chalmers," he said. Blankly, as if reciting names from a telephone directory.

The waitress whirled around, and Jake blinked. No wonder Dan had gasped in half the room's air. He had recognized his grandmother's voice. Or, step-grandmother ...

"Mrs. Romero." Jake's mind knotted at trying to merge the elegant woman eating lobster and steak in the Romero compound with the frowzy woman wearing a stained apron and holding an order pad in the Cuppa café.

But the eyes were the same. Eyes that bore the soul of a viper.

She bolted for the kitchen and disappeared.

Jake's breath exploded out of him. *She doesn't want to be recognized! What was she up to?* "Where's Eve?" he shouted at Henshaw.

The district attorney dropped heavily into his chair. "Y'said Miz Rumero." He chuckled. "Y'mean Laina. She said Eve'z sick. Said 'er son took Eve home."

Her son? Dread screwed hot bolts into Jake's stomach. "Did he have black hair, combed straight back?"

Henshaw's head wobbled.

"Yes," a woman in a booth called out. "He practically dragged her outside to a black limousine."

Jake snatched up Dan and ran for the door.

***

There was no limousine parked at Eve's house. Had a chauffeur dropped them off? Or had Ric Romero driven Eve somewhere else?

Jake shoved a twenty at the cab driver, whisked Dan-boy out, and hoisted the kid over the locked gate. "Hey," a man at the bus stop yelled.

"Call the police," Jake yelled back. He scaled the fence. If Eve wasn't here, law enforcement needed to be alerted.

The side door was unlocked. Jake's nerves sparked electricity across every synapse in his body. He signaled a shush to Dan and pointed at the door. "Ric Romero's inside," he whispered. He could all but see Dan's hair stand on end. "Go hide around the corner of the house."

Dan's chin quivered, but he crept away. Jake huffed a sigh of relief. He opened the door. Listened. At a noise from upstairs, he decided against checking out the living room and kitchen. Eve's bedroom was at the top of the stairs. Heart thundering, he dashed up the steps three at a time.

He stopped in horror at the sight of Ric. Eve lay in bed slack-jawed, eyes half open and rolled back into her head. Next to her stood Ric with a hypodermic syringe inches above her left arm. The memory of the teenage boy attacking Jake with a similar needle in the Philippines flashed into Jake's mind.

In the same split second, Ric spotted Jake and rushed to confront him.

Jake's training as a wrestler in college and the Marine Corps took over. He picked up the chair scooted under Eve's vanity and hefted it as a weapon, legs pointed out. Ric grabbed one of the legs and shoved it in a hard jolt against Jake.

But instead of resisting, Jake yielded and pulled Ric toward him. A look of surprise flicked over Ric's face. Caught off balance, he crashed chest-first onto the chair legs. At the same time, Jake rolled onto his back, slammed both feet into Ric's belly, and launched him through the air. Ric smacked in a hard landing against the wall and fell face down to the floor.

Jake sprang up to finish the job, but halted when Ric got to his feet, the syringe protruding from his abdomen. Jake winced. There was something about a needle buried deep in a person's gut that brought your breath to a standstill.

Ric stared at the syringe, fear casting a pall over his face. He pulled the needle out. Whatever it had contained, it had been fully deposited into his body.

Their eyes made contact. "I didn't inject her," Ric said hoarsely. "I just needed to make it look that way for my mother." He glanced at the closet, and Jake followed his line of sight. A hidden camera?

"Jake," Eve moaned. She rolled over and thumped to the floor.

Jake ran to her side, and Ric took off. Torn between lifting Eve back to bed or pursuing her assailant, Jake thought of Dan hiding outside. Ric's footsteps clattered down the stairs. The front door opened.

There was no choice. Jake sprinted after Ric. He arrived at the front door to see Ric race across the back yard, away from where Dan had hidden.

"Dan," he yelled. To his surprise, the boy crawled out from behind the living room couch. "What—what are you doing there?"

"It was cold, and I was s-scared for you." Teeth and body shook in confirmation.

"Here now, we're just fine." Jake swooped Dan into his arms and carried him upstairs. "But Eve fell, and she needs our help."

Dan raised his head from its snuggle on Jake's shoulder. "I saw Unca Ric run away. Did he hurt Eve?"

Jake gritted his teeth. "I'm wondering that too."

Chapter 22

Brad Henshaw had said Ric took Eve home from the café. Feeling as if he'd been poisoned, Jake lifted Eve from the bedroom floor to her bed and let Dan tuck her in. Question was, what kind of lead-time did Ric have before Jake arrived?

He stooped and picked up Eve's clothing. Coat, scarf, stocking cap. Socks, boots. Slacks and a sweater. Underwear.

Who had undressed her? Who had put on her nightgown? And what had happened in between?

"Jake." Eve peered at him with glazed eyes. "You're—home."

"I came as soon as I could." *But not soon enough.* His stomach clenched.

Dan squirmed his way in to stand between them. "Unca Ric was here and—"

Jake slid a swift shush-finger over the boy's mouth. "What happened, Eve?"

Her eyes, as if suddenly mechanized, swiveled from side to side, then slammed shut. The color drained from her face, and the same pallor that had accosted Ric floated into her skin like a visiting ghost.

Jake gasped and snatched up her wrist. Her pulse beat erratically under his fingertips. His throat constricted, and he felt his own heartbeat mimic hers. "Call 9-1-1," he shouted.

Dan looked up at him saucer-eyed.

"The telephone! Dial 9-1-1! You don't know how to do that?"

Dan's chin plummeted to his chest, accompanied by a quivering lower lip.

"Ahh, son!"

Jake plunged out of the room. A telephone was in Eve's office upstairs, another was downstairs on the kitchen wall. He raced down the hallway to Eve's office. Locked. All right then, downstairs.

Dan emerged from Eve's bedroom, tears dribbling from cheeks, nose, and chin. Jake pushed him aside and scrambled down the stairs. Before he could pick up the telephone receiver, a wail pierced his ears.

A double wail.

One from outside the house, one from inside.

He opened the front door as two screaming police cars skidded the sharp corner from South Hyde Park Boulevard into Eve's driveway. He hit the electronic lock to open the front gate and rushed to meet them. "Call an ambulance! It's Judge Eriksson!" He directed two of them upstairs to Eve and a third to the back alley where Ric Romero had vanished.

Inside the house, the second wail increased in volume and pitch. Jake dashed upstairs.

The second policeman blocked the doorway to Eve's bedroom. "There's a kid here says you pushed him."

Jake's stomach sank to his toes. "Dan," he called to the mop of curls crouched in a corner of the room. "I'm sorry. I had to get to a phone to save Eve, and I didn't want to run you over."

"I don't know 9-1-1," Dan shrieked. "And I didn't know about Puno's beard!"

Jake smiled weakly at the policeman. He didn't suppose it would do much good to explain the push wasn't a punishment for not knowing 9-1-1, much less about Puno's beard. He peeked around the policeman at Dan. "How about if I show you 9-1-1 now? We can practice on the kitchen phone and then go outside and look at the red and blue lights flashing on the police cars."

The policeman folded his arms across his chest and glared at Jake. "You are not calling 9-1-1."

Jake eyed the handcuffs on the policeman's belt. Dan had no idea he was setting himself up for a social worker if Jake was put in jail. And Crystal too, with Eve unable to look after her. "I'll hold the cradle down," he whispered.

"But this is the best way to calm him."

"Okay, Daddy." Dan, a cheery smile on his tear-stained face, squeezed by the policeman's legs and took Jake's hand.

Relief at a crisis averted—one of them, anyway—rolled over Jake. He craned his neck to look into the bedroom. "First, son, let's ask about Judge Eriksson. Is an ambulance on its way?" This was the love of his life. His heartbeat pounded as if ricocheting in an echo chamber between his ears.

The policeman looked irritated, but nodded. "While we wait, I have questions about this Ric your son told us about." He pulled a small notebook and a pen off his belt.

Dan tugged on Jake's hand. "You sa-id …"

"I did." Jake quirked his head at the human dam in the doorway to follow them, and walked Dan down the stairs and into the kitchen. The policeman's boots on the stairs thudded heavily behind him.

"Here you go, buddy." Jake stood Dan on a chair next to the wall phone and gave the boy the receiver, but kept the cradle depressed under the policeman's watchful eye. "9-1-1, attaboy."

The three of them jumped when the phone rang. Without thinking, Jake released the cradle. "Hello?" His eyes grew wide. "No, she didn't!" he barked. "Call them back and tell them not to let her go with him. I'm sending the police."

He smashed the receiver onto the phone base. "Let's go," he yelled. "That was Judge Eriksson's secretary, and she said a man claiming to be a cop was at Crystal's school to pick her up!"

***

Like, really? Crystal slammed her school locker shut. The bang reverberated off the vinyl flooring and row of metal lockers lining the empty hallway. Like, her mom was sick enough to send for her, and she had to get her books before she could leave? She took off at a run for the principal's office, clutching five books to her chest. Her nerves jittered like the tail of a rattlesnake, and she wanted to throw up. Something had to be desperately wrong for her mom to call her home.

She halted at the sight of the man waiting for her outside the principal's office. The hair on her arms pricked erect and a shiver scraped ice cubes down her spine. Had the school secretary called to confirm his story about picking her up? He didn't look like a cop. His graying hair lay in greasy furrows, probably combed with his fingers—fingers, she saw when summoned into the principal's office, that had dirt caked under the nails. His teeth were caked too, white guck sealing the spaces between yellowed teeth. And his eyes … she swallowed. His eyes ate her up. Her stomach contents lurched to her throat, and she took a step backward in the hallway.

He gestured for her to join him. "Don't be scared, honey. I'm under cover, and I know I look awful, but I was right by the school when the request came through, and it sounded so urgent I volunteered."

She didn't move.

He bared his teeth in a frighteningly friendly smile. "I don't know Judge Eriksson, but I know Brad Henshaw, talk to him almost every day, if that helps."

She clasped her books tighter.

"You can wait for someone else if you want, but sounds like things are bad enough you're gonna want to hurry."

Her heart thudded against her books.

"All right." The man shrugged. Pivoted. Headed for the front door.

She snuffed in tiny spasms of air. Moved one foot forward. Then the other. "Wait!" She ran after him.

He didn't wait. He broke into a trot, pushed through one of the two front doors, and disappeared.

She followed him outside to snow muddied on the front steps by student boots. Her skin prickled at the chilled air. She'd forgotten to get her jacket.

The man stood at the curb beside a black limousine. He opened the passenger door and hollered to her. "Hurry up if you're coming."

She hurried.

He slammed the car door behind her before she'd barely climbed in. She watched him dash around the hood and jump into the driver's seat. The limousine growled to life.

And then she heard it.

Click.

The noise that said she'd made a mistake. That said she was right, he was no cop.

The metal locks on the doors submerged out of sight.

Her books tumbled from her grasp, and she threw up.

Chapter 23

Run! Get out, get out, get out!

The words pounded in Crystal's head. She gulped in quivering shards of air. The driver opened the partition above the front seat and hungry eyes gazed at her in the rearview mirror. She shrank back in her seat and whimpered.

Get out!

She lunged at the door handle next to her. Beat on the window. Scooted across the seat to the door behind the driver and tried it. He laughed, and she burst into tears.

Get out!

The stench of vomit covering the schoolbooks at her feet assaulted her nostrils. She gagged, bit teeth and lips shut.

Get out! Get out! Get out!

Barely thinking, simply obeying, she seized the heaviest book. Tensed her muscles. Twisted head and torso to the right. Swung the book up to her left. Whacked the driver on the side of his head with all her might.

He yelped.

Next second, his right arm reached back, his face turned to her in rage. She grabbed his arm, braced her feet against the front seat, and pulled hard. She was barely aware of his fingers clamping onto her shoulder as she sank her teeth into his flesh and dug in.

The car swerved to the right, to the left. She hung on, teeth and hands locked onto his arm in spite of the pain of iron fingers crushing her shoulder.

A sharp jolt followed by a loud crunch of metal loosened her hold and threw her against the window. Through the front windshield, she saw the hood of the car spouting steam against a lamp post.

Click. Her heart leaped as the driver unlocked his door and fled.

The wail of a distant siren floated dreamlike to her ears. She watched her abductor disappear behind a building. Tested her own car door. Stayed inside when it opened. What had moments before been her prison was now her refuge.

She leaned out and spat the taste of vomit and blood textured with short, black hairs onto the pavement. A police car pulled up, red and blue lights twitching, siren reduced to a throb.

Run! Get out! A policeman emerged, then Jake. A sob throttled her throat. She got out and ran into his arms.

***

In the back seat of the police car, Jake hugged Crystal to his chest with both arms, head and heart dizzy with relief. On Crystal's other side, Dan cuddled up to her. She shook violently, her teeth chattered, her lungs released air in gasps.

She tried to talk, but Jake shushed her. Dan pulled Jake's arms away and crawled onto her lap to press tummy and head against her front. He slipped toothpick slender arms around her neck and patted a soft drumbeat on her shoulders. Jake's chest jerked recalling Emilio's photo of Dan covered in bruises, crouched in terror, face streaked with tears. The little guy knew exactly how she felt. Jake resumed his hold, this time around both kids, and Crystal and Dan sighed together.

Crystal's tremors slowed until at last her breathing leveled. An ambulance going the other direction passed them, and she twisted to watch it. "Mom! What about Mom?"

"She's okay," Jake said. "I hope to get you home before they take her to the hospital."

"Hospital? What happened?" Crystal's voice shook, and she struggled to free herself of her comforters.

Reluctantly, Jake withdrew his arms. "We think she was drugged. The doctors will test her and make sure she's okay."

"Mom on drugs?" Crystal's forehead knotted in bewilderment.

Dan hopped up, planted his feet on either side of Crystal's lap, his palms on her cheekbones, and his nose and eyes an inch above hers. "She was out cold, but it's okay, I think she was just sleeping."

Jake groaned inwardly and pulled Dan onto his lap. "She—"

"Unca Ric did it," little motor mouth said. "I saw him. 'Cept he's not my uncle anymore. But I saw him. I was hiding behind the couch and I saw him run away."

"Who is Unca Ric? And why'd he run away? And why were you hiding?" Crystal's voice rose in pitch with each question.

"Okay, let me explain," Jake put a shush-finger on Dan's lips. "Ric Romero. You knew him as Rock Giannopoulus." He paused at Crystal's gasp. "I stopped at the Cuppa Chocolatte Café to look for Eve and was told he had taken her home, apparently heavily drugged. So I rushed to your house, and told Dan to hide while I searched for them.

"They were ... upstairs ... and Ric fled before I could stop him." Jake halted as the bedroom scene flicked into his mind. "When the police came, Dan here"—Jake patted the boy's head—"confirmed Ric's identity and saved me from a trip to jail. Then Eve's secretary called about someone picking you up from school. The police let us join them in coming after you."

"What ... what were they doing? Mom and Ric?"

Jake couldn't help the grimace. "Your mom was in bed unconscious, and Ric was next to her, holding a hypodermic syringe." Crystal paled, and Jake grasped her hand and squeezed it. "I don't think he injected her, but that, and being drugged, and ... any other harm that happened, said she needed to go to the hospital."

An ambulance pulled out of Eve's driveway just as they arrived. "That's Judge Eriksson," Jake said. "Can we follow it?" The policeman grunted assent, and once again Jake enfolded Crystal and Dan in his arms.

***

Eve opened her eyes. Her head thudded with hammer blows. Skewers impaled her eyeballs. The inside of a chimney coated her tongue. She moaned as lungs and stomach joined the parade with their own pain.

"Judge Eriksson, can you hear me?"

A man in a white lab coat stood perpendicular to her, and she realized she was lying down. In a hospital bed. Ohhh, right where she belonged. She inhaled a stinging breath that squeezed her insides like the coil of a python. She exhaled a grunt in response to the man's question. "Yes."

"Do you remember what happened to you?"

A prick of alarm weaseled through her pain. Mushroomed. Swallowed her head. Shadows groped blindly in the furniture of her brain.

No.

She didn't remember.

Panic surged hot from her belly to her throat. "What happened? Tell me!" She grabbed the man's sleeve.

"I'm Dr. Cassidy," he said. "An ambulance brought you in with an overdose of Gamma-hydroxybutyric acid, a hypnotic depressant better known as GHB."

"GHB." A light went on, and she swallowed. "The date-rape drug." Her heartbeat pulsed in her ears. Her memory might be blank, but the implication was clear.

"You were suffering from respiratory depression, so we had to put you on a ventilator. You've been in a coma."

"How ... how long?" The shadows groping in her brain minutes ago began to take on flesh. Take on faces. Laina ... Ric ... Jake ...

Jake?

"Today is the third day. The effects of the GHB were compounded by the amount of amphetamine in your system. How long have you been addicted?"

"Addicted?" The word stunned her. "Amphetamine?" Her mind reeled. "I don't take street drugs. I don't take *any* drugs."

The doctor's lips flattened into a straight line. "I see." He fixed his gaze on her white-knuckled clutch of his sleeve. "If you don't mind, I need to continue my rounds. There's someone here wanting a private audience with you."

"Oh. I'm sorry." Heat flushed her cheeks, and she released his lab coat. He made a swift exit. Too late, she realized she hadn't asked him about whether Ric had taken advantage of the GHB.

Judge Martin, an ancient crony, and Andrew Perez, a colleague from the DA's office serving as Brad Henshaw's assistant, trudged with sober faces into the room. They shut the door.

This did not bode well. Whatever they had to say, she didn't like the disadvantage of being flat on her back to face them. "Please, would you mind raising the head of my bed so I can sit up?" Perez obliged, and she felt in better control—if not of her pain, if not of the accusation of drug addiction, if not of the threat from the GHB—of at least her ability to handle her visitors' mission.

The two men positioned themselves at the end of her hospital bed. Judge Martin spoke, his voice gravelly. "Judge Eriksson, you are a witness to the murder of Federal District Attorney Bradley Henshaw, and for your safety, we have entered you into the Federal Witness Security Program."

Chapter 24

Eve stared at the two men looming like thunderheads at the end of her bed. Whatever they'd said, a giant eraser had obliterated it. For a horrible moment, she thought she was dead. She heard nothing. Felt nothing. Comprehended nothing. She was just there … staring.

And then the sound came on. The pain cannibalizing her body tuned in. Comprehension clicked.

Bradley Henshaw was dead.

Murdered.

She struggled to sit all the way up. "When?" she blurted. "How?"

"Same day and way the Romeros went after you—a drug overdose three days ago," Perez said.

"They used GHB on Brad?" Wait! A light snapped on in her mind. Did Perez say it was the Romeros who had drugged her?

"Not GHB," Martin said. "Amphetamine. Appears the Romeros used your afternoon consultations at the Cuppa café to build an addiction in the two of you. Amphetamine in the cocoa," he explained. "Mrs. Romero posed as your waitress."

"Laina?"

"Roza," Martin said. "Roza Romero. No one knew who she was because she seldom appears in public and has never allowed photos."

Her good friend, the one she had trusted enough to share her heart with, had betrayed her? No, Eve realized with a pang. Her friend hadn't deceived her. Her *enemy* had. She fought back tears.

"Jake Chalmers recognized her. He likely saved your life, not only from the overdose but from whatever Ricardo Romero was going to inject you with. Chalmers saved Crystal too." Perez raised his eyebrows at her. "Quite the hero of the day."

Eve sat back. "I ... you've got my head spinning. Please, start over, at the beginning."

Perez talked slowly, allowing her mind to keep pace. He told her about Danny Romero's death in jail, which Henshaw probably was coming to tell her about at the Cuppa café. But she had already left with Ric Romero before Henshaw got there. Dimly, she recalled Ric's help. Help? Abduction!

She stopped Perez. "The GHB, did ... did Ric taken advantage of it?"

Perez dropped his eyes. "Yes. The doctor confirmed it."

The room quieted. Blood ebbed from her face. Spasms yanked air through her nose into her chest, exploded into jolts that shook her whole body. *Nooooo, God, no!* She buried her face in her hands. Body, soul, and spirit propelled great gasps of anguish from her lungs. Wails she barely recognized as hers thundered in her ears. A wall of pain fell in giant chunks to isolate her.

From a distance, as if materializing from shadows, arms encircled her. Warm and strong. Rocking her. Breaking down the wall. Murmured words drove away the wails, softened the spasms in her lungs. She spread her fingers to find Perez holding her against his shoulder.

She pulled away, sniffling, rubbing her face with the back of her hand. He handed her a box of tissues, asked softly, "Do you want me to continue?"

She nodded, mopped her face, blew her nose. At least Perez's account couldn't get worse.

But it did. Ric had tried to inject her with something in a hypodermic syringe.

She blinked. Tried to unravel his intent. A drug to kill her off once he'd had his way with her? At the back of her mind, she couldn't believe he would want to harm her. As Rock Giannopoulus, Ric had fallen in love with her—Eve was sure of it. The syringe must have contained some kind of drug.

At the news of Crystal's near-abduction, Eve's breath deserted her. When she found her voice, she all but screamed at Martin and Perez. "Where is she? I want her *here* with *me*."

"She's with Chalmers," Perez said. "He brought her to the hospital, right behind your ambulance. Since then, because she's his ward as well as yours, we've let her stay with him and his son in hiding."

His son. Eve felt her blood pressure skyrocket as every drop of blood in her body surged to her face. Two Romeros had sought to kill her, and yet Jake was insisting on bringing a Romero into the family.

Martin shuffled from the end of the bed to her side. "Judge Eriksson." His voice boomed, the tone stern. "Bradley Henshaw is dead—murdered—and your life is in jeopardy. We insist you go into Witness Security."

Perez cleared his throat. "We are asking for your cooperation."

Asking, she knew, because they couldn't force her to go into the program. "Six months ago I was appointed Drug Czar of Chicago." She clamped trembling lips onto the words. "I have a job to do, and I won't let the Romeros stop me."

"They already have." Martin took a newspaper clipping from his pocket and thrust it at her. "Mrs. Romero initiated a phone interview with the *Chicago Tribune.* It was published two days ago and has gone nationwide."

The headline read, *Widow Claims Feds Murdered Husband, Agents Use Drugs.*

In an exclusive telephone interview, Roza Romero accused the federal government of murdering her husband, Danny Romero, who was standing trial for drug trafficking. "They feared disclosure of feds at the top who are using the very drugs they claim my husband was selling," she said. Asked specifically who, Romero named the prosecutor on the case, US Attorney Bradley Henshaw, and the newly appointed Drug Czar of Chicago, Judge Evedene Eriksson. "The Department of Justice can prove me wrong by administering drug tests and making the results immediately available to the public," Romero challenged.

Martin took the clipping back. "Yesterday's headline featured Henshaw's death from an overdose of amphetamine and your hospitalization two days earlier for a similar overdose."

"We'll counter with the truth," Eve insisted. She flinched at the thought of bearing the label *duped.*

"That will be tomorrow's headline," Perez said. "We are arresting Mrs. Romero tonight."

Eve closed her eyes to make sense of the timing. "I was drugged with GHB three days ago. The next day, headlines claimed Brad and I had murdered Danny Romero and were using drugs. Day after that, yesterday, headlines featured Brad's"—she gulped—"death and my hospitalization from a drug overdose. And tomorrow, the big news will be the arrest of, of Roza Romero."

She swallowed as the recitation brought home the reality of Brad Henshaw's death. Her dear friend, her treasured coworker and mentor, was dead. Impossible to believe she'd never visit his office again. Never see the tall, craggy, Lincolnesque man folded into his oversized chair. Never hear the pondering rap of his fingers on wood. The pain already gripping her body channeled into a second tidal wave of tears.

When the flood abated, Perez, his own eyes misty, offered her more tissues. Judge Martin, however, was on a mission. With barely a pause, he demanded her attention. "Judge Eriksson, we have serious business to attend to. *Urgent* business. It must be dealt with *now*."

Eve blotted the tears from her face and straightened her backbone. Her heartbeat sent tremors throughout her aching body. Every beat shouted that her life was about to change.

"Your drug addiction has placed the justice department in a bad light." The gruffness in Martin's voice hit her like an iron gavel. "You will be removed from the bench until such time as Roza Romero faces trial for the murder of Bradley Henshaw."

Eve recoiled. "No! I'm not addicted. I have a brain tumor." Her protest sounded tinny, like a toy Christmas horn, next to Martin's boom.

"The doctor examined you for a tumor at Chalmers' insistence," Martin replied. "There is no tumor. Your symptoms and your blood tests show unquestionable proof of addiction to amphetamine."

Eve's head wobbled in a feeble attempt at dissent. She remembered the doctor's lips minutes ago flattening into a straight line, the lack of credence in her denial of taking drugs.

"You're our star witness against Romero," Perez said. "Your addiction lines up with Henshaw's—both of you were served cocoa laced with amphetamine at the café. With Chalmers' identification of Roza, we have an airtight case."

"Motive," Martin grunted. "You've got to add that potato to the stew."

"Pretty sure we got it," Perez said. "We believe she's behind her husband's death. She wants new management in the family—either herself or one of her sons. The newspaper interview as good as says all she needed was someone to take the blame for Danny Romero's murder."

Eve grit her teeth against the agony building in her body. "Why aren't I dead? Why just Brad?"

"You still work out at Ace's Gym?" Perez asked. "I recall your trekking over there most days at noon when you worked in the DA office. Regular aerobic exercise is the only known antidote for amphetamine addiction."

Martin folded his arms across his chest. "Doctor said GHB was your overdose. Which brings us back to why you need to go into Wit Sec. The Romeros have a fixation on you. They are not going to leave you alone. If you don't utterly disappear, we can't protect you, and in your current state of addiction you will be in the Romero's hands in no time."

Jake could protect her. Or did he need to go into the program too? "What about Jake?"

"Definitely," Perez said. "He needs protection too."

"But you must go now—this minute," Martin said. "Before we arrest Roza Romero. We delayed it until tonight so we could get you to a safe house. Once the news is out, the Romeros will be after you."

"No, please." Pain sucked at Eve with a throbbing tongue. "I need to stay here tonight. I hurt too much." She grabbed her stomach and curled into a fetal position as the pain mounted.

"That's your craving speaking, Eve." Perez stooped to line up his eyes with hers. "This is what we mean by being vulnerable to the Romeros."

"Okay, I'll go, I'll go," she moaned. "Just help me." The room swam as a fresh onslaught of need hit her. "My family ..."

"We'll get them on the phone tomorrow," Martin said. "Once you're at the safe house."

The safe house. Martin and Perez believed in it.

Trouble was, she didn't. The past three months had proved there was no safe place when it came to the Romeros.

***

"You told me there was an antidote!" Ricardo roared. He punched the Queen Anne wingback with the full weight of his fury, and it slammed on its back to the floor. For good measure he kicked the chair twice. His brothers jumped up from the couch and scurried to stand on either side of their mother.

She screamed right back at him. "Because you wouldn't have injected her otherwise, you love-sick fool! And now you've infected yourself instead of her!"

"Wait, wait, wait, you don't even know if you're infected," his brother said, stiff-arming Ric. "You gotta take the test and see. Just go donate blood and they'll find out for you."

"Yeah," his other brother chimed in. "They've probably got a treatment plan ready now that they've got a test."

"Rock Hudson died two weeks ago, and there was no treatment plan to save him," Ric snarled.

His brother huffed. "Well, yeah, he died because he was a homo."

"What, you think the virus has some kind of moral compass attached to it?" Ric snapped. "It's a blood disease, not a guilty verdict."

"C'mon, Ric, Ma said she wasn't gonna kill the judge, just make her life miserable. You shouldn't have waited and got stopped by her boyfriend."

"Maybe I didn't want to make her life miserable," Ric yelled. Spittle flew from his mouth onto his brother's outstretched arm. "Maybe I wanted to make her mine." *His*, before Chalmers got his claim in. And not just for this one time, but for later too. "I've got my plans," he bellowed. "*My* plans!" He glared at his mother. "But if I die of AIDS, I promise I won't die alone."

His mother's face reflected no fear. "Well then, lover boy, let's go get her for you."

Chapter 25

Hands shaking with a barely perceptible tremor, Eve blotted the sweat on her face and neck with the thin motel towel. The material was stiff, rough to the touch, and absorbed little of the moisture beaded on her forehead. A shower would feel good, would soothe the frazzled knots of her nerves. But not yet. If aerobics was the only antidote to amphetamine addiction, then the goal to build up to exercising several times a day must rule her life until she was cured.

She had no idea where she was. Only that last night an ambulance had swept her away from the University of Chicago Hospital. She had slept cradled in the comfort of pain meds and had no inkling as to how long they had traveled nor where they had stopped. When she awoke, she found herself in a cheap motel room attended by a tall, lithe physical therapist with strawberry-colored hair and freckled pale skin.

"I'm Mary," she said. She handed Eve a fast-food bacon-and-egg biscuit for breakfast, then hauled her out of bed to walk around the room. "I'm told you're a runner, so our goal these next few weeks is to walk till you can trot, and trot till you can run. Then we'll add aerobics." There was no sympathy for Eve's pain, no interest as to who she was. Front and center, Eve was a drug addict, of concern only because the government needed her as a witness.

She had no clothes, no cosmetics, nothing personal except her wristwatch. At noon, a nurse arrived with undergarments, sweat clothes and tennies, a heavy jacket, and a hairbrush, comb, and toothbrush. Cold air blew in the door with her, and Eve caught a glimpse of snow on the ground before the door shut. A minute later, Mary left for a break and left Eve with the nurse.

Anger pinched Eve's nerves, and she clenched her hands into fists. "Why haven't I received a call from my family?" she yelled at her new warden. With a sweep of her arm she shoved the fast-food hamburger and fries the nurse had brought onto the floor. Hunger for the sweet taste of cocoa shook her body from the inside out. She closed her eyes and pictured herself seated at the table in the Cuppa Chocolatte Café with Brad.

"The marshal will take care of that soon enough." The nurse picked up the food, plopped it back in front of Eve, and fixed her with eyes of steel. The aroma of meat, starch, and grease wafted from where the paper wrapping had come loose. "You want to get better, you eat. Get that done, and I'll give you something for that pain you're fighting."

The promise melted Eve into compliance and she ate what she could. "Please," she begged when she could choke no more down. So this is what it felt like to have no pride. Only a craving that sent her to her knees, willing to kiss feet, to lick toes. She recalled Perez's words, "That's your craving speaking, Eve. This is what we mean by being vulnerable to the Romeros."

She whimpered as the nurse gave her a shot of something that reduced the monster within to mere beast status. "What's your name?" she asked, ashamed at how her addiction had kicked her civility in the teeth. *I'm a judge*, she wanted to say. *I'm a good person. I was tricked into this.*

"Bertha." The nurse's tone of voice softened. "This will hold you until tomorrow. Mary will get you up and walking when she gets back in a half hour, then you can get cleaned up and out of that nightgown before the marshal comes."

Eve straightened her shoulders. "How long will I be like this—until I'm free of the addiction, I mean?"

Bertha's eyebrows shot up. "Oh, honey, you'll never be free. On top of it, yes, but always at risk."

Vulnerable. That's how Andrew Perez had put it. She inhaled a struggling breath. "On top of it, then. How long until I'm not ruled by these ... these cravings?"

"Eat well, exercise well. That will determine how long."

"Days? Weeks? Months?" Eve bit her lower lip to keep from screaming the questions.

"As bad as you've got it, weeks, maybe, to get weaned off the pain meds. Let me ask you something. Do you dream—daydream—about being back where you used amphetamine? The location?"

Eve's stomach twisted. "Yes. At the—"

"Stop. Don't tell me where. Don't tell anyone any information except the marshal. But this you can answer yes or no because it's medical."

"Okay, yes."

"Then my answer is months to get on top of it. Those daydreams are called 'conditioned place preference,' the longing to spend time where you used amphetamine. That says serious addiction. That says months before you're on top of it."

Eve's lower lip trembled. Rage spouted from her gut. Angst beat it into submission. "I don't want to wait for Mary," she said. "I want to put on the sweats and coat and walk outside, now."

"Not with the dosage of pain meds I gave you. But you can walk in the room, if that's what you want. And again when Mary returns."

She didn't walk, she bumbled, with Bertha holding her arm. "If you fall," Bertha said, "don't stiffen up and resist. Just go loose and crumble to the floor. I'll protect your head."

Nausea shortened her circumference of the room. "That's the pain meds," Bertha explained. "That's why we were waiting for Mary. Take a snooze and the nausea will settle down. Tomorrow the pain will dominate again, but you'll be strong enough to go outside and walk."

Eve blotted the sweat on her face and neck with the motel towel, then snoozed, and when Mary returned, she walked. Or, rather, bumbled. Before the marshal came, she sat on a portable bench in the shower and soaked head and body until Mary turned off the spray and handed her what looked like the same thin towel she'd used before.

Dressed and combed out, she nibbled at another fast-food meal. Her mind was clearer, and she contemplated the prospect of months of recovery, of abandoning her judgeship, and of forsaking the identity she had lost to amnesia three years ago and had struggled so hard to regain. Was that the price she wanted to pay, even with Jake and Crystal by her side?

She'd agreed to go into Wit Sec, but that had been under duress. She'd tell the marshal no. The cost was too high. Jake would protect her until the court case was over and she could resume her life with nothing lost but time.

She closed her eyes and saw herself seated at the table in the Cuppa Chocolatte Café. But it wasn't Bradley Henshaw who sat across from her. It was Andrew Perez. He leaned toward her and said one word.

Vulnerable.

The threat loomed over her like the sharp edge of a guillotine.

***

An hour later, Eve sat at the motel room desk with Deputy US Marshal Sims, a stocky man in his forties with thinning hair. One by one, the documents he wanted her to sign passed from his hand to hers, with no small amount of explanation. Most of the information was familiar, but she wanted to be sure of the facts now that their application would be personal. If she signed.

To go into hiding meant changing her name and history. No, not just changing them, but agreeing to utterly and forever expunge them from her life. Anything she retained of Evedene Eriksson, Sims emphasized, would be a clue for the Romeros to chase down until they found her. Eve's insides quaked at how close Roza Romero had already come to destroying her. Roza was not a woman to be underestimated.

On the flip side, Sims said, Eve would acquire a new name and a new history. Her name must be one she quickly got used to, so it was her choice. Her new history was Wit Sec's choice—where she came from, her educational background, what jobs she'd held. Her new identity would be validated with a birth certificate, social security number, educational diplomas, and job records—none of them, of course, connected with a law degree or employment with the government. Not one iota of Evedene Eriksson's past could cling to her new one.

She must sell her house and car and all her belongings. The Romeros would be keeping an eye on them. Although her finances would be transferred into new accounts under her new name, she must watch what she purchased and not repeat old patterns. No favorite vacation spots or retail stores.

All that was the easy part.

The hard part, the part that sliced into her soul, was to completely cut off all contact with family, friends, and colleagues. To communicate with them would be to shine her new identity in bright lights on a Hollywood movie marquee. The Romeros would be monitoring every one of her connections as their best bet to locate her.

"Your family is in jeopardy too," Sims said. "Your father and brother and Crystal will need to go into Wit Sec with you."

"My father? I don't know …" They had plans to get together in three weeks at Thanksgiving—she and Crystal and Jake were going to fly to New York to spend the holidays with her dad and brother. She blinked away tears. She'd planned to have her dad walk her down the aisle when she married Jake. "He's a rich and powerful man. He'll probably opt for bodyguards."

And never see his daughter again? Sims face said it although his mouth didn't. "I don't want to worry you," he said, "but bodyguards aren't much defense against a long-range rifle. We'll try to convince him."

She pressed her lips together and nodded. Two decades of estrangement from her father and brother had been put to rest only four months ago. Dread of losing them washed acid over her stomach. Their relationship couldn't be cut off again. "I'll try too."

The amphetamine craving peeked with hungry eyes over the top of her pain meds, and she inhaled softly to cram it down, to hide the monster from Sims. "Crystal will go with me," she asserted. "And Jake Chalmers. *If* I go," she added. "I need to talk to Jake and see what he wants us to do."

She hadn't talked to him since his arrival in the United States.

The memory of his presence in her bedroom four days ago suddenly surfaced. He'd fought off Ric for her, hadn't he? She'd seen him, had called out to him.

You were too late, Jake.

The need to blame him struck like a sledgehammer. He had stayed away too long. In fact, he never should have left in the first place. It all began with that boy. Emilio's son. A Romero.

She closed her eyes and once again found herself in the Cuppa Chocolatte

Café. Brad Henshaw sat across from her. Walking toward them, smiling, balancing a tray with two cups of steaming cocoa, was Dan-boy.

She jumped as Deputy Marshal Sims' voice brought her back to the motel room. "We can call Chalmers right now." He pulled the desk phone to him and punched in a series of numbers. "Rayburn, Sims here. You've talked to Chalmers?" He pressed the receiver to his ear and listened intently. "All right." He looked at Eve and handed her the phone. "Here you go."

Before she even heard Jake's voice, she broke down crying.

Chapter 26

Jake's heartbeat accelerated at the sound of Eve's tears. "Eve, are you okay?" It angered him that the marshals had blocked him and the kids from visiting her and then had whisked her away from Chicago without telling him. It was understandable she was upset. The kids sure were. They sat huddled together on the couch across from him, lips and eyes pinched with worry. "Do you know where you are? I'll come get you."

Gradually, Eve's voice hushed into ragged hiccups. The rasp of breaths in and out of her mouth indicated her lips were hovered close to the phone's mouthpiece. Was she trying to whisper? He pressed the receiver tighter to his ear.

"They won't tell me. They said I'm in a safe house, but it's only a cheap motel somewhere with snow on the ground." She caught her breath. "Do you know where you are? Is Crystal there? I want to talk to her."

"We're in Michigan, a couple hours out of Chicago. Crystal is here, and she's fine. But before you talk to her, demand to know where you are. You aren't a prisoner."

A deep voice muttered in the background, then Eve spoke. "The marshal says he can't tell me—that he's not allowed to. He has papers he wants me to sign."

"To go into Wit Sec?"

"Yes. With Crystal, my dad and brother, and you."

"Not with me." Jake let the three words sink in. "Before he died, Bradley Henshaw signed an order that you and I couldn't go into Wit Sec together.

127

Only separately. To different locations."

Eve's inhale rattled in the phone. "Because of the Romeros and that boy." It was a statement, rigid with resentment—and right on the mark.

"Yes."

There was a pause, then, stiffly, "Brad's dead, so the order can't hold. I know his assistant, Andrew Perez. I'll talk to him."

"I already did, and he's sticking with Henshaw." Relief flooded him that at least Eve hadn't asked him to ditch Dan so the two of them—three, including Crystal—could enter the program without the boy. "But it doesn't matter, we don't need Wit Sec. We'll go to the Philippines and disappear until the trial."

"Jake"—Eve's voice came across the line in shattered fragments of pain— "I can't. I'm sitting here shaking. I'm addicted to amphetamine, and I want it so bad, I—" Her voice shut down in jagged breaths. "I need help," she cried. "I can't trust myself. There's a nurse here, and a physical therapist ..."

"We can do that too, Eve. We'll hire everyone you need. We'll get you through it."

"I was raped, Jake! What about that?" Her voice shredded into jerking gasps. "What if ... what if I'm pregnant?"

"We'll get you through that too. I love you, Eve. There's nothing to keep us apart." He spoke with a passion that was fervent, that he felt with all his heart. "We're a family. We don't desert each other when bad things happen."

Eve broke into sobs. "Okay," she said at last, "I won't sign. I'll go with you. I love you too, Jake. I love you so much." When at last she subsided into sniffles, she asked to speak to Crystal.

Crystal took the phone in hand. Her eyes were glazed. Ever since seeing Eve in the hospital, she had been unusually subdued. Not even Dan, her "favorite bro in the whole world," could rouse her. Knowing her mom was fine and that they'd be getting together soon would be good for Crystal. A fifteen-year-old girl needed her mother.

"Mom, don't come," Crystal said. "That man will come after me, and you need to stay away so he can't find me. Sign the papers."

She slapped the phone onto its cradle and sat down on the couch, arms folded, nostrils flared. "Sorry, Dad," she said. "It's her or me."

The US Marshal shrugged. He wasn't going to help.

It took a minute before Jake could trust himself to reply. When Eve didn't call back, he said in as even a tone as he could manage, "Looks like I've been outvoted."

PART 3

Chapter 27

November

Bertha removed the tin foil from Eve's lunch, and the aroma of home-cooked turkey, dressing, green beans, and mashed potatoes with gravy floated to Eve's nostrils. The plate was china, and the folds of a white linen napkin placed beside it held a silver fork and knife. Tears spiked Eve's eyes. "You're going to make me cry." This was a reward, but did she deserve it?

"I just wish they had let you join my family yesterday," Bertha grumped. She emphasized her words by smashing the tin foil into a tight ball. "Well, given that, the least I could do today was lift you above fast food and plastic." She smothered Eve with a quick hug. "I can't tell you how proud I am of you. You're off the pain meds a week earlier than I said was possible, and Mary told me you've been running a bit. You deserve a feast!"

Eve sniffed back tears, sliced a bite of turkey, and dipped it into the potatoes and gravy. The weight of real silverware in her hands felt extravagantly indulgent, the home-cooked food a feast. How long had it been since she'd eaten a normal meal, been treated like a normal person and not simply a project? "Thank you for going to all this trouble. It means a lot."

She tried not to think about how she had expected, instead, to be at her father's yesterday for Thanksgiving with Jake and Crystal. About how delighted she'd been that her father had invited Jake's two children and son-in-law to join them for the holiday. About how everyone in her family and Jake's would have been there. Her lower lip trembled. The timing would have been perfect for Jake to propose to her.

She stopped, smashed the thoughts into a tight foil ball. "Tell me about your family tradition for Thanksgiving," she said to Bertha. She speared two green beans and poked them into her mouth. They were cold now, chewy, as if rubber bands had replaced the vegetable.

Bertha eagerly took a seat across from her and began with a list of family members.

Eve tried to listen, but her thoughts kept straying to her father and brother. Where were they? She'd been right that her father wouldn't go into Wit Sec. Instead, Sims informed her, they had disappeared on their own to wait out the Romero trial.

She corralled her thoughts again and redirected them. "Does your family take sides or root for the same football team?" She tried not to aimlessly push the food around on her plate, but, truth was, she had no appetite. Only the same overwhelming, horrible craving that Bertha had told her she'd fight for months.

Eat well, exercise well. Bertha's advice had become Eve's mantra. She forced down several more bites. It was snowing today, but a run would feel good when Mary returned from her lunch break. Or maybe, if Mary felt it was too icy outside, they could start on aerobics. She was ready.

"My husband is a master at carving the turkey," Bertha said.

Would Jake be a master carver? And Crystal—would she set a fancy table? Eve caught her breath at the loneliness their absence evoked. Where were they? In the Philippines? Sims refused to tell her, said it was safer for her not to know. She closed her eyes, and immediately Jake and Crystal were embracing her. The warmth of their love washed over her as they each took her hand and walked her to a table in the Cuppa Chocolatte Café. Jake pulled out a chair for her. Crystal set a steaming cup of cocoa in front of her. The rich smell of chocolate rose to her nostrils. Her hands trembled in anticipation of the amphetamine smoothing away all her troubles.

"Eve."

Startled, she opened her eyes. Bertha was standing over her, hand on Eve's shoulder. "Where do you want to be, Eve? Picture someplace else. Someplace safe."

Eve buried her face in her hands and sobbed. This was too hard. The physical pain might be gone, but not the yearning. It wouldn't go away. Perez had pegged it. *Vulnerable.* That's what she was: weak, defenseless, helpless. There was no safe place. No one who could help her.

Eve. A sweet inflow of Breath pierced her.

And she knew.

Knew the exact location of her refuge.

In the throne room of God. In the warmth of His love. Seated at His table.

Only she didn't want it. Everything spiritual inside her had been scraped away. Everything life-giving squashed. The only thing left was hunger.

And it wasn't for God.

***

Jake woke Crystal and Dan for the landing at Clark Air Base. A sergeant had given them blankets to sleep with, and the kids had cradled their heads on their arms and stretched out on either side of Jake on the long jump seat attached to the wall—one advantage, at least, to flying on a military transport versus the upright seats of a commercial plane. Remarkably, the kids had adjusted quickly to the thumps and whine of the C-141 Starlifter's uninsulated hydraulics. The noise had created a quiet space for Crystal to cuddle with Dan and whisper the entire length of Rudyard Kipling's *Jungle Book* into his attentive ear.

Given no choice, the US Marshals had agreed to Jake's disappearance plan. The Romeros would not be watching military flights out of the country, he argued, and Clark Air Base in the Philippines was the perfect destination. It was huge, the largest American military base overseas, with a population closing in on 13,000 to disappear into. In addition to the usual base exchange and commissary, there was a shopping arcade, branch department store, hotel, miniature golf, cafeterias, zoo, riding stables, and, of course, schools. The kids were excited.

The plane bumped to a landing, and Dan nudged Crystal with a gleeful "We're here!" She shrugged and cast a blank stare out the window.

Jake pressed his lips together to cover a sigh. Change that to one kid who was excited. For the most part, Crystal was numb. An unsmiling apparition that haunted Jake's heart. If it weren't for the marshals forcing Jake to disappear, he would be after the man identified by the police as Blue. Would be displaying the brute's face, black-and-blue, behind bars to Crystal.

Not that that would be enough for Crystal. Time would soften the trauma, but vanquishing its immediate control was a challenge not easily met.

The plane hummed with a million vibrations as it taxied to the terminal. Within minutes, the three of them would deplane—minus one passenger who should be with them. Eve.

He grit his teeth. Crystal wasn't the only one who needed help. Eve needed it too—their help, not Wit Sec's. His mind flashed back to his and Crystal's last conversation with Eve …

"Mom, don't come," Crystal had said. "Sign the papers." And *wham*, just like that, Crystal had slammed the phone down and cut Eve off. Cut him off! And of course the marshal wasn't about to reestablish the connection. Wit Sec didn't want him and Eve together. They wanted control of her. Until the trial was over, they said, neither he nor Crystal would be granted access to her …

Stop! Every muscle in his body was taut. He closed his eyes, breathed slow and deep. *He loved Crystal, he understood her fear. God was in control, not Wit Sec. Not him. God would enable him to do whatever He handed him.*

The plane lurched to a standstill, and he opened his eyes. Crystal and Dan were staring at him. "Ready, guys? I am." He gave them a genuine smile. "Grab your bags and let's go."

Dan slipped his knapsack on and wormed a cold little hand into Jake's warm one. "Can we go to the stables and ride horses now?"

Jake sighed. The kid was fixated on going horseback riding. "Hotel first, bud. And you know what my nose says."

"Showers." Pronounced with full disgust and a drawn-down mouth. "Then can we go?"

"You know what my stomach says?"

Dan giggled. "Yeah, I'm hungry too, Dad." One breath and then, "After that can we go?"

Jake glanced at Crystal, sweater sleeves pushed to her elbows, jean legs rolled to her knees. "What do you say we stop by the Post Exchange first and buy some summer clothes for Crystal?" For the first time since leaving Eve at the hospital, Crystal smiled. Yep, for sure when it came to Eve and Crystal, a shopping spree was definitely the way to a woman's heart.

An enlisted man summoned a courtesy car to take them from the airport to their hotel. The air base had guest rooms at the officers' quarters, but Jake didn't want to identify himself as military. Too easy to trace if someone wanted to find him.

The day started off well with showers and a cafeteria meal where the kids could select what they wanted to eat. It got better with a haul of summer clothes and sandals for Crystal and two bags of popcorn to pace Dan's patience. At the stable, Dan pointed to a brown and white pinto for him and Jake to share, and a pretty bay mare which Crystal, the wardrobe princess, happily consented to ride.

In spite of Jake's warning that an hour-long trail ride guaranteed sore muscles once they dismounted, Crystal and Dan insisted they were up to it. The rhythmic creak of saddle leather, the earthy smell of horse flesh, Dan's laughter when the pinto trotted, the look of contentment on Crystal's face— Jake would happily have extended the ride another hour. Here was a measure of healing. Here was a venue for restoration. He would bring them back.

The next morning, Crystal and Dan moaned they couldn't possibly walk anywhere. "You check out the schools, we'll read another book," Crystal pleaded. She patted the small space next to her in an overstuffed chair, and Dan crawled into it. He snuggled up and handed her *Peter Pan* with an appealing smile at Jake.

The cuddling looked therapeutic, and, to tell the truth, a few hours to himself wouldn't be hard to take. "I'll bring back lunch," he promised, and called a taxi. There were several elementary schools Dan could attend, but only one high school. He'd start there.

The cab drove past the middle school gym and pulled into a parking lot fronting Wagner High School. Students in short skirts, slacks, and jeans dodged past him in the hallway until he finally got one to direct him to the principal's office. Inside, three students stood in line waiting for the attention of a middle-aged secretary already looking tired and in dire need of coffee.

Jake picked up a 1985 yearbook and leafed through the first several pages for details he could share with Crystal. Featured after a picture of the school and its mascot was a photograph of the principal. Jake froze, closed the book, and hastened back to the waiting cab.

By noon, he was back at the hotel with a used pick-up truck. "Change of plans," he told the kids. "Pack up."

Chapter 28

"You sa-id …" Dan sniffled. "… we'd live here."

"Where there are horses and a zoo …" Jake said. He was going to have to eat that promise, wasn't he? He pulled out of the hotel parking lot and headed west. How do you tell a five-year-old you have to flee because there are people out to harm you?

"And that I could go to school here." The sniffling continued.

Crystal, shoulders slumped, stared silently out the pickup window.

"You'll still go to school," Jake said. "You can start tomorrow."

"But I don't like the kids at Puno's. They're mean."

Jake sighed heavily. "Meaner people are looking for me, Dan. If we stay at the air base, they might find me."

Crystal's head whipped around to face Jake. Yesterday's peace vanished in a snap.

"It's okay, hon. Nobody's found us. It's just that when I went to the high school, I discovered the principal was a Marine Corps buddy from Nam. He's a good guy, but it's safest if absolutely no one knows we're in the Philippines. I'm not even telling Detective Lee."

"The US Marshals know," Crystal muttered.

"Yes, so I can be a witness at the Romero trial. And meet up with Eve"—the words pricked a bitter taste on his tongue—"since we don't know where she is." He flinched when Crystal stabbed him with a glare and turned back to the window. Why was it so hard for him to let go of Crystal banishing Eve into Wit Sec?

"Is Unca Ric the mean guy looking for you?" Dan asked.

"He's looking for our whole family," Jake said. May as well hang it all out there. "We need to hide and not draw attention to ourselves."

Dan sniffled again. "Maybe Crystal can help the kids not be mean to me."

"Or maybe help you not be mean to them," Jake countered.

Dan squirmed. "They start it."

"Then you end it!" The words came out sharper than Jake intended. Or were they? Before returning to the United States, Dan had gotten into fights with practically every boy in the village within two years of his age. Nothing Jake said or did seemed to make a difference. And he was not looking forward to more of the same.

Maybe Eve was right about the Romero genes.

They drove in silence, Crystal with a rigid back, staring out the window; Dan with a jutted jaw and folded arms; Jake with teeth in a clench that ended in his colon. When at long last they arrived at Iba, the two kids sat stubbornly in the truck while Jake opened a bank account and bought gifts without their help for Puno and his family.

An hour later, they turned off Highway 1 onto the dirt road leading to their new home. The monsoon rains of September and October had softened the sunbaked ruts into mud pits that sucked hungrily at the pickup's tires and created a breathtaking slide down the steep hill toward the village. Rows of green rice seedlings poked through the water on either side of the elevated road. In four months, the plants would be a foot taller and the fields would be drained for the crop.

The harvest—that's what the mission compound was about, wasn't it? The training of workers to go into the spiritual harvest. But even more important was another harvest God had called him to. A personal one. He straightened, took in a deep breath, and reached sideways to give a quick pat to Dan and Crystal. "Hey, kids. I love you, no matter how tough it gets for us, and I'm very, very happy you're with me." He let the words water their souls. "You two and Eve and me—we're a family, and that means that nothing, not even a long time and a long distance, can separate our hearts."

Dan's arms slowly unfolded. The tightness in Crystal's shoulders melted.

A moment later, Dan scooted closer to lean against Jake's side and Crystal shifted to face the front window.

"We love you too, Dad," Dan said.

"And Mom," Crystal added. "You know, I'm glad we're going to Puno's. And I'll help my bratty little brother become an upstanding citizen." She punched Dan's arm. "Won't that be fun, dude, to make the mean kids like you?"

Jake glanced at the look of doubt on Dan's face and chuckled. What woman didn't love to reform a wayward man?

He took the road that skirted the village and drove straight to the mission compound, where he parked beside a building marked Administration. The one-story building consisted of bamboo-stick walls, a palm-branch roof, and large windows open to the breeze. Jake had purposed the design to be simple for the seminary students to learn to construct and easy to add onto as the need arose. Skills they could use wherever they went in Asia.

The slam of the pickup's doors must have attracted Puno's attention. He appeared at the doorway of the building before they had hardly exited the truck.

"*Mabuhay*," Puno said, his face alight with pleasure.

"That means 'welcome,'" Dan yelled. He ran with open arms to Puno, who braced himself for impact. "We're gonna live with you, Puno!"

Jake grinned at the jump of Puno's eyebrows. "At the compound if there's room," he clarified. He peered to the left of the administration building. "Looks like both Admin and the dormitory have expanded."

Puno nodded. "Yes, blessing of more students, more instructors. Come, we will tour. But first, *mabuhay*, Crystal. You are a rose"—he placed his hands on Dan's and Jake's heads—"between two thorns."

Crystal laughed. "Like, totally!"

With Dan clasping Puno's hand, the four of them trooped around the left end of the administration building and stopped. Puno pointed to the addition of a small office. "Two more instructors, so new office on each end."

Perpendicular to the admin building was a dormitory of the same construction materials. Dan shrank into Puno as ten students emerged in response to Puno's call. Jake shook hands with them, but lost track of their names when ten pairs of eyeballs flitted to Crystal.

"Perhaps rose needs protection from other thorns," Puno whispered as they continued the tour. "Perla good at pruning thorns. Good housekeeper, good cook too."

Ah, Perla, the cousin of Puno's mother, who had hosted him and Puno and Dan in the village a few months earlier. "Would she be willing to help? She has to be in her seventies."

Puno smiled. "Age a sharp blade in Filipino community."

"Then yes, if she will come." Warmth radiated from his heart and filled his chest. His little family was off to a good start.

They crossed to a line of three bamboo huts on the other side of the admin building. Puno halted at the third one. "Chalmers hut, for family of four."

Dan pushed open the door and ran inside. "It's just the three of us," Crystal blurted. "Eve's in witness protection until the trial."

Puno's head jerked in surprise.

Jake cut in with a quick explanation. "Her illness turned out to be the Romeros drugging her—both her and her former boss, when they met in a restaurant to discuss the Romero trial. The drugs killed him, so now there's a murder trial with Eve as a witness."

Dan stuck his head out the hut's door. "C'mon, guys!"

"Problems here too," Puno murmured. "With students." Concern cut a furrow across his forehead. "But first we tour, then talk."

Jake trailed the group into the hut, a feeling of unease stirring his gut. The mission was just getting started, and already they had problems?

Inside, he viewed the hut from Eve's perspective. A total of three rooms, with two beds apiece in the two bedrooms, and a large table and several chairs in the common room. Anything more would have to be added by the occupants. The island-Eve would have easily adapted, but the city-Eve, who had no recall of the island, how would she do?

"You have to potty outside," Dan giggled.

"Dude, I survived a year on a jungle island," Crystal snorted. "I know how to live without electricity and plumbing."

Outside again, they ambled a fair distance to the two-story, cement-block auditorium Jake had spent August and September constructing. The bamboo buildings on the compound might suffer damage during the typhoon season, but not, Jake was determined, the auditorium.

While Jake showed Crystal around, Dan dashed ahead to examine the storage sheds that completed the campus behind the auditorium. Within minutes he was back, breathless from running. "Dad, come look!" He tugged Jake into a trot out the auditorium door and through a fledgling garden to a pen attached to a simple shed. The odor and flies gave Jake a hint as to the occupant.

Dan poked his head between the rails. "Look, Dad! It's a funny-looking lit'l horse. Maybe I can ride it."

"Dude, it's a donkey," Crystal exclaimed. She entered the pen but stiffened to a halt when her brand new sandals squished into the donkey product layering the ground. "Ewwww."

Jake stifled a laugh, although mind, body, and soul hungered for the relief of releasing—even if just for a second—the day's accumulated anxieties. Puno's disquiet added to the burden.

"Okay, kiddos, how about running ahead and moving our stuff from the truck into our hut so Crystal can change sandals. I'll catch up with you in a bit."

When at last the kids were gone, Jake questioned Puno about the students.

"Two men from Islam faith," Puno said. "Hamza and Muhamoud from island of Mindanao. Claim to be converts, but evidence falls short."

"Such as?"

"Cold hearts—toward Scripture, toward instructors, toward other students."

Jake chewed his lower lip. It was hard to discount Puno's concern. "Perhaps they find us cold, and we need to be friendlier." He shrugged in consternation, remembering the hardness of the Muslim population at Salonga Prison. "I imagine moving out of the Muslim culture into a Christian lifestyle has its challenges. How long have they been here?"

"Arrived day after Detective Lee came to tell you about Eve's illness."

"That's hardly three weeks." Jake gazed at the green tinge of rice seedlings on the distant fields. "You know, Puno, Muslims are part of the harvest we seek. What do you say to our practicing on Hamza and Muhamoud?"

The furrow in Puno's brow softened. "Yes. Our practice may reveal their purpose."

Their purpose? Jake stared at his friend. Why else would Hamza and Muhamoud be here if not to learn about Christianity and how to spread the gospel?

Chapter 29

December

Sleet beat against the motel window as if it too were miserable and wanted in where it was cozy and warm. But warm toes a merry heart does not make, Eve grumbled. She stared despondently at the blanched landscape. During the Thanksgiving holiday, her loneliness had been dulled by the craving for amphetamine. But now, at Christmas, the craving had flip-flopped. With the chemical yearning diminished, it was her longing for Jake and Crystal that consumed her.

She needed to get out of here. Go join them. Escape.

Before today's snowstorm, she had been running at least a mile out and a mile back with Mary. Along the route was a gas station where truckers stopped. She'd hitch a ride, fly to the Philippines, and get Detective Lee to drive her to Jake's compound … assuming that's where he was hiding.

The plan clicked. Simple. Doable. Easy. Her heart danced a jig.

Neither Mary nor Bertha had arrived at the motel yet, which made her escape a breeze. No doubt they were eating cinnamon buns and opening Christmas gifts with their families before taking up their vigilance over Eve. Good for them for getting that precious time. Soon she'd be doing that too with Jake and Crystal.

She emptied the chest of drawers and closet onto her bed. Not much there. Sitting on a chair, she pulled on jeans then sweat pants over them, layered three tees and a sweatshirt up top, and squeezed two pairs of socks onto her feet before crushing them into her tennies. Underwear and the rest of her socks she stuffed into the pockets of her coat, slipped it on, and tugged the knitted cap and leather gloves on that Mary had provided for their runs in the cold.

Her heartbeat ticked like a time bomb buried in a cocoon of clothes. This must be how a refugee felt when fleeing with her meager possessions before the authorities showed up.

One step away from opening the door, it struck her that she had no purse to sling over her shoulder. No wallet to go in the purse. No money to go in the wallet. No bank account to get money from. No I. D. whatsoever.

She had given up her identity as Evedene Eriksson. As good as killed and buried her.

She stood stunned. All her joy, all her resolution, sank like the *Titanic* to the bottom of the Atlantic Ocean. Shuddering breaths scraped the lining from her trachea and exploded a barrage of fist-sized gasps from her lungs. Who could help her? Not Andrew Perez. Not anyone at the DA office. In fact, no one in Chicago.

Then it hit her. Of course! George Peterman, the chaplain who had befriended her when she first lost her memory and who had remained her ally and confidante since then. She would call him collect, and he would come get her. He would be the refuge from which she could force Wit Sec to release her from their contract and turn over her assets.

A surge of laughter—a *guffaw*, as Jake called it—burst from her lungs and inflated happiness into a hot-air balloon that swept into a cloud-free sky. In a matter of days, a week at the most, she would be hugging Jake and Crystal and never, ever leaving them again!

The door banged open, and Deputy US Marshal Sims stomped snow prints onto the carpet. "You have ten seconds to grab what you want, and we're outta here." His eyes widened as he took in her apparel. "Looks like you're ready to go." He grabbed her arm and hustled her out the door to his car.

Sleet stung every bit of exposed skin on her face with needles of ice. She barely got the car door shut before Sims raced out of the motel parking lot onto what she hoped was the road. "What's happening?" Her heart hammered a hundred beats for each word.

Without slowing down, Sims leaned as far forward as he could over the steering wheel to peer through the sleet-battered windshield. She could only trust he knew the lay of the road, for all she saw was a blur of frothing white.

"Got word a thug called Blue sniffed you out," he said, his voice tight. "We're moving you to a new location." The front wheels veered off the road, and he grunted, swung to the right, and made contact with the cement surface again. "This storm will hide our tracks—unless," he hissed, "we slam into him coming our way."

Blue.

Eve shivered. With him this close on her tail, there was no way she'd head for the Philippines. Wit Sec was her only refuge ... and Crystal's continued protection.

***

For Christmas, Jake gave Dan-boy a setting hen and ten chicks. Over the next two days they built an enclosure to prevent escape until the new denizens adapted to their home. Dan's rapture turned to disgruntlement after his first hour with her in the pen. "She won't let me be nice to her," he whined.

Jake sympathized. He had the same complaint with Hamza and Muhamoud. "What's she doing?"

"She keeps running away and won't let me hold her or her chicks."

"So if she's running, she's afraid of you. Why do you think she's afraid?"

"Cuz she doesn't know how nice I am." The corners of Dan's mouth drooped toward his toes.

Jake forbade his own mouth to tweak into a smile. "How can you show her that?"

When a shrug and brimming tears joined Dan's downturned mouth, Jake crouched to Dan's eye level. "It's a secret. Go spend the day by sitting very, very still with her, and see if you can discover it."

Immediately the sun rose on Dan's soul and lit up his eyes. Giggling, he ran for the pen.

Jake chuckled and folded his arms across his chest. Now if only he could discover the secret for winning over Hamza and Muhamoud's friendship.

Inside the Chalmers hut, Crystal and Perla were preparing *sinaing* for the evening meal and *patis* to flavor the rice once it was cooked. He put his arm around Crystal's shoulder. "I'm going to town. Want to join me?" Even though it was too early for Roza Romero's trial, he liked to keep a check on it, and Crystal enjoyed going with him if she wasn't in school.

He grinned at Perla, whose job included looking after Dan. "Our boy is spending the day with his hen—"

"Choc'late Brownie?" Perla tittered. For Christmas, Jake had given Perla a large box of baked goods from Iba, and the brownies had inspired Dan's name for the russet hen.

"Yes, so maybe you'll get a break." Dan was still tussling the village boys, but Perla, who owned the coveted donkey in back of the auditorium, held learning to ride over Dan's head as a reward for good behavior.

Jake and Crystal took the pickup to Iba, where he put a call through to the number the marshals had given him. "Nothing new," he told Crystal afterward. He always asked the marshals about Eve, and they always had nothing to share. Their silence was a cold, dark room for his soul. The best he could do was assume no news was good news.

At least on Christmas Eve the marshals had put him through to his children. Brett, Dana, and her husband, Bentley, were all serving tours in Afghanistan. Jake huffed at the sad fact that at least over there they were safe from the threat of the Romeros.

"How's school?" he asked on the drive home. The smell of brine and roar of the ocean through the pickup's open windows helped to walk him out of the dark room the call to the marshals put him in.

"Okay." Crystal picked at her fingernails, a sure sign something was troubling her. "The kids say those two guys aren't really Christians," she said at last.

"Hamza and Muhamoud?"

She nodded. "They say Muslims from Mindanao are killed if they convert to Christianity, so they're, like, bogus."

"What do you think?"

Crystal frowned, pressed her lips together, screwed one side of her mouth into her left cheek. "You know, moving here was harder than I thought it'd be. On the island it was tough, but we didn't have to live by some other dude's rules. We just made up our own, and we sorta liked what we decided, and we all got along. Well, except for Eve sometimes."

They both laughed.

"I figure it's like that for those two guys. They've got rules they're used to, and now they gotta live by new ones." She shrugged. "I think that's Dan's problem too."

"You mean, new rules of meanness to learn?"

Crystal slid right over his joke. "Yeah. Bummer he has to wait till he's seven to go to school, but I think I found a way he can make friends." She fluttered her eyelashes at him in an exact imitation of Eve that made his heart jump. "But I want to show you and Dan at the same time, so you'll have to wait."

He voiced a loud hurumph, but her promise encouraged him.

Back home, Dan came to supper with a long face. "There's no secret," he moaned.

Jake poured him a cup of ginger tea and piled the boy's dish with rice. "What happened?"

Dan answered in one long breath. "I sat real still like you said and after a while she came over and I didn't move and the chicks came too." He inhaled reinforcement oxygen molecules and turned sad eyes on Jake. "But when I tried to pet her she cackled real mean and ran away."

"Hey, buddy, you got half the secret—good job!" Jake stopped short of patting the sulky kid on the head. "You found out that with some friends you have to wait until *they* come to *you*—you know, build some trust between you first." Is that what he needed to do with Hamza and Muhamoud, build trust?

Dan's expression shifted from frustrated to pleased to skeptical. "But she ran away, Dad."

"What did she do after that?"

Dan scowled and stuffed rice into his mouth. "She chased bugs and pooped a lot."

"There you go, the other half of the secret! She wanted something from you to prove you're a friend, and you didn't give it to her."

"I gotta catch bugs for her?" Dan actually looked delighted.

"Table scraps from dinner good," Perla said. "Put in bowl on lap and she come."

"You think that would work with Hamza and Muhamoud," Jake asked after Dan zipped out the door with his peace offering. "Don't pressure them but find out what they want to befriend them?"

Perla hobbled close to Jake's face until they were literally eyeball to eyeball. Her breath was heavy with the smell of fish from the *patis*. "Muslims don't be-friend. Better you send them away before you and family and village hurt."

"Perla," Jake sputtered, "they're here for the gospel. We can't turn them away."

"You be sorry, not be-friend." She sniffed and proceeded to collect their dishes amid much clatter.

"Told ya," Crystal whispered.

Jake grimaced. Puno, Perla, apparently the whole village—it was hard to ignore their ill ease when, way back in his own brain, alarms had sounded ever since he met Hamza and Muhamoud.

He sat back and folded his arms. It was time for him and Puno to confront the two men.

***

Jake decided the simplest way to smell a rat was to make it stink.

"After classes today," he announced the next morning from the auditorium podium, "we will share a meal." The ten students greeted the invitation with a cheer that reverberated against the cement-block walls. Although both genders in the Philippines were taught to cook, who didn't enjoy food prepared by someone else's hands? Especially when the shared fare was more abundant than one's usual meal.

Perla happily conspired with Jake and Puno. After all, she had a point to prove, didn't she? Hamza and Muhamoud were Muslims, not Christians, she declared with a toss of her head, so even though *adobo* was made from either pork or chicken, she would limit the meat to pork. The same with the *lumpia*—she would forego shrimp and stuff the fried egg rolls with pork only.

"*Adobo* is national dish, everyone like," she said. "Muslims not eat pork, so not eat my *adobo* or *lumpia*. You watch. They eat only mangoes and bananas and guavas."

Puno added to the rat trap by lecturing that day on the Trinity. The Father in the morning, the Son after lunch, and the Holy Spirit in the late afternoon. Muslims denied the Trinity and rejected the divinity of Christ, he pointed out, so he'd watch to see if Hamza and Muhamoud squirmed.

After the final lecture, he whispered his observations to Jake. "No face flinching, no body tics, no revelation of loathing," he said. "No smell of rat."

It was good news. But Jake found the tension in his shoulders wired tighter than before. He needed more evidence.

With classes dismissed, the students dispersed in the blink of an eye to retrieve bowls from their dorm rooms. The aroma of Perla's cooking beckoned from across the clearing where she and Crystal and Dan had set up tables of food outside the Chalmers' hut. Perla beamed as student after student declared her *adobo* and *lumpia* to be *masarap*, delicious.

Crystal joined Jake and Puno at the end of the line after all the students and instructors had helped themselves. "Three didn't take any *adobo* or *lumpia*," she reported. "One instructor and two students. The two students were John and Muhamoud."

"Hamza took pork?" Jake darted a glance at Puno and back to Crystal. "Did he know that's what it was?"

"Perla pointed it out." Crystal giggled. "You should've seen her face. He just nodded and took more."

"Let's see if he's actually eating it." Jake heaped his bowl and sauntered over to sit between Hamza and another student.

"*Masarap*. Thank you for generous meal," Hamza said. The other students and instructors murmured in agreement. Hamza waited for Jake to dig in, then took a bite from his *lumpia*. On the other side of Hamza, Muhamoud chewed on a banana and talked to a student on his left.

Huh. No stink, so no rats. In fact, it seemed he had copied young Dan with his bowl of table scraps. He had successfully befriended Hamza and Muhamoud.

Chapter 30

January 1986

In November of 1985, Evedene Eriksson disappeared from the face of the earth. In January of 1986, Genevieve Wertz appeared out of nowhere in Lincoln, Nebraska, full-blown, fully formed, the same height and weight as Evedene Eriksson but with a birth date two years earlier and a birthplace in the backwoods of Arkansas.

"This is the best you can do?" Eve, in her new label as Genevieve, balked at the last bit of assigned identity held in her hands. The tiny rented bungalow she stood in and the rusty Ford parked in the weed-pocked gravel driveway were bad enough, but this ... this assignment of Genevieve's level of education ... was beyond acceptance. "A General Education Degree? What kind of a future do I have with a G.E.D.?"

"It makes you harder to trace, easier to hide." Deputy US Marshal Shari Kane, short and brawny as a bear in her brown uniform, took the certificate and placed it on the table, next to a Nebraska driver's license and a social security card bearing Genevieve's data. "That's our goal, not your upward job mobility."

She added a typewritten sheet of paper to the collection. "This lists your job history and past addresses, which you'd do well to memorize. Your new job starts tomorrow, so better practice your name too." She dropped the keys to the Ford on Genevieve's persona pile. "Check in with me every morning when you leave, and every evening when you get home."

"You couldn't find a tighter leash?" Eve snapped.

Kane's eyebrows rose. "You need another month in a motel? I told Sims this was too early to release you."

"No—I'm over the drugs!" Eve's blood pulsed against her temple at the half-lie. "It's all this close surveillance. This, this degree of control over my life, and my lack of say in it." The only thing she'd been allowed to choose was her first name, which she picked because it ended in *-eve*. "I want options. I want in on the choices."

"Honey, the reason we make them for you is because you'd make bad ones." Kane stepped next to her and pointed at their reflections in a mirror over a scarred buffet. "Tell me what you see, Genevieve."

Eve shrugged. A haggard woman and a burly marshal. "I'm a mess. I need a haircut and my skin is dried out and I have bags under my eyes."

Kane's mouth twitched a smile. "You are pitiful, but you know what the world sees? It sees a beautiful woman. Taller than the average female, with the bearing of a proud warrior. Open your mouth, and you're articulate, confident, used to being in charge. What happens if we put you before the public? Even behind the scenes, will you go unnoticed?"

"Blue," Eve whispered. "Blue would happen."

"Now don't you worry—we've got our eye on him and we won't let him get close to you. But the Romeros will cast a wide net, and they won't quit looking. You've got to hide, and that's what we're doing for you."

Don't worry? Eve's chest was so tight she could hardly breathe. "I'll call you," she choked out.

She followed the marshal to the door, locked it, and went back to the mirror. She stared long and hard. Beautiful, tall, articulate, confident. Genevieve Wertz was due a makeover.

***

The job was a joke. Really, Genevieve was a weld repair operator? Eve had never held a torch, much less made a repair with one. But Deputy US Marshal Kane only reiterated over the phone the next morning that Wit Sec knew what it was doing. "Go, and don't be late," she said. So Eve—Genevieve—went.

The Eve-to-Genevieve makeover was simple. Her mane of hair had always been an eye catcher. Not anymore. She chopped it off to bare ponytail length and pulled it straight back in an elastic band so the ugly scar above her right eye was no longer hidden. No application of mascara and eyeliner, either, to make the hazel brown of her eyes stand out. With a hard swallow, her lower lip pinched between her teeth, she had dared to shave off her eyebrows and pencil in thin brown lines to replace them. The dry-skinned, cosmetic-free, stark-eyed woman who stared back at her in the mirror made her want to cry. No one would call her beautiful.

She drove the Ford to work and discovered her transportation, like her, was also in masquerade. In spite of all its rust, the vehicle was in top working condition. Wit Sec had seen to it that she had transportation that wouldn't break down on her and that provided a speedy getaway if she needed it.

But they had missed the boat on the job assignment. Her lungs tightened into two clumps of knots. She shouldn't have let Kane bully her into it.

The marshal's directions led Eve downtown to Lincoln's Haymarket District, where the city's old manufacturing sites were under renovation. She passed several offices housed in cleverly spiffed-up warehouses, but the buildings got shabbier the farther she drove. Her destination, Midwest Welding Parts, was a middle-sized, one-story red brick building with several entrances. The trampled snow at the back parking lot identified the main employee entrance. She parked, locked the car, and joined the other workers trudging with icy breaths to the double doors.

Beautiful, tall, articulate, confident, Kane had said. Eve clamped her jaws. She couldn't do anything about the *tall,* but last night she had scalped the *beautiful.* Now to destroy the image of *articulate* and *confident.*

"Genevieve Wertz?" A mustached man in jeans and a yellow flannel shirt greeted her at the door. Anxiety pounced on her chest like a roaring tornado. Within minutes they would see she couldn't tell the upside of a welding machine from the downside. What good was a disguise if her skills didn't back it up? Why hadn't she stood up to Wit Sec?

The man extended his hand. "Welcome to Midwest W-P. I'm Ray Litner, and I'll be your on-the-job-trainer for the next four months."

The tornado vaporized in a burst that snatched Eve's breath away. She covered the wobble in her knees by pawing off her gloves to shake his hand and give him a mute nod. *Maybe Shari Kane was right. Wit Sec knows what it is doing.*

"Let's start with a tour to get you acquainted, then we'll go to your booth and you can hang up your coat." Litner pointed to a blue footpath painted on the floor a few feet away. "Wherever you go, stay on the blue path. You'll see we have a diversity of machines crowding the floor, and sticking to the path protects both you and the machine operators."

Genevieve's job history mainly listed factories—this, in spite of the fact that Eve had never stepped inside one. She had pictured factory work as a repetitive job performed at a conveyor belt, but at Midwest W-P everyone worked alone. Her exposure to coworkers would be limited to a few people. Again, kudos to Wit Sec.

Litner explained that Midwest W-P was a small stamping facility that made exhaust system parts for cars. The back half of the plant consisted of the press-line area, where raw coiled steel was pressed and shaped into the parts clients wanted. The smaller presses made two parts, left and right, that were sent to the front half of the plant for welding. That was where Genevieve's job came in. When the machine welding proved imperfect, she and other weld repair operators fixed them.

"This is your booth." Litner stepped off the blue path and led her to a tall, narrow, tent-like structure. Eve almost laughed. In size and shape, it looked like an outhouse.

They entered through a door of eight plastic strips that overlapped each other, much like the entrance to a meat locker. Inside, the other three sides consisted of plated steel to keep weld sparks from flying out. A metal desk took up half the space, a chair and a narrow locker the other half.

Litner opened the locker. "Let's exchange your coat for your safety wear."

Self-conscious of her makeover as Genevieve, Eve shrugged out of her coat and with a little guidance by Litner donned her factory attire—a leather apron that reached to her ankles, a lightweight welding jacket, a bandana to cover her hair, and protective gloves.

Litner reached into the locker and removed a pair of safety glasses and a helmet that looked like what an astronaut might wear and set them on the metal table. "Get yourself some leather boots and denim pants with no cuffs, and you'll be all set," he said. "Today we'll look at what you'll be repairing, and tomorrow we'll introduce you to the Tungsten torch."

The tightness she'd been carrying in her chest since last night loosened, the nausea that had hovered all day dissipated. Okay, she could do this. She'd learn how to wield a torch, and she'd shape Genevieve into a quiet, unassuming, melt-into-the-background persona.

For the first time since leaving Chicago, she felt safe—buried inside four pods of protection like nesting dolls: welding attire inside a booth inside a factory inside a small midwestern city.

On the way home, she'd stop and get boots and jeans, pick up a few items at a pharmacy, and buy groceries. Maybe she'd even remember what it was like to drive and sing.

But no, she still had another problem to face. Crisis, really. Tonight she'd have to ask Deputy US Marshal Kane to find her a doctor.

Chapter 31

"No news." Jake opened the truck door and climbed in, reminding himself once again at the loud screech of the hinges that he needed to oil them. He had purchased the old truck to avoid flaunting wealth in the faces of the villagers, but at times he regretted the care the vehicle took.

"I could tell by your face," Crystal muttered. "And your stoop. And pretty soon the sighs."

Jake swallowed his irritation. More and more, the visits to Iba to check on Eve were ending in an exchange of jabs between him and Crystal. It wasn't as if he meant to use the occasion to remind her that Eve wasn't with them because of her. The weekly trip to Iba was simply an opportunity to get one-on-one time with her.

Without thinking, he sighed. And maybe to not be alone when the lack of news about Eve reached deep into his soul with sadness. Regrets dipped like a wooden bucket into the deep well of his misery. Every week he hauled them up: If only he hadn't delayed marrying Eve. If only he hadn't insisted on making Dan part of their family. If only he hadn't promised Emilio he'd take care of the boy.

He heaved a second sigh. Six months ago he'd left Salonga Prison with hopes stacked high. Marriage, family, a return to normal life. Then the ground split open and the hopes tipped into an abyss.

No. He brought himself up short. It was only a matter of months before he'd be called as a witness and he'd see Eve. This time he wouldn't let her disappear. They'd get married and together they'd face what to do about Dan.

He started the truck and shifted gears … and topics. "What's the latest on the villagers concerning Hamza and Muhamoud—you know, now that the two are friendly with the other students?"

Crystal shrugged. Her moods didn't swing easily from icy to warm. "Nothin's changed."

"Any reason?"

A second shrug. "Like, yeah, they blame the Muslims for destroying their crops."

"They aren't Muslim anymore, and it was pigs that trampled the crops." Frustration crisped the edge of Jake's voice.

Crystal's shrug shifted to the twist of one side of her mouth into her cheek. "Someone let the pigs out."

Sourness rose from Jake's gut and settled on his tongue. "I'm tired of this. Today two students left because they didn't want to work crops and construct buildings. They told me they came to learn how to preach, not to gain skills to survive." Bitterness swelled like viper poison in his veins. He missed Eve, two of his students were accused of malice, and now two of his students had deserted the program. He spat out the last, and most vexing, of his rancor. "And Dan—that boy has me at the end of my rope. I don't know what to do about his constant fighting."

He almost slammed on the brakes. "You don't think he let the pigs out, do you?"

Crystal whipped startled eyes at him. "No, Dad. It wasn't him."

Dad. When was the last time she'd called him that? His throat constricted, and he felt a sweet calm infuse his body.

"I think I have a solution." Crystal rubbed the palm of her hand up and down his arm as if calming a jittery horse. "I was going to save it until Dan's birthday next week, but I can give it to him now and we can invite a few of the village boys over for his party." Jake frowned, and she hastened to explain. "It's a way to compete without fighting each other. I'll show you when we get home."

When they arrived, they found Dan and Angelo, Perla's youngest grandson, sitting with glum faces at the table under Perla's stern visage. Dan sported a black eye, and bruises tattooed Angelo's upper arms. The viper poison swelled in Jake's veins again. The kid was almost six years old. What would he be like as a teenager?

He didn't attempt to hide his exasperation. "All right," he snapped, "what happened?"

"All I did was tell him"—Dan darted fierce eyes at Angelo—"that my chicks would beat his in a cockfight when they got bigger and he said all of them were girls and would only wear skirts and lay eggs."

Jake stared in disbelief at the boys. "You got into a fistfight over chickens?"

"He said my chickens were sissies." Dan jutted his chin at Angelo.

Jake pursed his lips. Cockfighting was a Filipino passion, had been for centuries. The birds were specially bred, cared for, and prepared for the sport. Some owners paid high prices for them, and even hired famous handlers to train them for hours each day.

"Listen, boys. Roosters are daddies and protectors of their flocks. But fighting cocks are different. They're like warriors specially trained to attack and kill. They fight till one of them is dead, and the fight takes only seconds. One, two, three … eight, nine, ten"—he clapped his hands in a loud pop—"and one of them is dead. Is that what you want for your chickens?"

Dan paled. Tears beaded his eyes, and he wiped them away with the backs of his hands. "I don't want my chickens to be like my other daddy. We're Chalmers, not Romeros."

"Dudes." Crystal jumped into the fray. "If you each had a warrior, would you let them fight for you and not fight each other?" The boys glanced at each other, then nodded in solemn assent. She narrowed her eyes. "Even if, like, your warrior loses, you won't fight?" Their heads bobbed in unison. "Okay then. Angelo, do you have your spider with you?"

Surprise flicked across Angelo's face, followed by a wide grin. "Yeah." He dug into the deep pocket of his shorts and brought out a matchbox. "I got two of 'em."

"Hold on—don't open it till I get Dan's." Crystal ran from the room and returned with a matchbox similar to Angelo's. She handed it to Dan. "Meet your warrior, dude."

Seconds later, two black, eight-legged warriors faced off on a stick held straight out by Angelo. Jake watched in fascination as the two arachnids went at each other with fangs.

"I learned about this at school," Crystal whispered. "Totally grody, but as rad with the boys as cockfights are with the men. Wish I'd thought of it sooner for Dan."

Before Jake could answer, Angelo's spider fell and crumpled onto the floor with legs in eight upside down Vs. Dan crowed and thrust a fist over his head.

"Uh-uh, I got another warrior," Angelo shouted. He opened his matchbox to loose a spider from a second compartment. This time, Dan's warrior fell.

"Plenty more warriors in chicken coop," Perla said. She swept the boys out the door and the dead spiders after them. "Smart girl!" She patted Crystal on the head and planted a kiss on each cheek.

Jake released an elated guffaw. "Perfect solution—a substitutionary sacrifice!" He caught Crystal in his arms and swung her in a circle to her delighted shrieks.

They trailed Dan and Angelo outside to the chicken coop and watched the boys capture prospective champions among the webs cloaking the fence.

Jake blinked. That's it! He and Puno would set up a vigil outside the compound's dormitory every night to see if they caught Hamza and Muhamoud sneaking out to damage the villagers' crops. That should settle the issue once and for all.

***

Eve buttoned her shirt and adjusted her clothes. She sat primly on the edge of the examination table, her legs dangling with no support, to wait for the doctor to return to the room. He couldn't just tell her the results. Noooo, he wanted to talk to her about them.

The walls and tile floor were white and reflected the brightness of the florescent light overhead. The sheet on the examination table was white, as was the crumpled gown she had discarded onto it. The metal stand holding the doctor's instruments was white without scratch, chip, or dent. Everything was white except the doctor's stool, which had a black cushion and black wheels. White, everything white, no doubt to convey the impression of pristine examinations … and results … and advice.

She wanted to throw up that she even had to be here.

The door cracked open and a cheerful "Ready?" slipped through. Without waiting for an answer, the doctor entered and plopped a generous derriere onto the stool. A white medical jacket cloaked an equally generous waistline. Above the jacket, sagging jowls bracketed a round chin. He smiled and peered at her with the kindest blue eyes she had ever seen.

No question about it, the "talk" would be fatherly.

"Between the ultrasound and the October date you gave me, you are ten or eleven weeks along."

"I don't want it." She flung the truth at him. Bad enough that Jake wanted to include Dan Romero in their family. Adding another was out of the question.

The doctor continued as if she hadn't spoken. "All the basic physiology is in place now, and the little body is almost fully formed. It can bend its tiny limbs and kick and stretch. A few more weeks and you'll feel it."

Eve swallowed and tried again, louder. "I don't want it."

The doctor nodded, eyes pensive on hers, and reached to hold her hand between his big soft ones. "Someone else would love to have it."

"I was raped. And on drugs." She meant it for her defense, but the words came out crumpled between convulsive sobs.

"I'm sorry." The doctor hopped up and wrapped her in a bear hug, pressing her head to his chest. "I'm so, so sorry."

Tears flooded her eyes. When had anyone last hugged her since Ric's assault? She had been too high on drugs to care at first. Then too into recovery to want anything but a fix. She shivered—then too frightened of Blue to think of anything but safety. Yet, underneath, like a victim buried in an avalanche, her soul had been crying out for comfort. She wanted Jake. She wanted Jake's arms around her.

She drove home still snuffling. Deputy Kane's unmarked car stood parked to one side of the driveway so Eve could pull in and not block her. Probably fearful the news from the doctor would send Eve on a hunt for drugs.

They sat in the living room and Eve gave a clipped report. "I'm eleven weeks pregnant and I'm told I have three options: accept, adopt, or abort."

Kane pressed her lips together in an obvious attempt to keep her face passive. "Tough decision."

"Yeah." Eve clasped her knees and leaned toward Kane. "Let me put those in personal terms. I can keep a baby I don't want, I can cast my responsibility for a drug-addicted infant onto someone else's shoulders, or I can kill off a Romero." She sat back. "Which do you think I'd like to do?"

Kane's eyebrows flicked high. "What did the doctor say?"

"That he'd support me, whatever my decision." But the kindness in those blue eyes had said what he wanted her to choose.

But how could she?

Chapter 32

February

"Father, allow me to kill our enemy. Every day I have opportunity." Muhamoud slapped a *kris*, its ornately molded hilt glinting in the office light, onto his father's desk. The dagger's blade was long, straight and slender, easily identifying it as a *jihad* weapon of choice for executing infidels.

Twice in Mindanao, Muhamoud had watched the condemned kneel before an executioner, a wad of cotton placed on their clavicle area and the *kris* blade thrust through the padding to pierce the subclavian artery and the heart. Death came within seconds. Upon withdrawal, the cotton wiped the blade clean.

"You have been patient," Amir replied, "and your wise conduct has allayed suspicion." His eyes told Muhamoud he was pleased, and Muhamoud held his chin high as a swell of pride rippled up his chest and tightened his throat.

Amir's expression changed, and he took the *kris* and rested it on his flattened palm. "But Allah has said no. Three times he has spared this infidel from the hands of assassins. Though I wish for revenge, I must conclude that Allah has other plans. His will is for bigger things than the death of Jacob Chalmers."

Muhamoud stiffened. "We will not avenge Salmid's death? How can we not give him this honor?" He knew of his young brother's dream to join Osama Bin Laden in Afghanistan and their father's stern insistence that Salmid respect the family and submit to serving it as an accountant. His cheek twitched. Even as a small boy Salmid had bucked the chain of command. How good that the wisdom of Allah placed the oldest brother in charge of the family and not a wild, young one like Salmid.

But to die in *jihad* in Afghanistan was preferable to the death that had shamed Salmid. An assassin's bullet had taken his innocent brother instead of Jacob Chalmers. Only the death of the intended target would restore honor. "Every night, Father, Chalmers and Puno watch for Hamza and me to slip out to damage the villagers' crops. The darkness would hide the end of our enemy's life."

Amir leaned across the desk. "Allah wants more than one man's death. You must find opportunity to end all lives on the compound."

Muhamoud's heart leaped. He had never been assigned a mass murder before. It was all he could do not to hug his father. "And Hamza? He is accepting their lies."

Amir slid the *kris* back to Muhamoud. "Then he must face his betrayal and die the death of a traitor."

Unspeakable joy shook Muhamoud, and his hand trembled as he took hold of the *kris*. All these months of listening to lies, of living the filth of a Gentile life, of pretending to take the enemies of Allah into his heart—at last *jihad* was his and he could bring honor to his brother, to his family, and to the only true god.

***

Eve drove by the church five times before she could bring herself to climb the snow-trampled steps and enter. The congregation was singing *Just As I Am* with voices sober and tremulously grateful. Her breath caught in a tight clamp in her lungs. How long had it been since she had sung in a church choir? She snuffed a quick intake of air, shuffled into a seat at the back of the small sanctuary, and swiped at the wetness in her eyes. She wouldn't cry, she wouldn't, even though it sure seemed like God had just taken her into His arms and told her He loved her.

Would these people accept her just as she was? Pregnant, husbandless, a lost and bedraggled sheep roaming the hinterlands? She bore no cause for their esteem—she was a weld repair operator, not a judge. She was rich—but hid in poverty. She was beautiful, articulate, confident—but remade into humble. She had nothing to offer but a strayed heart that loved Jesus and wanted back into His family.

With trembling hands, she picked up the hymnal and let God's arms enfold her.

***

The next morning, she gave in to her waistline and went to her job with jeans unbuttoned beneath an untucked flannel shirt. Naked before the bathroom mirror she could see the slight bulge in her belly, but, fully clothed, it was not discernible. She resisted the urge to flatten her fingers on the area where the doctor said she would feel the flutter of the growing child. The parasite. The Romero leech. She couldn't bring herself to kill it, but she didn't have to love it.

The parking lot at Midwest W-P was slick with ice, and she half-walked, half-skidded to the entry doors. Two months on the job, and she was getting good at welding. It didn't require a rocket scientist, just skill. She hid the ease of her progress, though. Didn't jump to the head of the line, made sure she made mistakes, reminded herself daily of the deputy marshal's words: *beautiful, articulate, confident.* More and more, humble Genevieve Wertz was none of those.

She could switch jobs before the leech was born, Kane told her. Wit Sec gave her that freedom. She could buy a house. Buy a better car too. But never, Kane emphasized, without consulting the US Marshals. Always and forever, till death did them part, Wit Sec needed to protect Genevieve, to guide her into good decisions, to sculpt her life as nondescript Genevieve Wertz.

The thought ate at her all morning until she found herself gritting her teeth. Wit Sec wanted to be her big brother and rule her life, didn't it? Well, she didn't want to be part of its family. She didn't want the Romero leech in her family, and she didn't want Wit Sec as her big brother. Once she completed her obligation as a witness at Roza Romero's trial, she would ditch these problems, switch families, and escape with Jake.

Last night, Kane had told her the Romero case had made it to the grand jury and that Roza was indicted but released on bail. "She will be stepping up her search for you," Kane warned as the two of them prepared Eve's deposition. Ric, too, was free. Absent the syringe, there was no sustainable case against him.

Eve ended the workday feeling as though she had sucked lemons all morning. She slammed her locker door just as Ray Litner stuck his head into her cubicle. "Bad day?"

"Complicated," she answered. She stuffed her mood out of sight with a half-laugh. "Nothing a good shopping spree can't fix."

Which, come to think of it, wasn't a bad idea. She needed clothes for her expanding waistline, and her wardrobe for church could use a little spiffing up. She strode across the now-slushy parking lot and headed the car for a small, out-of-the-way mall. Maybe pick up some groceries, too, and invite the pastor and his wife over for a meal this week. May as well discuss her pregnancy right off the bat.

Forty minutes and two shopping bags of clothes later, she drove downtown, spirits definitely lifted. Parking spaces at the grocery were sparse at that hour of the day, and she had to walk from the back of the lot to the store. The checkout line was long too. Otherwise, she might have missed Paula on her way out the door.

"Eve?" The voice hesitated with her name.

If only she hadn't turned around, she might have avoided recognition. Could have walked away. Could have denied acknowledgement and left Paula wondering. But she did turn. Her name captured her as surely as if a lasso had settled over her head. She spun around and responded before the noose could choke off Paula's name from her lips.

Paula Beauchamp, coach of Crystal's high school volleyball team, stared agape at Eve. Behind Paula, a gaggle of teenage girls gawked with eyes and mouths equally wide.

Eve froze, heart stuck in her throat. She had been discovered.

"I'm sorry," she blurted, "but I've got to run." And she did.

Straight to her car.

Straight home to call Deputy US Marshal Shari Kane.

"They recognized me," Eve whispered. "They'll tell everyone."

"Pack up," Kane barked. "A marshal will arrive in half an hour to escort you to a safe house. You'll get a new assignment from there. Good luck, Eve."

And just like that, Deputy US Marshal Kane was out of Eve's life. The church and its open arms were a puff of smoke. And the kindly, blue-eyed doctor would not see her child born.

A new location, a new job, a new identity would put their stamp on her. But she knew the ropes of Wit Sec now, she could handle it. What mattered was that Roza must not find her.

Chapter 33

June

Eve stiffened, telephone receiver clamped to her ear, until a static burr replaced the US Marshal's voice. She hung up, goose bumps prickling her body. The marshal's message settled in slow reality, so that she had to inhale several breaths to absorb it. Roza Romero's trial had a date. Eve must return to Chicago.

She bumbled into the kitchen and with trembling hands set the kettle on the stove for a cup of tea. Country Peach or maybe Black Cherry Berry. Definitely decaffeinated. Her insides were already shaking.

She told herself she was ready. Keen to get on with it. Eager to get the trial off her plate and move on with the life she wanted.

A downright lie. Half a lie, anyway.

Chicago held enemies waiting to kill her. Twice they had outsmarted her. First with Ricardo Romero posing as Rock Giannopoulus, then with Roza Romero posing as Laina. They knew Eve's vulnerabilities. Had known how to schmooze her. And they would know how to use the vulnerabilities of the court system. Know how to schmooze the jury.

And … she was eight months pregnant. She plopped onto the hard wood of a kitchen chair and put her feet up on another. Acid washed the back of her throat at the thought of Ric watching her cross to the witness stand, his eyes widening at her pregnancy. Surmising, correctly, that the child was his. She ground her teeth.

And Jake? Would he do a double take? Would he remember telling her it didn't matter if she were pregnant? "We're a family," he had claimed passionately. "We don't desert each other when bad things happen."

The kettle whistled, and she got up, made the cup of tea, sat back down at the table with paper and pen to make a to-do list for quitting Wit Sec. Pack—a no-brainer. She'd use a small backpack and leave her suitcase in the garage. Passport—check. Wit Sec provided one "just in case." Give notice at work—nah. Wit Sec had relocated her to Arizona and given her a job shelving books in the musty stacks of a local library. She wouldn't be hard to replace.

The rental house and car belonged to Wit Sec, so she could just leave them. And her doctor? He'd simply shrug his shoulders when she didn't make appointments. Truth to tell, no one here was interested in her life. She sniffed. Suited her. She hadn't expected a quick-and-easy severance of relationships to be part of Wit Sec, but now she knew to protect herself against the hurt.

She added *Buy cosmetics* to her list. Given Paula's recognition of her, Eve had abandoned the failed makeover and let her hair and eyebrows grow out. Still no makeup, though. Until now. In Chicago, she would appear in the courtroom as Judge Evedene Eriksson.

And she would be reunited with Jake.

She knew the trial date had to have been set a while ago, that Wit Sec had waited to inform her until it was time to go. Still, it took her breath away that in a week a US Marshal would pick her up, fly with her to Chicago, and stay by her side every minute she wasn't in the witness stand.

Would his protection be enough in Romero territory?

***

Eve unbuckled her seatbelt, struggled into her carry-on backpack, and lumbered down the plane's narrow aisle behind Deputy US Marshal Goins into O'Hare Airport. With no need to pick up luggage, they made a beeline straight to the Everett Dirksen Courthouse. Her heart pounded against her throat on entering the building that had once been her second home as an Assistant US Attorney and then as a federal judge. The click of high heels on marble floors, the wafts of air against her face as people with stern visages and clutched briefcases dashed by, the doors of familiar offices and courtrooms and meeting rooms—all were intimate acquaintances of a life to which she was no longer privy.

But it was the fear of Roza Romero that held Eve's emotions tight in her chest. The grip of the marshal's hand on her arm down the long courthouse hallways was a rudder to weak knees. He steered her to a small room, assured her he would be on guard outside the door, and left her to settle in for what she knew would be a long wait.

She dropped the backpack to the floor and sat gingerly on the couch. The last occupants of the room must have brought in popcorn. The buttery smell turned her stomach. She unwrapped a stick of mint gum and tossed the wrapping into a plastic-lined wastebasket. So, that's where she the offending popcorn bag was. She loosened the plastic liner and tied the top into a knot to kill the smell. If only all her other problems could be so easily resolved.

She sat and put her feet up. Chewed her gum. Wished she had a cup of tea. Earl Grey. Definitely caffeinated. Her nerves had already exhausted themselves and she needed a pick-me-up.

The room was stark—white walls, gray carpet, two armchairs, and the couch she was sitting on. And a wastebasket. She had brought a book to read, but that required a focused brain.

Somewhere nearby was Jake, probably also sequestered as a witness. They would not be allowed to meet before their courtroom appearances lest they connive to match testimonies. She huffed at the safeguard. Okay, it was a legitimate precaution, but so totally unnecessary in their case. She would just have to wait until each of them had testified and they were allowed to sit in the gallery. They would sit side-by-side, Jake taking her hand into his, and together they would observe the triumph of Lady Justice over their archenemy.

And Jake would reassure her that her pregnancy by another man was not a problem.

***

Andrew Perez took his seat at the US Attorney's table and shed fifty pounds of relief with a long sigh through his nostrils. Eve would have been pleased with his opening statement, he was sure. As a young lawyer in the Chicago office, he had made it his task to attend every lawsuit she tried, had taken copious notes, and afterwards had discussed the strategy with her to confirm he was on target. He considered it an honor and a privilege to win this case for her.

He was well prepared to walk the jury to a guilty verdict. He would present four pieces of evidence, he told them, that beyond a reasonable doubt would prove Roza Romero's guilt. Number one: the physical evidence of an amphetamine overdose found in Henshaw's cup of cocoa. Numbers two and three: the testimonies of two witnesses—Jake Chalmers and Evedene Eriksson — that Roza Romero had disguised herself as a waitress to serve the tainted cocoa and had done so minutes before Henshaw's death. And, most importantly, number four: the eyewitness testimony of the waiter turned federal witness who had assisted Romero in the two-month buildup to addiction that finally killed Bradley Henshaw. Every face in the jury had been attentive, some openly intrigued. Perez smiled to himself. What could the defense offer against this?

A chair scraped, and the Romero lawyer rose to his feet to present the defense's opening statement. Emerson Farland, gray hair a tad long, curling ever so slightly on the back of his neck, stepped to the podium placed in the middle of the courtroom to address the jury. Perez felt his own eyes and no doubt everyone else's in the courtroom drawn to the tall, slender man clothed in a perfectly cut Emporio Armani suit. Perez grimaced at the image of success, power, and authority prepared to battle him for the jurors' souls.

For a moment the courtroom seemed to hold its breath. Twenty people were in attendance—the twelve-member jury and an alternate, a Deputy US Marshal, the judge, bailiff, and recorder, the defendant, and the two defense and prosecution lawyers. It was a closed trial. No media circus muttering in the gallery. All witnesses sequestered.

"Ladies and gentlemen of the jury—" At the defense attorney's voice, the courtroom recharged. Lungs inhaled oxygen, clothing rustled, the court recorder tapped on keys.

Farland's brow furrowed into a thoughtful pose. "Have you ever felt wounded in your heart because you befriended another person, were kind to them and went out of your way for them, only to have them turn and betray you?" His mouth tightened into a thin line at the very idea. "This trial is an attempt to make Roza Romero the scapegoat for the improper actions of others. In this proceeding, we are going to bring before you person after person who will testify to the fact that they observed multiple acts of kindness on the part of my client toward Ms. Eriksson and Mr. Henshaw.

"Why were these acts of kindness performed? It was not for any financial gain or benefit, but simply as a demonstration of the kind of loving person Roza Romero is. You see, Roza has no daughter, and in her heart she adopted Ms. Eriksson and treated her like the daughter she always wanted.

"I'm not going to speculate on why these two powerful people turned on Roza. But the facts of this case will show that she was convenient—convenient through the location of her little café close by the federal building where Ms. Eriksson and Mr. Henshaw worked. Convenient for their lunch breaks where Ms. Eriksson and Mr. Henshaw could slip the drug of their choice into the hot chocolate featured by Roza's Cuppa Chocolatte Café. More importantly, convenient in case their addiction was discovered by Roza, because of the threat they represented from putting Roza's husband in jail, where he was mysteriously murdered before he could face trial."

Farland paused, and Perez rolled his eyes at the man's drama. He noted Farland's reference to Eve and Brad by their last names to create distance between the jury and them, while referring to Roza Romero by her first name to create a sense of familiarity.

"The undisputed facts of this case," Farland continued, "will show that Ms. Eriksson and Mr. Henshaw had an illegal drug problem. Let me be more specific. When examined by health personnel, they both had amphetamine in their systems at a level that said their bodies had made a significant adjustment to it—the kind of adjustment that happens when you take amphetamine over a period of time and not just for a one-time use. The evidence points to Ms. Eriksson and Mr. Henshaw as habitual drug abusers." Farland's voice rose as he emphasized the last word. "*Abusers* by their choice. *Abusers* who conspired to meet for a buzz over lunch. *Abusers* who shielded themselves behind the wife of a man they had put in jail."

Again, Farland tightened his lips into a thin line. "Yet the Assistant US Attorney would have you believe that Roza hid the drug in their food and beverage at the café over a two-month period of time. He would have you believe that Roza disguised herself to trick them into trusting her, when all she was doing was avoiding the loss of business the Romero name might cause. And he would have you believe a waiter speaks the truth when he points to Roza as a murderer. A waiter with a huge gambling debt he can now avoid paying by bargaining with the government to testify against his employer. In exchange for what? For refuge in the Witness Protection program where his creditors can't find him.

"Why is Roza Romero here today on trial? Not because she is a murderer, but because she refused to be the shield that Ms. Eriksson and Mr. Henshaw expected to hide behind. Because, instead, she exposed them. She dared to write a letter to the *Chicago Tribune* to publicly demand drug tests for these two high-powered public servants—a US Attorney and federal judge, mind you—who were betraying the trust of those they were supposed to protect."

Farland turned his head to gaze at Roza Romero, seated demurely at the defense table. She cast her eyes down as she became the focus of the courtroom's attention. Farland pursed his lips and turned back to the jury. "Ladies and gentlemen of the jury, Roza Romero is innocent. She is here on trial, not because she is a murderer, but because she is a scapegoat."

Andrew Perez's heart ticked ten beats for every step Farland took returning to his seat beside Roza Romero. He swallowed, rose, and addressed the judge. "I call my first witness, Dr. Robert Stein, Medical Examiner of the Cook County Institute of Forensic Medicine."

The bailiff moved the attorneys podium from its location near the jury to its new placement near the witness stand. Perez, forcing his face to express a confidence he didn't feel quite as keenly after Farland's opening statement, walked to the podium to wait for Dr. Stein to be sworn in. *Chin up*, he reminded himself. He had hard evidence to win over the jury, whereas Farland had only drama.

Lady Justice would not fall target to the Romeros at this trial.

Chapter 34

Minutes dragged with leaden feet into an hour. Eve squirmed on her chair, shifted positions, rubbed her swollen belly. The discomfort wasn't just that of the Romero leech stuffed tight against her guts and waistline. It was the disquiet of forced separation from the courtroom. Of not knowing what was happening. Of having to trust someone else with her destiny.

It was vital that Roza Romero be convicted of murdering Bradley Henshaw. Not only for the sake of justice in the death of her friend and mentor, but also for the sake of Eve's life and the safety of those she loved. To convict Roza was to chop off another leg of the Romero crime organization, to render it lame and even further disabled after Danny Romero's death in October.

Equally important—perhaps more so now—to convict Roza was to free Eve. Long enough, anyway, to flee the confines of Wit Sec and hide with Jake.

She got to her feet awkwardly and began pacing. Andrew Perez was the Justice Department's lawyer—she'd at least been told that much. And she'd caught a glimpse of Dr. Stein, the Medical Examiner, in the hallway. Surely Perez had witnesses from the Cuppa Chocolatte Café lined up. If they'd talk.

She put herself into Perez's shoes, walked herself through the strategy he'd use. After years of mentoring him, she knew how he thought, knew his presentation would be linear. First he'd establish the buildup of amphetamine in Henshaw's body—use the medical examiner's autopsy for that. Also use the ME to share the forensic evidence of the overdose of amphetamine found in Henshaw's cup the day he died. Next, Perez would bring in witnesses from the café—waiters, kitchen staff, the cashier—to identify "Laina" as the server who always waited on Henshaw, the server who had the opportunity to consistently slip the drug into Henshaw's cocoa.

And finally he'd bring in her and Jake. Her, probably first, to testify to Laina's deception of who she really was. Perhaps, as well, for Eve to testify to the slow buildup of her own symptoms of amphetamine addiction over the two months. And no doubt to the GHB administered to her on the day of Henshaw's death that removed her from the scene.

Jake would be an even stronger witness. He had been in Roza's home and had therefore instantly recognized her at the café. His arrival at the Cuppa sent her fleeing, leaving behind a woozy Henshaw already in the process of succumbing to the drug overdose in his cocoa.

But all this was circumstantial. What Perez really needed was an eyewitness.

***

Troy Rollin's guts pinched into a razor wire of knots when the security guard halted at his holding cell. All morning Rollin had watched other prisoners be escorted into the Dirksen Courthouse basement, warehoused in individual cells, and eventually led in handcuffs to the prisoners-only elevator and on up to the courtrooms. It was his turn.

He swallowed against a leather-dry tongue. He could hardly believe he'd made it this far. Every day at the Metropolitan Correctional Center, he'd fed off anxiety in expectation of a Romero-executed revenge. Even in solitaire he hadn't felt safe. Who dared to defy the Romeros and expect to live? But given the odds of the Romeros versus the mob and the huge gambling debt Rollin owed them, he'd taken his chances on outmaneuvering the Romeros. And now here he was—all he had to do was testify against Roza and he'd be under the protection of the US Marshals, hidden away in the Witness Protection Program.

"Let's go, pissant." The security guard unlocked Rollin's cell, cuffed his hands behind his back, and shoved him toward the elevator.

Freedom! It really was going to happen! Rollin's heart rose in giddiness. Once he stepped into that courtroom—into that fortress of the law that not even the Romeros could invade—he would step out on the other side a free man!

The metal doors of the elevator slid shut with only the two of them inside. But the guard, instead of punching the Up button, turned his back to the doors and dug into the right trouser pocket of his uniform. "I got a present here for ya from Roza."

Rollin felt his eyes go wide and the blood drop from his face. He hadn't counted on a bribed law officer. He struggled against the cuffs. No one would hear him yell for help.

The guard brought his hand up and pointed a miniature spray bottle at Rollin's mouth. "She thought two milligrams of fentanyl would help ya relax at the trial. Say *ahhhh*."

Two milligrams was a death sentence. Rollin pressed his lips together and whipped his face to the side.

"Now, now, can't keep them waiting." In one swift movement, the guard punched the Up button and at the same time smashed his boot hard onto Rollin's foot. Rollin's mouth flew open in a wheeze of pain. He closed it with the deadly spray invading his tongue and the insides of his cheeks with an intense euphoria.

He heard the elevator doors grumble open, felt the guard's grasp on his shoulder to steer him toward a man in a suit standing by a closed door.

"The bailiff will take you inside, and you'll do just fine." The elevator doors grumbled again and, *poof*, just like that, the guard evaporated.

The bailiff mumbled something … maybe about removing the handcuffs before entering the courtroom? Rollin's arms swung free. The door opened. The bailiff nudged him forward.

The first thing he noticed was the air conditioning. Good thing, cuz he was suddenly sweaty. And, look, there was Roza. Seated at a table. Face deadpan. Eyes glued to him.

He should say somethin' but his windpipe had narrowed, as if someone had put a sieve over his air intake. His lungs had to work harder with the sieve limiting his oxygen. He opened his mouth wider, and shallow breaths ballooned his chest in and out.

He stumbled and someone steadied him. But then his knees caved. The lights dimmed. His eyelids fluttered, and darkness drifted over him.

***

Eve jumped when the US Marshal flung open the door to the waiting room. The set of his jaw and the length of his stride shot her heartbeat into double time. Something was wrong.

Before she could ask, he had ahold of her elbow and was hustling her out of the room. "The trial has been postponed, ma'am. I'm taking you to a safe house."

A safe house? Not a hotel where most sequestered witnesses stayed? Three steps into the hallway she stopped and refused to budge. "Tell me what happened," she demanded.

The marshal urged her forward but leaned down to mutter in her ear. "US Attorney's key witness entered the courtroom and dropped dead. Judge has locked down the courtroom to investigate the cause."

Eve gasped a breath that pierced her lungs like a sharpened arrow. *Roza!* She had manipulated this!

"Eve?"

The familiar voice jerked her head to the left. Only the marshal's restraint kept her from leaping at Ricardo Romero with flailing fists.

Ric rose from his seat on a hallway bench. "Our baby," he exclaimed. "You're carrying our baby!"

When his eyes shifted suddenly to a figure across the hall, Eve, a sickening feeling in her stomach, followed his gaze.

Jake.

His face said it all. Shock. Dismay. Revulsion.

The marshal all but picked her up and carried her. "We've got to go, ma'am."

Eve shook her head violently as he rushed her away. Her legs stumbled in protest, but it was only her heart she was aware of. The pain that clutched it cried out to the still figure that didn't move. Didn't follow after her. Didn't chase down the love of his life.

I told you I might be pregnant, Jake! You said it didn't matter, that we're family and we don't desert each other when bad things happen!

But it did matter, didn't it?

Because the man she loved had just deserted her.

Chapter 35

Jake blinked as Eve disappeared around a corner. His brain rumbled to life, spitting and hissing like a machine operating on fumes. He broke into a run. He'd waited all these months to see her, pined for her every second of every day, and he'd let the surprise of her pregnancy knock him to his knees? He gritted his teeth. No, more than that, much more than that was the sight of Ric Romero next to her.

"Stop." An iron hand landed on his shoulder. He spun around to face the Deputy US Marshal who earlier had escorted him to a waiting room. Jake's Marine Corps training to respect authority halted his feet. He forced himself not to swipe the marshal's hand off his shoulder.

"I need to catch up with her." He pointed down the hallway. "To Eve. Eve Eriksson."

"I'm sorry, but you're a sequestered witness, and I've been told to escort you to a secure hotel room."

"But I haven't testified yet." Had Eve? Why was she leaving? A glance at his watch told him it was barely past noon. "Is this a break for lunch?"

"The trial's been postponed until tomorrow. In the meantime, your meals will be provided in your room." The marshal removed his hand from Jake's shoulder and indicated they move forward.

But the next morning, the marshal told him the trial had been dismissed, and that he was free to go. And that with Roza free, Eve had been whisked away by Wit Sec. Neither a telephone call nor a letter to Eve were options at Jake's disposal.

His only hope was that she would think to contact him through Detective Lee in the Philippines.

***

Only pride, clutched tightly to her bosom, kept Eve from bawling her heart out on the flight back to Arizona. The deputy marshal, stiff and silent in the seat next to her, knew she was Judge Evedene Eriksson, and there was no way she was going to place herself on exhibit as weak. But when she unlocked the door to her rental house, she left the lights off, crawled into bed, and let loose.

Imprinted on the inside of her eyelids was Jake's face. His feelings had been on display like roadkill guts. Over and over, her mind reviewed them. Shock—dismay—revulsion.

If only he had called out. Or run after her.

But he had let her go.

"There's nothing can keep us apart," he'd told her. But he hadn't known his own heart then, had he? Hadn't known a flawed wife fell short of what he wanted. Hadn't known he'd be tested and the truth revealed.

Revulsion. That said it all.

She called in sick the next day. What did she care about shelving library books?

***

What did she care about anything? Minutes passed into hours passed into days. A hard lump of coal crowded her insides as if she were a Christmas stocking and Santa had checked her off on the naughty list. The frontal lobe of her brain ached with weariness behind eyeballs wrung out with tears. She cried to God, but her wails fell on deaf ears, and a thick mist darkened the landscape of her mind. Was there no one to help her?

A week later, in July, the library let her go because she shelved the wrong books on the wrong shelves. She sat at home in front of the TV and gazed numbly at shifting shadows garbling unintelligible words. Even *Night Court* failed to elicit a response from her. When she began to wish Blue would find her and put her out of her misery, she knew she had to do something.

She called George Peterman.

The deep rumble of the chaplain's voice released the lock on her inner jail. She couldn't help but smile, his face as clear in her mind as the day she'd met him four years ago. Intense blue eyes, halo-white hair combed straight back, leathery skin around eyes and mouth that crinkled into a thousand tiny grins when he threw back his head and laughed. He'd been her anchor since the time she awakened from her coma with no memory. "Eve! I feared you'd vanished from the face of the earth!"

She explained to him that, indeed, she had disappeared. And with her, everything that mattered—her judgeship, her family, Jake and Crystal, her independence, a life that had meaning. Her very identity. She told him about the pregnancy and that she was giving up the baby for adoption. "I'll be put under anesthesia and never see it," she said. "I don't want to know if it's a boy or a girl. I don't want to know if it's healthy or affected by my addiction. I'm sending it off into its own little Wit Sec program, out of my life and out of my mind."

When every gut had been spilled and every tear shed, Eve hushed. The silence that followed told her Peterman was praying. "Help me," she pleaded.

"I'm sorry for your troubles," he said softly. "God's providence is mysterious, but sometimes He lets us unravel it. Go to Him and event-by-event trace the bad on back to when things changed from the good. Then talk about the *why* to Him."

She agreed, although frankly it sounded like a bother rather than a help.

"One more thing, Eve. Take spiritual responsibility for your baby. Before you send it away, hold it in your arms and pray for it. Pray for God's blessing on it, and for a destiny that ends in Heaven."

She swallowed hard on that one. "I don't know …"

"You'll never regret it."

"It's a Romero, I don't care how young or helpless it is …"

"Care this one time, that's all."

She didn't make any promises. But when she hung up, though the pit of her stomach remained rock hard and the frontal lobe of her brain equally leaden, the sadness around her heart began to lift.

***

"Your baby is coming early." Dr. Como's face was sober.

Eve's breath stopped. Was something wrong?

"You're dilated to three centimeters. Go home, pack a bag, and set it by the door. It could be tonight, it could be a week from now. Do you have someone to take you to the hospital?"

Her breath rushed from her lungs. "A taxi?" She couldn't expect the marshal to take her, could she? If only Marshal Kane were here, she'd take Eve.

"Taxi is fine. You have my number. Call me when your contractions are five minutes apart."

She wanted to ask if this was the effects of the amphetamine. Was the damage showing up now, causing her baby to come early? *Her baby.* She recoiled. No. It wasn't her baby. It was Ric's. It was his leech, and at last she would be rid of it.

"You still want to proceed with your plan?"

"Yes." She answered emphatically. "Put me under, and bring me out when it's all over."

***

She lay at the end of her living room couch, feet elevated, television off, shades drawn, and waited. Nothing happened. Only a dark, heavy ache that started at the back of her throat and crept down to a cavern deep inside her that wrapped the interior of her chest. Loneliness, sadness, emptiness chipped away at her heart. She longed for an end to it all.

"Trace events back to their beginning," George Peterman had said. "From the bad to when things changed from the good." She worked at it, but there was no anchor to her soul, and she drifted on great swells of a hollow ocean.

The events were tiny tugboats that hauled her like a disabled ocean liner to a port she'd never aimed for. Working backwards from Wit Sec, she ticked off the tugboats: her rape and the murder of Bradley Henshaw ... before that, Roza's deception as Laina ... her and Brad's amphetamine addiction ... their meetings at the café ... sending Jake away ... his foolish contact with the Romeros ...

She sat up. That was it! Jake's decision to make Danny Romero's grandson part of their family!

Her heartbeat reverberated like crashing lightning bolts in her head. Without question, that was the event that had changed the good to the bad! Jake's dogged determination to include a Romero in the family had shipwrecked their marriage plans. She laughed bitterly at the irony—and what goes around comes around: her getting pregnant with a Romero had shipwrecked the plans for Jake.

She wrapped her arms over her chest and rocked back and forth. It was all so clear now. She and Jake had been on course, and happily so, to marry. It all changed when he went to the Romero compound and extracted the boy. Jake knew the Romeros were her archenemy, yet he had proceeded anyway, had returned expecting her to simply fit in with his wishes. As if their hearts would be one.

But there was no room in her heart for a Romero—and most certainly not as a family member. Family was about loving and protecting and prospering each other. The Romeros had not only destroyed her life, but had demolished countless other lives through drugs and trafficking, not to mention murder and rape. The world was best off getting rid of them.

She stood, suddenly aware that the couch cushion was damp. Her water had broken.

Hands shaking, feeling all alone and for all the world that nobody cared, she called Dr. Como, then a taxi.

Chapter 36

Pain that moments before had been two on a scale of ten climbed swiftly. At the hospital, Eve submitted gratefully to the capable hands of Nurse Alexis. "We're keeping Dr. Como informed of your progress," Alexis told her, "and the anesthesiologist is on his way to talk to you."

"What? Why? I'm not changing my mind!" Eve's tone of voice made it clear she was not open to discussing her decision about the baby.

"Why? Because we're nice around here." Cheerful eyes backed up a genuinely happy grin. "All of us in the hospital introduce ourselves. It's part of caring for our patients."

"I'm giving the baby away," Eve growled. She didn't want nice. "So put me under, and don't anyone tell me what sex it is or what happens to it."

Alexis patted Eve's arm. "I trust you have good reason for your decision, and I have no problem with it."

Eve swallowed. The kindness was harder to take than the nice.

A short, balding man strolled into the room, arm extended for a handshake. His smile said the shake would be a hearty one. What was it with these people? Their cheeriness only made her want to bite them.

"Dr. Weber, your anesthesiologist," he said. "Just a few questions and we'll get you ready to go."

Eve gulped. He had the same compassionate eyes as her doctor in Nebraska. "I—"

Chaplain Peterman's request pinched her conscience. "I've changed my mind. I want to hold it … bless it … before I send it away. Just a few seconds, that's all." Her breath shuddered in her lungs. *It's still an it, a leech.*

Weber's eyebrows jumped in coordinated delight with an upward curve of his mouth. "Absolutely! Shall we bring the baby to you after you wake up, or do you want to stay awake, maybe use another anesthesia?"

"Stay awake." She groaned as a contraction seized her body. "But give me something … anything … to minimize this."

What seemed like a century of pain later, Alexis placed a tiny bundle on Eve's chest. Eve automatically folded it into her arms. She peered inside the blanket. A pink little face scrunched its nose and eyes and issued a howl of protest. Vernix, mixed with blood, smeared the baby's scalp and neck and chest. Eve's heart thundered a joy she had never known before.

In a flash she remembered something else Peterman had urged her to do. Not to just trace the bad back to when everything had changed, but to talk to God about it.

She hadn't done that.

She shivered as light filled her soul. *What am I to see, Lord?*

The answer smote her, hard and swift: It wasn't Jake she should fault, but herself.

Her breath stilled as the thought took root.

She had complained to Peterman that she had lost her identity. Yet God had brought her into His family, not as Evedene Ericksson or as a judge or as a future wife or mother. Certainly not as someone worthy of being included— not in God's perfect family.

But she was accepted because she was God's beloved. That was her true identity. Didn't matter if she was a judge or a weld repair operator, in Wit Sec or Chicago, living in a mansion or a clapboard rental house. God wanted her, had saved her, had taken the initiative to bring her into a relationship with Him. She was family—forever.

That's what Jake had done with Dan. But not her. She had rejected the child as unworthy. Had relegated him to a destiny of wickedness simply because he was a Romero. Had denied any chance of a relationship between them.

Her breath went out of her stony, came back trembling, shaking her.

Could she love the boy? Treasure him as God treasured her? Make room for him as God had for her?

Shame flooded the pit of self-righteousness that had been holding her soul hostage. Her breath exploded into heart-wrenched sobs.

"Are you okay?" Face etched with concern, Alexis hovered over her. "Should I take the baby now?"

"No," Eve choked out. She heaved in two breaths of air, swiped at her tears, and snuggled the squalling infant against her cheek. She didn't have access to Dan, but already she loved this little Romero. And if God brought young Dan back into her life, she would snuggle him into her heart too, grateful for the privilege.

She blinked wet eyes at Alexis. "Is it a boy or a girl?"

"A girl. As perfect as can be," Alexis gushed.

No, not perfect—but like her imperfect mother, totally beloved. "She's family," Eve said. "She's staying with me."

***

September

Blue set the mailer of audiotapes onto the makeshift desk Roza had provided in the storage shed. She'd said no one could see what he was doing hidden away like this, but she sure hadn't thought about the temperature being in the eighties, had she? Sun beating down like that, it was twice as hot inside the shed as outside. More sweat rolled down his chest and back and legs than the five-minute shower he'd taken last Saturday. He wondered that the flies didn't drop dead at the stench. But he'd promised he'd locate Eriksson, and he'd face the heat of hell before he'd fail Roza.

He snorted. Yeah, and things just might've gotten easier now that Eriksson had a tater tot in the oven. Ric had said she looked like she'd burst any minute. She might be hiding in Wit Sec, but no way she'd keep the news to herself once the kid popped out. Someone dear to her would get a phone call, and Blue was confident his spies had wiretapped every one of those dears.

He opened the mailer and dumped out the tapes recording George

187

Peterman's calls. Their plastic casings clattered on the wood. His cohort had numbered them consecutively by date, one through thirty-one for July, the same for August. The kid had to have been born sometime during then, and maybe Eriksson had called her chaplain friend. If not, Blue still had more mailers to sort through.

He selected July fifteen, inserted it in the tape recorder, and punched the Play button. Tape by tape he moved forward until at July twenty-nine, *Bingo!*

Target acquired.

***

Ricardo Romero flipped the TV news to a different channel. His stomach spat bile to the back of his throat. Impossible to watch the news without hearing about the blasted HIV virus. They were calling it the gay plague. Insult, in his case, added to injury. He would never forgive his mother.

His brothers entered the den and scooted to chairs a safe distance from him. Their eyes fastened on him as if he bore a skull-and-crossbones flag above fully loaded cannons aimed their way. His meals, his dishes, his laundry were separate from the family's.

Their fear hurt. He scowled at them, sorely tempted to bite them and put them in his camp.

The tap of his mother's cane on the hall floor revealed the reason for his brothers' presence. Mother dear had news. His scowl deepened into a glare of pure hatred as she limped in and barricaded herself behind his brothers. Her mouth puckered into a tight smile that said she was pleased with herself.

"We found Eriksson," she announced.

Ric sat up straight. "Where?"

"Wellton, Arizona. On the east side of Yuma. Blue caught her on a wiretap and is on his way there now."

Alarm frizzed Ric's hair. "To do what?"

"To find her." The answer was curt, as if he were stupid. "We don't have a specific address."

Petulantly, Ric waited for her next step. When she remained silent, aiming to provoke him no doubt, he said, "Has she had the baby?"

188

His baby. A prick of happiness surprised him. Who would've thought? Eve and the child—he wanted both.

Roza's pucker thinned into a wide smile. "She gave birth to our perfect instrument of punishment. Your daughter, Daddy-boy"—she inserted a full sneer into the title—"will save Eriksson from the death she deserves and provide the perfect substitute. She will never get over it."

Over my dead body, Ric thought ... *or yours.*

Chapter 37

Done. Jake stepped back from the 60-kilowatt generator he'd purchased in Iba and labored all morning to install. Now to test the results. He strode eagerly into his hut and laughed at the sight of Perla, Crystal, and Dan hovering around a small white refrigerator as if it were an egg ready to hatch. "Is it humming?"

Dan put his ear to the door. "Yep! Can I try the light?" Without waiting for an answer, he dashed to the one switch in the common room and flipped it. A lone light bulb centered in the ceiling emitted a bright glow, and the four of them cheered.

"Like, totally gnarly, dude!" Crystal hugged Jake. "Mom will love it."

Jake flinched at the expectation. He had told Crystal and Dan little of what had happened at the trial. Certainly nothing about Eve's pregnancy. "I don't know, we're pretty basic here. No running water, an outhouse for a toilet, no air conditioning … she might not fit in so well."

"She'll love it cuz she loves us," Dan crowed. He joined Crystal in a group hug and giggled.

And that was another problem—Eve's revulsion to Dan. Jake swallowed back the bitterness that burned his stomach. After all that sullenness, here she was, adding her own contribution of Romero offspring. A very personal contribution.

The memory of finding Ric in Eve's bedroom launched like a bazooka rocket into Jake's mind. *Eve in bed, slack-jawed, eyes rolled back in her head, Ric standing next to her. Eve's clothing piled on the floor.* The missile pierced, red-hot, trailing smoke, screaming into Jake's heart. Bloody pieces hurled skyward from his soul.

Is this what marriage to Eve would be like? Fending off assaults, defending the family from constant threats of evil? Ricardo Romero, Roza Romero, Blue … were they only the beginning? Were they God's three-alarm fire shouting at him to escape?

A thought slammed him like a sledgehammer to the knees: had God all along been protecting him and Crystal and Dan by not allowing the marriage to go forward?

His heart froze at the thought.

Crystal, as if sensing his struggle, pulled back from him, her brow furrowed. "Mom doesn't think I don't want her to come, does she? You know, what I said on the phone? I only meant for her to stay away until the trial was over." She bit her lower lip. "I really miss her, Dad."

"Me too." Dan tightened his squeeze on Jake's leg.

Jake pushed himself through a wall of lead to reply. "She knows to get ahold of Detective Lee. Like she did last time. Until then we've got to wait." It's on her, he told himself.

For all he knew, she had decided to go with Ric Romero. He was the father of her baby. Allied with him, the threat to her life would no longer exist. Was that what they'd been talking about in the hallway at the courthouse?

Was she debating between him and Ric?

He tightened his jaw. Maybe, behind the scenes, God was directing him to an alternative as well.

***

Muhamoud wheeled his Suzuki into the lengthening shadow of the compound's auditorium and parked it where it was handy for a quick getaway. Pushing the four-wheel cart from the dormitory to the double doors at the front of the auditorium, however, was not as easy. The position of the metal 55-gallon barrel of petrol—purchased bit by bit, ostensibly for his motorcycle—was precarious and sloshed tsunami-sized waves against the barrel's sides. He should have thought of the rough terrain and not filled the barrel so high. But the fuller it was, the higher and wider and deeper the blast would go.

He halted the cart in front of the auditorium's double doors and stepped away quickly. In spite of the protective mask covering his mouth and nose, he gagged at the fumes and barely stopped short of retching. Sweat beaded his forehead and ran into his eyes. His whole body was wet with perspiration and his clothing stuck to him.

Hamza should have been here to help! His absence infuriated him. Instead, the man who was supposed to serve him for the love of Allah was inside worshipping with the infidels. Muhamoud spat on the ground. He had been wise not to share his plans with Hamza. Not after he saw the way Hamza paid attention to the lectures and asked questions and accepted the infidels' customs.

Muhamoud fingered the *kris* secured at his waist. This morning Hamza had confirmed his destiny. He had partaken in the Christian ritual of bread and wine from the visiting pastor. Clearly, Hamza had crossed the line. Death as a traitor was required.

He took in a breath of clean air and calmed his soul. Everything was ready. Thanks to the considerable damage he had secretly wreaked inside the auditorium a month ago, heavy steel hasps with padlocks had been installed on the exteriors of the four entries. Robbers could not enter, and now, with Muhamoud padlocking the hasps only moments ago, the Christian worshippers could not exit. Except Hamza, soon to slip through the front doors Muhamoud had left unlocked to meet together before the worship songs began.

"It is urgent you come," he told Hamza. "Alone, at that exact time."

Then he would overpower Hamza, tie him up, and complete the final steps of his plan: burn the Christians alive and execute the traitor.

"Can I ride your motorcycle?"

Muhamoud jumped at Dan's voice. The boy stood next to the Suzuki, petting its smooth side as if it were a horse. For a moment, panic jammed Muhamoud's heart. What was the kid doing out here?

In a flash—almost a vision—he saw Dan in instance after instance over the last month sitting apart from his father, distancing himself from Chalmers, and the man not noticing.

"What bothers the boy?" Muhamoud asked Hamza.

"He sulks because Chalmers doesn't retrieve his bride and is gruff when asked about it."

Immediately Muhamoud knew how to answer. "I am going for a long ride. Can you hold on to me?"

Dan nodded eagerly.

"Then run, quick, to the front of the administration building and wait for me."

The boy sprinted at top speed past Muhamoud and disappeared around the corner of the admin building. Muhamoud's heart leaped at the unexpected triple victory that would now be his: not only a massacre of infidels and the death of a traitor, but the kidnapping and conversion of an enemy's child. How apt that Chalmer's son would be an exchange for Amir's son!

Hamza emerged quietly from the auditorium, almost catching Muhamoud off guard. "What is this?" he hissed at Muhamoud, peering at the reeking petrol barrel.

Muhamoud beckoned him closer and knocked the unprepared man to the ground. Quickly he sat on his chest and bound his hands. "This morning you took part in the infidels' ritual. You have shown yourself a traitor to Allah." He removed the *kris* from his waistband. "For this you must die."

Hamza's eyes widened at the sight of the weapon. "No, Muhamoud." His voice did not shake as Muhamoud expected. Instead, it was steady, as were his eyes on Muhamoud's. "I have shown myself loyal to Jesus. The ritual is commanded by Him to remember His death on the cross."

"Gods don't die," Muhamoud snapped.

"You are correct. And so Jesus rose from the dead. He rose into the heavens and sits with the Father to answer our prayers until He returns."

"You believe a lie," Muhamoud snarled.

"He loves us," Hamza said. "He died for our sins so the Father will forgive us. Forever, Muhamoud! Only believe."

Muhamoud raised the *kris* high and centered his vision on where he would plunge the knife into Hamza's chest. He was surprised that Hamza didn't resist him. The meekness stirred rage in his soul. "You will die for your sins"—he spat the words at Hamza's face—"with no forgiveness."

"Wait."

Startled by the plea, Muhamoud stayed his hand.

Hamza turned his head toward the auditorium doors. "What are you doing with that petrol?"

Sudden pleasure that Hamza would suffer over the infidels' fate suffused Muhamoud. "While they are singing their infidel songs, I will open the two doors and tip the petrol inside, light it, and lock the doors. The balcony and roof will enflame and there will be no escape because all doors are locked."

His boast ended in a surprised gasp as Hamza abruptly bucked him off and he landed on his back. He twisted to his side to grab hold of Hamza, but Hamza rolled out of his reach. Both men pushed to their feet. Muhamoud, *kris* in hand, lunged at Hamza. The man dodged the weapon but didn't flee. Instead, he landed a powerful kick in Muhamoud's groin. Muhamoud managed a slash across Hamza's thigh before, head spinning, he doubled over in pain.

He caught his breath and straightened to a stand in time to see Hamza limp to the auditorium doors and fling them open. Hamza's scream for help silenced the worshipers mid-song.

Terror hotter than the flames meant to consume the infidels engulfed Muhamoud. He dashed to his motorcycle, grateful he had parked it in the darkness of the auditorium's shadow. When he shot out from the side of the building, he saw the infidels had spilled out of the auditorium doors and were milling around the barrel of petrol.

They shouted after him and gave chase. He sped around the corner of the admin building to the front and stopped. "Dan," he called, "are you ready?"

The boy emerged from behind a tree but didn't run to him.

Muhamoud patted the small square of leather behind him. "Come, jump on. We will ride to the land at the end of the sea, and you can become family, my little brother."

Chapter 38

"Where's Dan?" The narrow escape at the auditorium had flared Jake's adrenaline sky-high. With no telephone available in the village, he had dashed to Iba to contact the police. Time was of the essence to catch Muhamoud while he was still in the act of fleeing. Hamza, his leg wrapped in bandages, joined Jake to help with the details of Muhamoud's family and their home address. Crystal, Jake figured, would look after Dan.

At his question, Crystal rose from her seat at the kitchen table, her face ashen under the glare of the room's single light bulb. "I didn't see him anywhere, so I … I thought he'd gone with you."

From their chairs around the table, Puno, Perla, and her three youngest grandsons stared wide-eyed at Jake. "I did not see him at worship service," Puno said. "Perhaps search of village will reveal boy playing hooky."

"I know where he is." Angelo, the youngest of the grandchildren, jumped up eagerly from his chair. "Collecting spider warriors in the fields. There's a big contest tomorrow."

Perla rose and urged her other two grandsons to their feet. "Okay, we search village while Angelo hunt fields." She shooed the two boys out the door. The high pitch of their excited voices marked their speedy departure toward the village.

"Crystal and I will accompany Angelo for favorite hideouts and spider dens," Puno said. "You look in compound, Jake, but with eye glued here should *Yun Sun Dan* return home."

Jake ran to fetch Hamza from the dormitory to wait in the hut in case Dan came back, then formed a posse of the other students to methodically search every inch of the compound from the admin building at the front of the compound to the donkey pen at the back. Darkness hung like a heavy curtain over the campus by the time everyone reassembled at Jake's hut.

Inside, Hamza sat alone, his injured leg propped on a second chair, his face grim as one by one the searchers entered.

Crystal slumped into a chair, fighting tears, while Angelo took a seat next to her, his mouth curved downward at their failure to find Dan. Puno's shoulders sagged from the exertion of tromping for an hour over stubbled fields. The last to arrive was Mark, Perla's oldest grandson, with news of a fruitless search in the village as well.

Jake stood under the naked light bulb, his brain numb, his throat tight, his heart barely beating. *Please, God.* His knees gave way and he sank to the floor. "Pray with me," he choked out. He should have had them do that first, not last.

The rustle of clothing and the soft thumps of knees joining him broke the lock on his soul. "Heavenly Father," he gasped, "help me. Help me find my Dan-boy and bring him home." Murmured pleas surrounded him and lifted him on a cushion of love and concern until a certainty that God would answer grabbed him in a tight embrace.

He opened his eyes to find Mark rising to his feet, his eyes downcast. "I am sorry to leave," the boy murmured, "but my grandmother will worry if I don't return soon with her donkey and Angelo."

"Her donkey?" Jake felt a jolt of electricity slash through him. "The donkey pen was empty."

Immediately Puno's eyes caught his. "Dan," they said at the same time.

Jake ran for the door. "He must have fallen off and is hurt."

"Wait!" Hamza called. "He may have run away."

A second jolt of electricity stopped Jake. He blinked in confusion at Hamza. "Why?"

"Find him and talk to him." Hamza's tone of voice was gentle. "Only he can tell you why."

Jake's protest halted at Puno's nod of affirmation. "Go, Jake. At edge of northeast field is trail to Zimbales Mountains. Best guess, that is his path."

Crystal appeared at Jake's side and handed him a flashlight. Her face was sober. He blinked again, surprised she didn't ask to go with him.

Did everybody know what this was about except him?

"He's got a two-hour start," he said. "On a tireless donkey." As fast as he could, he exchanged his sandals for tennis shoes and took off at a run. "Pray for me," he yelled over his shoulder.

Apparently he needed it for more than just finding Dan.

***

In the dark, the northeast field seemed to stretch to eternity. Jake's heart pounded as he raced over the stubble, casting the glow of the flashlight back and forth, back and forth. He couldn't see the Zimbales mountain range or anything at a distance. What if he took the wrong path? Millions of stars glittered overhead but were useless for offering light. *Lord, help me.* The prayer, repeated over and over, kept him focused.

When at last the flashlight revealed what looked to be a barely-trampled pathway, he halted and gasped in air. Was this the trail?

His sides heaved painfully as he caught his breath. He squinted into the black landscape. How did he know Dan was even out there? What if he'd been misled, was wasting precious time? What if Dan had headed for the beach instead?

Dryness in his throat hampered swallowing. A migraine attacked his eye sockets and temples. He doubled over and vomited.

When at last his retching ceased, an angry buzz filtered into his ears. He spat, wiped his mouth on his arm, listened. Nose and ears made connection and he blinked, sorted out the smell, the noise, their intersection.

Donkey dung.

Blowflies.

He shone his flashlight down the path to a dark pile swarming with flies and whooped. He was definitely headed in the right direction.

"Dan!" The boy was probably too far ahead to hear the shout, but every affection, every delight, every bit of joy Jake had ever felt for the little guy swelled his heart with love. Yeah, he'd have to chew him out for running away, but first … first he'd sweep him up in his arms and hold him and thank God over and over again for the gift of this precious son.

He settled into a pace that lacked the panic of his earlier run and allowed the flashlight to confirm the meandering trail's direction. Additional donkey deposits offered supporting documentation.

The night hushed into the thud of his footfalls, the chirrup of insects, the breath of the wind over rustling vegetation. Gradually his night vision distinguished shades of gray, shapes of lumps, the dips and rises of the terrain. He didn't break the rhythm to call out Dan's name. Every bit of energy was dedicated to his speedy arrival and a full restoration of father and son.

He had no sense of time. No thoughts. No percolating emotions. Only a body, a vehicle pounding turf to carry him to his destination.

And then he saw them. Two dark shapes, one with four legs and two long ears perked in his direction, the other curled into a fetal position on the ground, head resting on his right forearm. A lump rose from Jake's stomach to his throat and stuck.

His drive dissipated, his muscles liquefied, his bones melted. He forced his feet forward when all he wanted to do was fall headlong onto the ground and weep in gratitude to God.

"Dan." He crouched and caressed the boy's cheek, not wanting to startle him. Soft snores fluttered from Dan's lips. The donkey nuzzled him, and Jake saw the reins were wrapped around Dan's arm. "Dan," he said louder. "Wake up. It's Dad."

Dan's eyelids popped open. Eyes roved over Jake, the donkey, the ground, until recognition rocketed him to a sitting position. "Dad!" He propelled himself into Jake's arms.

Jake scooped him in tight. When Dan's wails had subsided into hiccupping sobs, Jake released him and positioned the two of them face-to-face. "Why are you out here, son?" Hamza and Puno seemed to think Dan had run away, but that made no sense. Had Jake promised a hike to the Zambales and forgotten?

"To find … to find … a new home." Dan's chest jerked a snuffle with each word.

Jake sat stunned. "You don't like the compound?" he finally asked.

"I want my real daddy back." Dan's lower lip protruded into a determined pout. He averted his eyes from Jake.

The words cut hard. "Why, son? I love you."

"Cuz I'm a Romero. Doesn't matter how much I try, I can't change."

"You don't have to change, Dan. You change families, that's all. I adopted you and now you're forever my son."

Anger contorted Dan's face and he raised glaring eyes to Jake's. "Uh-uhhh! There's no fam'ly. You say that but you don't bring Eve back and you don't dop Crystal and you don't want me neither. Nobody's good enough for you! There's no fam'ly!"

Nobody's good enough for you.

Everything in Jake stilled. He wanted to protest, but his mind refused his control. Instead, it transported him back to the afternoon he and Eve had invaded Bradley Henshaw's office ... to Henshaw's revelation of Eve's relationship with Scott Ryker ... to the sick feeling afterward that had chased Jake back to Indy and eventually to the Philippines.

But I came back the minute she needed me, he argued. Again his mind wrested control and this time whisked him to Eve's bedroom ... to Ric at her bedside ... to her telephone call days later from Wit Sec: "What if I'm pregnant?"

I meant what I told her, he insisted—*that I love her and wouldn't let anything keep us apart!*

Again his mind took charge, overrode his objection, and plunked him down in the hallway of the Everett Dirksen Courthouse. He felt himself wince anew at the sight of Eve pregnant and, once again, Ric Romero at her side. Felt revulsion pinch his face. Felt his heart turn to ice as the marshal rushed Eve past Jake.

The rising intensity of his reactions raised a mirror to his soul. And he understood. God was showing him his hard heart. Deep down, Jake had found Eve wanting. Damaged by previous relationships. Not worth a family that came at the cost of an imperfect bride. But it wasn't Eve who was unfit, was it? It was Jake Chalmers.

"Dan." Jake grasped his son's hands. Dan pulled away, but Jake curled his fingers around Dan's slender ones so they couldn't slip out. "You're right, Dan. My love hasn't been big enough for us. Not big like Jesus's love. He died on the cross to make sure His loved ones would be in His family, but my love was too selfish." The confession shredded him. He had counted himself good enough for Jesus's love, but Eve not good enough for his.

Dan crept onto Jake's lap and snuggled up. "Muhamoud wanted me in his fam'ly, and said I could ride his motorcycle, but—"

"What?" Jake exploded.

Dan shrank back. "But I ran away from him cuz I'd rather live in the mountains where I can come 'n' see you. And Crystal." He sniffled. "And Eve if you'd stop being selfish," he mumbled.

It took several minutes for Jake to calm at the news of the near-kidnapping. He stood and lifted Dan onto the donkey's back. "We're going to make a deal, son. You and Jesus and me. No more running away, and no more selfish love, okay?" He handed Dan the reins.

"We're gonna be a fam'ly?"

"Yes. We're going to the States to find Eve, and Crystal and you are going to be the bridesmaid and the ring bearer in a very special wedding!"

"Deal!" Dan crowed.

Jake bowed his head. *Deal, Lord? Please?*

Chapter 39

Eve vacillated between being a Nervous Nellie and a ferocious she-bear. At all costs she wanted to protect her precious baby. Crossing paths with Ric at the aborted trial in Chicago had shown not just mild interest on his part that she was pregnant, but, unexpectedly, his delight. She had no question but that he would try to chase her down.

The marshal assigned to her insisted she was safe in Wit Sec. "We haven't failed you, and we aren't going to," he promised. No one had followed them from the Chicago trial. No one could access her Wit Sec information. She was safe. Period.

Still, she debated relocating on her own. Or hiring a fulltime bodyguard to augment the marshal's intermittent check-ins. Or maybe even getting her own firearm. After mulling over every possible pro and con, she settled for a top-notch alarm system and, as a backup, an escape route and a ready backpack.

She wanted to name the baby *Lana* after Eve's mother, but would that alert the Romeros? Finally she decided to name it Alexis after the cheerful nurse who had attended her birth. Did it really matter? They'd probably have to change her name several times anyway to hide from the Romeros.

Although tests showed no effects from Eve's addiction, Alexis proved a fussy baby. Sensitive skin demanded perpetual diaper changes. An over-the-top startle reflex demanded swaddling so no loose limbs set off screams of alarm. Insomnia demanded endless rocking or mile-long stroller rides.

Eve was exhausted. If only she could be with Jake and Crystal and, yes, little Dan. Alexis needed a family to care for her. Eve needed them! For the hundredth time she considered calling Detective Lee to verify the family was in the Philippines and take her to them. But every time her hand reached for the phone, Jake's face at the courthouse floated to her mind as a reality-check. Shock. Dismay. Revulsion. He was done with her. He hadn't chased after her, and he wouldn't welcome her chasing after him.

"Here you go, sweetheart." Eve lifted a sleepy Alexis from the stroller and dashed into the house to the kitchen to quickly transfer her to the baby swing and set it in motion. Success! Alexis didn't bat an eye. Eve sighed, sorely tempted to brew a tea before hauling the stroller inside and arming the security alarm. She turned toward the stove and shrieked.

Roza Romero stood in the doorway.

***

Ric waited until his mother entered the house before sneaking inside after her. No telling what she would do. Nothing grandmotherly, for sure.

He shivered, remembering her words that the baby would be "the perfect instrument of punishment." When Blue had finally informed Roza of Eve's address, Ric went behind his mother's back and put out a contract to be rid of the wretch once and for all. Then he booked a private plane, beat her to Yuma, and had a rental car ready to follow her into Wellton.

Eve's front door opened directly into a living room. His mother's voice came from a room to the right, which a quick peek showed to be the kitchen.

"We must let bygones be bygones," his mother was saying. Oh so sweetly. He could picture the insincere smile that accompanied the words. Would Eve fall for it?

She didn't. "Get out of my house," Eve yelled. A click followed by the dull rattle of a dial tone followed.

Ric licked his lips. She could be calling 9-1-1 … or the US Marshal in charge of her protection. Should he step into the kitchen, or hide and come back later now that he knew Eve's location?

"Put the phone down, dearie. I just want to hold my granddaughter. I don't suppose you named her Lana after your dear mother?" Roza's titter was sure to be a slap in Eve's face.

The faint tones of three taps on the digital phone pad stopped suddenly with the crash of plastic against a hard surface. "I said put it down," his mother barked.

The sharp cry of an infant pierced the air. "Get away from her!" Eve cried.

Ric whipped out the pistol tucked in the back waistband of his trousers. A second crash punctuated by a moan from Eve brought him in two giant leaps into the kitchen. Eve lay crumpled on the floor, holding her head in both hands. Over her stood Roza, cane in one hand at the end of the arc where it had contacted Eve's head, and the baby, howling, dangling upside-down by one leg in Roza's other hand. At the sight of Ric, she dropped the cane and snatched a knife hidden under her blouse. Swiftly, she raised the brutal weapon to plunge it into the screaming infant.

Ric fired.

★★★

Stars circled Eve's head. Brain, throat, stomach were numb. Leaden air bubbles collided in her lungs. From a galaxy far, far away, a missile launched and hit her chest in a screaming explosion.

"Eve, are you okay?"

A hand shook her shoulder. Picked up the screaming missile. Crouched at eye level next to her. "Eve, can you hear me?"

"Ric!" She sat up. He was holding her baby. She snatched Alexis from his arms. "Don't you dare touch her!"

Ric stood and took a step back, giving her room to clutch Alexis and push to her feet. She turned to flee and stumbled against—she screamed—Roza. Flat on the floor. Blood darkening her blouse. Eyes staring at the ceiling.

Eve caught her balance and backpedalled into Ric's arms.

He pulled her against him, but more like a shield than an embrace. "I shot her," he mumbled. A hard swallow punctuated the confession. She felt the hammer of his heart against her back, the tremor of his arms against hers. "She had a knife ... the baby ..."

The horror in his voice sent shivers down her spine. She gasped as Roza's intent became clear. "She wanted to kill Alexis?" She twisted away from Ric but halted at stepping over his mother. "Is she dead?"

"I thought she wanted to kidnap her ..."

Eve whirled around to face him. "How did you know about Alexis? And where I live?"

Ric pulled his gaze from his mother's body and focused dizzy eyes on Eve. "Blue. He wiretapped everyone close to you."

She drew in a quick breath. Peterman. He was the only one outside Wit Sec she had talked to. If she had to disappear, she couldn't go to him.

Ric shook off his daze. "Eve. We need to go. Someone may have heard the shot."

"No way. I'm not going anywhere with you!" Alexis's shrieks seeped into her consciousness. The screaming missile—it must have been Alexis, dropped on top of her when Ric shot his mother. Was she hurt? She held Alexis straight in front of her and did a quick lookover.

"She's okay. She landed on top of you."

Blood rocketed to Eve's face. "You could have shot her," she yelled. She clasped Alexis to her shoulder and stepped across Roza, hoping to death the woman was dead and wouldn't grab her leg.

"Or I could have let Roza stab her," Ric snarled. He grabbed Roza's knife from the floor and held it up for Eve to see.

It stopped her cold. "Ric ..." The huge knife shredded every nerve in her body. She felt herself sway, felt her stomach lurch. She reached out and steadied herself against a kitchen chair. "Please, go away. Don't let your family near us. Never contact us. For the sake of your daughter."

"No." Ric held out his hand in entreaty. "You have to come with me, Eve. It's the only way I can protect you. We'll get married and no one will hurt you or"—he hesitated—"Alexis."

Eve studied his face. Every breath she inhaled hurt, every heartbeat stabbed—she'd never be free of him, would she?

"I have a suitcase in the garage," she said. "See to your mother."

Chapter 40

"How are we going to find Eve in Wit Sec? Like, she could be anywhere."

Crystal's question brought Jake out of his reverie. Exactly the problem he had been chewing on during their flight to the US. He held up a finger for her to wait and nudged Dan awake. "Hey, son, we're about to land. Want to watch it out the window?" Best to get him peering out now before the stewardess approached and made the boy sit with his seatbelt fastened.

Dan popped up wide-awake and kneeled face flat against the window. Jake put his seat upright and fastened his own seatbelt before turning to Crystal. "In an hour we'll be home, and I hope to find her there."

Crystal's mouth dropped open. "What?"

Jake shrugged, grinned foolishly. "Well, it's a hope, nothing more solid than that. But at least twice in July when we got back from the Philippines, we mentioned going to my house to meet up with Brett and Dana. Maybe she remembered that and is hiding out till we show up."

"But why not just tell us she's there?"

"What's our telephone number and address to get ahold of us?" He chuckled when Crystal scrunched her nose at him. "She could have called Detective Lee, but I checked and he hadn't heard from her." Did she fear having her call traced? Or had she hooked up with Ric Romero? Once again he pushed dread of the possibility aside.

"What if, after the trial ..." Crystal's voice quavered.

"You're her ward and heir. If anything bad happened"—Jake swallowed the lump that rose to his throat—"the US Marshals would contact you."

"They don't have a phone number and address for me either," she grumped.

"If Eve isn't at the house, notifying them will be our first item of business tomorrow, I promise."

Crystal grabbed his hand, and he gripped it tightly.

***

The house was dark when the Indianapolis Express taxi pulled into the driveway. Jake put his arm around Crystal's shoulders and gave her a squeeze, as much for his own comfort as hers. At seven o'clock in the evening, most likely Eve would have been home if she were living here. "We'll find her, no matter what, sweetie." Crystal clamped her jaws and scooted stiff-shouldered out of the cab.

They recovered the spare key from its hiding place in a fence post and entered through the back door into the kitchen. Jake checked to make sure the electricity and water were on—an agreement he and the twins had made to avoid having to turn utility services on and off every time they used the house—and checked the other rooms. Dan ran to his bedroom and staked his claim. "Here's my room. Wanna sleep with me?" he begged Crystal.

There was no sign of Eve having been in the house.

Crystal let her two suitcases slam to the floor. "What you told me was bogus, Jake." Loathing curdled every word. She stomped down the hallway after Dan.

Not Dad, but Jake. Yeah, he should have kept his mouth shut instead of raising false hopes. He'd just been so sure …

Sleep had evaded him on the twelve-hour flight home, and the kids hadn't done much better. Food and bed were a must. He shuffled to the fast-food phone numbers posted on the refrigerator door, selected Pizza Hut, and plopped onto the living room couch to wait delivery. He woke to Dan's prodding—"Dad, a friend brought us pizza!"—and a half-hour later, with stomachs happily stuffed, Dan and a slightly more cheerful Crystal tucked in for the night. Jake breathed a sigh of relief. So, today was Thursday. Three more days to adjust to the time change, and hopefully the new normal would have settled in.

The next morning, he called the US Marshals. Their reception to his inquiry about Eve was, as usual, guarded and uninformative. Did they actually record the contact information he gave them for Crystal? "We'll go to Chicago on Monday to make sure," he told Crystal. "Maybe you can get them to send Eve a letter from you, or maybe even call her."

For sure, he would look up Deputy US Marshal Jackson. He had been assigned guard duty at Eve's house and might be willing to steer them in her direction.

Errands to make a second house key, a gas station to service Brett's Land Rover Defender stored in the garage, and a grocery store to stock up on food were barely tolerated before they retuned home exhausted. After a simple dinner of grilled hot dogs and potato chips on the patio, Jake remembered to return the spare house key to its hiding place.

"Wait, something's stuck in there," Dan said. His little fingers pried out a wad of cellophane from the carved niche. He extracted a tiny piece of paper and gave it to Jake. "What's it say, Dad?"

"*Lost*, I think." Jake turned it over. In spite of the protective wrapping, moisture had blurred the ink.

"Can I see?" Crystal took one look. "That's Mom's writing!"

Jake inhaled every molecule of oxygen in the backyard. "You sure?"

"Yeah! And it says *loft*, not *lost*."

Jake examined the word. "*Lost* makes sense, *loft* doesn't."

"Mom's not lost," Crystal insisted. "She knew how to come here, didn't she? What about the loft in the garage?"

They ran to the garage and climbed into the loft. Nothing but dust-covered bicycles.

Jake looked at the paper again. "Maybe the word is *last*."

"Last what?" Crystal scoffed. Her face brightened in a light bulb moment. "It's a clue, Dad, something only you'd know, in case someone else found the note."

He smiled at the restoration of *Dad*. Definitely not the time to admit he was clueless. "Tell you what—I'm tired, and a good night's sleep will make all the difference in the world. Let's start a list of ideas tomorrow, talk them over at lunch, and follow them up after that."

He put pen and paper on the table, dished out three bowls of ice cream, and went to bed praying that, be it *last*, *lost*, or *loft*, God would grant him a clue.

"It's got to be where she's working," Crystal declared the next day at lunch. She beamed and ate a whole PB&J sandwich without complaint. "The phone book gives three places."

Barely daring to hope, Jake drove them into downtown Indianapolis to check out a bakery, a clothing store, and a restaurant. None of the employees recognized Eve from the photo Crystal showed them. The kids returned home in silence.

"The clue is still good," Jake encouraged them. "We just need to figure it out."

That night they forced themselves to stay up until normal bedtimes. Sunday, he told them, they'd have to rouse and attend church.

They arrived the next morning, groggy and late, and slipped into seats at the back of the sanctuary. The familiarity of the worship service and long-time friends warmed Jake's heart. In spite of his intention to focus fully on the sermon, he found himself scanning the backs of heads for Eve's. Had he mentioned the name of his church to her? He had hoped they would get married here.

When the sermon ended, he hung his head. He hadn't heard a word of it. He had come to worship God, but had fed his flesh instead of his spirit. His shoulders sagged.

Lord, forgive me. My need is for You, to hunger and thirst after You. To rest in Your will.

His throat constricted. He swallowed against the air pinching his lungs.

O God, please! Help me to yield to You, to not look to my strength, but to Yours.

In Your timing, bring my bride to me—
Even as You brought Eve to Adam—
And Your bride, the church, to Christ.

The choir in the loft above him began its closing hymn, and Jake felt his spirit ease, his throat and chest relax. He sank back in his seat and let the music envelop him.

A solo soared like the voice of an angel from the choir, and Jake sat up. Next to him, Crystal sprang to her feet.

They gaped open-mouthed at each other. The *loft!*

Chapter 41

Eve didn't seem the least bit surprised to see them. He had wanted to dash out of the sanctuary and up the stairs to the choir loft, but restrained himself—and Crystal—until the song was done and the pastor had said the benediction. By the time Jake got to the narrow stairway, the choir was already descending. Eve spotted them right away and nodded an oh-there-you-are smile at them, as if of course it made sense they were standing there waiting for her.

Crystal flung herself into Eve's arms, and Dan followed suit. The tears that sprang to Jake's eyes were matched by Eve's, and they smiled timidly at each other like teenagers who had shared a first kiss and were now abashed. So many obstacles had torn them apart, and their relationship was no longer clear. He was ready to move forward, but was she?

Then joy burst fully upon him and he swept Eve and the two kids into his arms and, to his utter horror, wept without restraint every emotion he had stuffed into cracks and crevices in his heart over the past fifteen months. Eve broke down with him, then Crystal and Dan.

When the tears ended and tissues had blotted faces dry, Jake squared his shoulders. He wasn't done yet, was he? Now for the touchy part.

The baby.

Had Eve kept it or put it up for adoption? He didn't dare ask in front of the kids in case Eve hadn't kept the baby and didn't want them to know. And if she had kept it? How would Dan and especially Crystal respond? The surprise and the fact that he had known but not told them would not go over well.

Worse, how had Eve taken his reaction at the courthouse? He flinched remembering how she had looked back at him, her face pleading for him to chase her as the marshal hurried her away.

"Eve, at the courthouse …" His mouth went dry.

She pressed her lips into a tight line, lightly touched his arm, then took Dan's and Crystal's hands into hers. "I have someone I want you to meet." She led them down a hallway to a room marked Church Nursery. She waved at the nursery attendant, who nodded and left the room. "This"—she picked up an infant from a small crib—"is my daughter, Alexis."

Crystal's and Dan's eyes widened, followed by exclamations of glee on Dan's part and horror on Crystal's. "Mom, I didn't know. I wouldn't have told you to—" Crystal choked.

"—to stay away? Yes, you should have, and I'm glad you did." Eve gave her a quick hug. "I needed to deal with my addiction, and it helped to know you were safe."

"But isn't Ric the—"

"Yes. As it turns out, Jake and I are each contributing a Romero to the Chalmers family." She turned to Jake and spoke softly. "Am I right?"

His heart leaping at the words *Chalmers family*, Jake took the small bundle from her and clasped the baby against his shoulder so her head nestled in the crook of his neck. He inhaled Alexis's sweet fragrance and remembered the words God had compelled when he first held Dan-boy. The same tenderness swelled his heart. "I love you, little 'Lexis," he whispered. He patted the tiny back and kneeled to show her to Dan. "Meet your new sister, son. Think you can handle two of them?"

Dan put his face into Alexis's and kissed her cheek. He grinned at Jake. "Another baby rabbit for Momma Cat, huh, Dad!" He spun around and hugged Eve's legs. "Thanks, Mom!"

Jake hastened to explain the cryptic reference. "When Dan and I went camping last summer, we met a mother cat that had adopted an abandoned kit into her litter."

"And we're fam'ly, just like them," Dan said.

"Kits and kittens." Eve knelt beside them. "That sounds like just what I want in a family."

Jake's heart swelled. Those were words of love. Something had happened to change Eve's attitude toward Dan. Alexis grunted, and he kissed her head. *Yes, Lord, I'm holding the reason, aren't I?*

Dan pointed at Alexis and snuggled into Eve. "Can I hold her and you hold me?"

"Hey, son, how about if we go home and cuddle Alexis there?" Jake stood and handed Alexis back to Eve. He wouldn't mind a bit of Eve-and-Alexis-cuddling himself. "Crystal has chili waiting for us, remember?"

"I'll take my sister," Crystal declared, "and you too, bro." She held a hand out to Dan and looked pointedly at Jake before taking the baby and exiting the room.

"That was her *talk-or-else!* look," Eve murmured.

"Don't I know it." Jake picked up Alexis's car carrier. "But first, at the courthouse—"

"I'm over it, Jake. The sight of my eight-month pregnancy was understandably disquieting. I get it."

"It wasn't just the pregnancy, Eve. It was Ric Romero right there next to you."

She startled. "Ric? You thought—?"

"—you were together, yes."

Eve blinked several times. "He didn't know ... he was just there and saw me ... and then you were standing there—" Her chest jerked on a sharp intake of air. "You didn't come after me." It wasn't an accusation so much as it was an outcry of deep pain.

Jake groaned as remorse cut into his heart. "I was wrong—so very, very wrong not to chase after you." Gingerly, as if she might break, he pulled her into his arms. "I promised to love you and take care of you, and instead I let jealousy trip me up. I let it create a wedge between us and then let it grow until, when I saw Ric with you, all I wanted to do was punch him in the face."

"It was more than that, Jake." Eve pulled back enough to look him in the eye. "Admit it, my pregnancy defined the moment."

The corners of his mouth ticked down. Trust the lawyer-judge to pierce to the heart of the matter. "The pregnancy was hard," he admitted. "Both the cause and the effect."

She put her head back on his shoulder. "So what do we do now?" Her tone was weary.

That he knew how to answer—had hoped and prayed and prepared for this moment. "Why, we create our own special family!" Beaming from ear to ear, his heart firing off cannons of joy, he knelt on one knee and took Eve's hands into his. "I love you with all my heart, Evedene Eriksson. Will you marry me, and"—he kissed her hands—"before that, forgive me?"

Her facial expression became a battleground of surprise, delight, and confusion. "A special family how?" she asked at last.

"Special parents—that's you and me." He kissed her hands again. "Special kids—Crystal, Dan, Alexis, all fully adopted, Romero name obliterated." He stood up, ready to target her lips if, when, forgiveness was granted and his proposal accepted.

"The Romero genes won't disappear, you know. Nor, I suspect, Ric." Eve's mouth thinned into a hairpin slash at the mention of Alexis's father.

"Challenge acknowledged." Jake tipped up her chin. Waited.

She shrugged, looked at the ceiling, looked back at him. Her mouth twisted to avoid a smile, but her eyes danced. "Okay."

Not good enough. He waited, raised his eyebrows.

"Yes." Her mouth spread into a smile.

And waited.

"Okay, a second yes."

"Atta girl!" He leaned forward and kissed her tenderly. "More of that to come," he whispered. "But first, we'd better find the kids."

The hugs and tears of their earlier reunion had not gone unnoticed in the church. Friends of Jake, and more recently of Eve, crowded around them and the three children. Thankfully, explanations were shortened by Alexis's hungry wails.

Twenty minutes later, around steaming bowls of chili garnished with cheese and onions, Jake told Crystal and Dan about his marriage proposal and Eve's acceptance. He grinned at their loud cheers.

"How soon is the wedding?" Crystal asked. "Please don't say six months."

"How about tomorrow?" Eve arched her eyebrows at their laughter. "I'm serious. I've had a lot of time on my hands, so I got everything planned except which suit Jake will wear."

"Totally rad, Mom!" Crystal planted a noisy smooch on Eve's cheek. "Does that include a wedding gown and bridesmaid dress?"

"Waiting in my closet. Clothes for you too," she said to Dan. "Church building is available at 1:00 every day, and Pastor Phillips is on standby. In the morning, we can pick up flowers, cake, and the ring I selected."

Jake burst out laughing. "Should I have bothered proposing?"

"That essential I left to you." She smiled sweetly. "God and I are on good terms. 'Hope does not disappoint,' and I hoped for the best."

"Aha," Jake exclaimed. "That's why you didn't seem surprised when you saw us this morning."

"Believe me, my heart jammed into my throat at the sight of you three."

"What about guests?" Crystal interrupted. "Grandpa and Uncle Dax and Aunt Dana and —"

Eve's face fell. "No family. We can't chance contacting them. Roza is dead, but Ric and his two brothers might still be looking for me. After the wedding, we need to disappear."

The room fell silent. "Is that why you didn't stay at Jake's house?" Crystal asked.

"Yes. I rented an apartment. I didn't think they knew about Jake's church, so"—she shrugged—"I risked it. It was my only chance to cross paths with Jake, and I needed a spiritual family."

"What if they're watching us now?" Crystal wrung her hands. Jake knew she was thinking about Blue.

"How about the traffic-control cop we use when church lets out," Eve suggested. "Nathan Patterson. Can we hire him to sit out front in his police car for the night?"

"Perfect solution!" Jake exclaimed. "He's a Nam buddy. He'll do it in a heartbeat."

The tightness in Crystal's face and shoulders relaxed. "Rad, Mom!" She planted another smooch on Eve's cheek.

"Hey." Dan poked Eve in the arm. "Can you wake up 'Lexis and you and me and her cuddle now?"

"Whoa, family-cuddle time, dude," Crystal cried. "Last one on the couch gets buried." The four of them broke from the dinner table and raced into the living room to pile in a laughing heap on the sofa cushions.

Jake made sure he was last. With growls and groans, he fought them off until at last they succeeded in burying him under cushions and sweaty bodies.

Oh yeah. Best bachelor party ever!

Chapter 42

Jake sat up with a start. He hadn't slept a wink once the thunderstorm started. Not after Eve told him details about her encounter with Roza Romero and Ric, and that she had fled the Wit Sec program. Every crash of thunder, every slash of rain on the windows, every creak and groan of the wind-battered house sounded like an intruder.

Next to him, Eve, Crystal, and Dan slept on mattresses he had dragged into the living room. "Family slumber party!" he had proclaimed. No way he was letting anyone sleep out of his sight, even with Nathan Patterson parked out front.

He must have nodded off once the storm abated. He rose and slipped away to check the house and yard. Inside, nothing was amiss. Outside, the wet asphalt of the street shone in the morning light like a highly polished boot. Trees bowed branches laden with clinging raindrops. Puddles dappled the lawn. Nothing amiss. Tranquility seeped into his soul and lifted his heart. Today, he exulted, was his wedding day!

He returned to the living room and chuckled at the sight of Alexis, tightly bundled and snuggled against her mother's side. Would it wake Eve if he picked up Alexis? He had crooned the little sweetie to sleep last night, which Crystal, poking fun at his inability to carry a tune, had rolled eyes at. Jealousy, nothing but pure jealousy.

"Good morning." Eve peeked at him through sleep-pinched eyelids. "Coffee ready?"

He hurried to the kitchen to punch the coffeemaker's On button. He'd take a cup out to Nathan and catch up on local events.

A shriek erupted from the living room, and Eve stumbled into the kitchen with Alexis. "Forget the coffee. Bottle ready?" She thrust the howling baby into Jake's arms, mumbled what sounded like "First dibs on the shower," and disappeared. So much for coffee with Nathan …

A long hour-and-a-half later, after a few hastily contacted guests, the pastor, and the pianist had been put on notice, the Chalmers crew, Jake's suit in hand, crawled into the Land Rover and headed out to piece together a happy wedding. Everyone had a part. Outrageously gorgeous ring set already selected by Eve, totally rad flowers selected by Crystal, Bugs Bunny cake selected by Dan, and credit card selected by Jake. Lunch at McDonald's. Then the last stop, Eve's apartment to pick up the wedding attire.

At twelve-fifteen, they arrived at the church. Jake blew out a breath. They'd done it.

He let Eve and Crystal out at the back door to the bridal dressing room to feed Alexis and do girlie wedding-prep things, then parked at the front to take in the flowers, cake, and his and Dan's clothes. He patted his pocket to check on the wedding rings in a small velvet bag. Must. Not. Forget. Rings.

After freshening his morning shave and deodorant in the groom's suite, he changed into his suit and dressed a reluctant Dan. "Is this what a ring bear wears?" Dan surveyed the outfit Eve had chosen—checkered black-and-white knickerbockers held up by black suspenders over a crisp white shirt, ideal for any six- to seven-year-old whose size you didn't know—in a full-length mirror.

"Ring bear?" Jake chuckled. Why take away the kid's fun? "Give me a growl so I can be sure." The enthusiastic deep-throated response definitely rated a ten out of ten. "Best ring bear ever," he exclaimed. "Let's check it out with Crystal."

They trotted to the foyer, where they found Crystal checking the flowers they had purchased. Moisture sprang to Jake's eyes. She wore a dress that coordinated with Dan's outfit, a soft-flowing, simple, knee-length white sheath with checkered black trim at the hem and sleeves. Her hair, honey-blonde like Eve's, was braided in a wreath at the front and loose at the back.

Black earrings and black heels completed the ensemble. Funny how you saw people differently when they applied a bit of spit and polish, as his dad used to say. Crystal was beautiful.

Dan ran up to her, and she slapped her leg. "Look at you, dude! We match! Totally choice!"

He giggled and gave her a sample growl. Jake grinned. Did she know he was a bear?

"Hey, I've got a job for you." She handed the box of flowers to Dan. "I'm supposed to talk to the pianist when she comes, so how about if you take our bouquets to Mom. Walk slow and don't drop them. Pretend you're walking down the aisle as the ring bearer."

"Ring bear," he corrected her. Face sober, he stepped out at a measured pace toward the back of the church building.

The pastor and pianist arrived at the same time. While Crystal talked to the pianist, Pastor Phillips went over the simple ceremony with Jake. The guests arrived, and Jake peeked at his watch. Fifteen more minutes and he would meet Eve at the altar. He opened the front door and checked on the location of his car. Last evening's rain had perked up the grass and trees around the church, and the air seemed washed clean, shimmering with sunshine and good will toward men.

Yeah, he was feeling good!

Crystal nudged him in the arm. "I'm going to get Mom and Dan now. You'd better get up front."

Right. Inside the sanctuary, guests sat in the front pews, the pianist played softly, and Pastor Phillips stood at the altar.

He halted as an ear-splitting shriek crashed forward from the back of the church like a thrashing tsunami wave. Wow, Alexis had achieved a new high with that wail! The guests turned and stared at him, the pianist halted, the pastor took a step back. Crystal rolled her eyes at him and took off at a trot down the hallway.

Jake hesitated. Should he wait until Alexis calmed down?

Crystal returned at breakneck speed. "It's Dan!" she yelled.

The boy limped into view, shirt disheveled, hair in disarray, blood on his left knee. "He pushed me!" he screamed at the top of his lungs.

Jake ran to him and knelt to examine the bloody knee. "Who? What happened?"

Crystal sprinted toward the bridal suite. "Dad!" she hollered back. "Mom's gone! And Alexis!"

Jake leaped to his feet, stumbled as Dan clutched his leg. "Unca Ric took 'em," he bawled. "Mom opened the door and he stuck something in her face and made her fall down and grabbed Alexis and hit me."

Crystal ran up, colliding with Jake. "I looked out the back door, and they're in a van driving away!" She pushed him toward the front door and burst into tears. "Hurry!"

"Call the police!" Jake sped down the hallway and out the front door to his car. He glimpsed a gray van turning a corner a block away. The only other traffic was headed toward him. He peeled out of the church parking lot after the van.

His heartbeat thundered a prayer. *Don't let him get away, God, don't let him get away …*

Three intersections later, he slowed to check which direction the van might have gone. It was nowhere in sight.

Chapter 43

Jake clutched the steering wheel. The van's route had been south, toward Greenwood. Was it headed for Interstate 65? He clenched his teeth, debated. He knew a shortcut to the nearest on-ramp. Should he take it?

No. Not if he could catch sight of the vehicle. An affirmation to his decision appeared on County Line Road. At a green light one stop ahead, a car turned right and revealed the gray van continuing straight.

Jake gunned it.

Traffic buried the van from view once again and forced Jake to slow at intersections to see if the vehicle had turned. Did Ric know Jake was on his tail? It would be easy to lose a pursuer with short, quick turns. Four fast rights could lose a tail in a snap and put you back on route.

He passed the Greenwood Municipal Airport on his right and too late saw the van pulling up to a small plane. He did a hasty U and shot a left into the tiny airport. The twin turboprop was a King Air C90. Its propellers were turning, its door folding shut. Perspiration broke out from every pore on Jake's body as the plane taxied toward a runway. There was only one way to stop the aircraft.

He put the pedal to the metal and the Land Rover's engine roared to full life.

Keeping to the left side of the taxiing plane, he raced ahead of it. Feeling like the tiny pebble launched from the shepherd boy David's slingshot, Jake veered sharply to the right and hurled his car straight at the plane.

His breath stilled. His heartbeat accelerated.

At the last second, he jerked the steering wheel toward the tail. Ducked. Covered his head with his arms.

The top of the Land Rover plowed into its target. Tail and car scrunched in a mighty jolt. The disabled plane spun away in a half-circle. The Land Rover's air bag inflated.

The bag smacked Jake like a sack of cement and deflated. Stupefied, he pushed against the car door. When it failed to budge, he crawled into the back seat and out the shattered rear window. Shards of glass dug into his hands and knees as he tumbled to the runway. In the distance, a siren screamed. Airport authority—no doubt targeting him, not the real villain. He staggered to his feet.

The fist almost caught him. He shot his left arm up in time to block the blow. *Ric.* Jake slammed his right fist into Ric's neck, and the man stumbled backwards.

"Eve's mine," Ric hissed. "I put my claim on her with my daughter."

Jake launched his left fist with his full weight behind it. It landed squarely on Ric's jaw so that, head wobbling, spit and blood flying, Ric toppled to the asphalt. "You took what wasn't yours," Jake snarled. "What will never be yours."

Hands grabbed Jake from behind. He spun around to fend off the attack, but stopped when he saw the airport security uniform. "Arrest that man," Jake barked. "He kidnapped my bride. She's on the plane." He resisted the security officer's effort to handcuff him.

Holding his jaw, Ric struggled to his feet. "Crazy lunatic! He crashed my wedding, chased me here—did you see that? He drove into my plane!"

"Check out the passengers and crew," the officer ordered one of the men. "Meanwhile, we'll just let you two hang out with us until the police arrive and settle this little love triangle." He gestured to two security guards to station themselves next to Jake and Ric.

Jake caught Ric's glance at the gray van still parked on the tarmac. Caught Ric's slight tip of the head to the driver.

Jake gritted his teeth. He didn't put it past the slime ball to attempt a getaway. "Check out the gray van too," he said. "The driver is part of this."

To Jake's satisfaction, the officer immediately ordered the van apprehended.

"Boss." The guard investigating the plane emerged with two men Jake assumed were the crew. "Best order an ambulance," he called. "The woman is vomiting and badly disoriented."

Jake broke away and raced to the aircraft. Behind him, leather boots slapped the runway as guards chased him. The guard from the plane blocked him at the door, drew a pistol.

"Please, I need to see her," Jake pleaded. "She's my bride."

"Step back, hands on your head, drop to your knees," the guard shouted.

The memory of his arrest at Eve's over a year ago flickered into his mind. *Not again, Lord!* Stuffing his frustration, Jake complied, allowed his hands to be cuffed behind his back, let the guard haul him to his feet.

The officer in charge strode up to them. "Jacob Chalmers?" When Jake nodded, the officer ordered his cuffs removed. "Show me I.D. and you're free to join your bride. Police are on their way, said they received a call from your family and pastor about the kidnapping."

Jake whipped out his I.D. then rushed into the plane. Eve sat in a seat fully reclined, eyes closed, stomach contents smeared on one cheek. The smell of vomit lingered in the air. Regardless, Jake kissed her gently on the lips. "Eve?"

She opened her eyes. "Jake." She attempted to sit up but collapsed back onto the seat. "Where's … Alexis?" The question was halting, feeble.

"Next to you. In her carrier, safely buckled into the seat." He smoothed Eve's tussled hair. "How are you feeling?"

"Things're spinning." She closed her eyes.

"We've got an ambulance coming. You're going to be okay." He leaned over to kiss her again but drew back when she regurgitated more stomach contents. "Ric's in custody. You're safe, sweetheart. All of us are."

She grunted, swiped at the dampness on her face. "Wedding …" she murmured.

"Church building's available at one o'clock every day, and the pastor's on standby, remember? When you're ready, we're ready."

She smiled. "Wake me 'n time." Her body relaxed, and Jake released a tortured sigh.

Surely nothing else could happen.

***

That evening, the four of them crowded around Eve's hospital bed. Alexis snuggled on one side of her, Dan on the other. Jake and Crystal sat on each side of her legs. After all the trauma of the day, idle chatter was hard to come by.

Crystal didn't dilly-dally in bringing up hard questions. "How did Ric find us?" she asked, "and who else is looking for us?" She spoke boldly, but Jake didn't miss the tremor in her lower lip.

Us. He knew Blue was on her mind. "Danny and Roza Romero are dead, and the marshals found Blue dead two days ago." He watched the stiffness in Crystal's shoulders melt. She inhaled a big breath and looked around the hospital room as if seeing the world with new eyes. "That leaves the three brothers," he continued. "Ric, at least, will be in prison."

"How did he find us?" Crystal persisted.

After a few seconds of silence, Eve spoke. "My guess is that Ric wiretapped Jake's phone, and when Jake called the marshals with your contact information, Ric found out Jake was home and searching for me."

Revulsion at Ric's ability to invade his privacy and use it to harm him made Jake's blood boil. "When I talked to the marshals today, they asked if we wanted to hide out in Wit Sec."

Eve and Crystal synchronized a resounding *NO!*

Relief flooded him. The idea of anyone controlling his life—Romeros or the government—was repugnant. "Where then?"

They didn't brainstorm for long before they reached a consensus. Puno's compound, bare bones as it might be, was paradise compared to hiding anywhere else.

"Next decision," Jake said. "When do we resume the wedding?"

"I don't care if I'm in a wheelchair," Eve said. "Tomorrow at one o'clock gets my vote."

Smiles all around affirmed the vote was unanimous.

A half-hour later, Jake herded the three kids out of the room so Eve could get a good night's sleep. Tomorrow they would turn a corner. Start a new day. Begin a new life.

Five people a family at last.

Chapter 44

Jake stood at the altar. The pianist segued into the wedding march. The pastor straightened. The guests rose to their feet.

It really was going to happen! Jake inhaled through his nose, blew out softly through his lips. His heart fluttered tremors in his throat. His limbs quivered. His eyes burned tears. He closed them, focusing on every physical sensation, every emotional rush. Packing them into his memory. Treasuring them.

Today was his wedding day!

He had waited so long.

He opened his eyes and smiled as young Dan stepped into the back of the sanctuary. Knickerbockers hid his scraped knee. Suspenders clasped the loose waist. A freshly-ironed shirt was tucked in place—for the moment. Dan crouched, shoulders forward, his pace in measured stomps. A small, velvet bag on a string dangled from his right hand. He was the ring bear. Snarling not allowed, but soft growls permitted. Jake chuckled.

He had waited so long. To what end?

This. This boy. Redeemed from the darkness of an enemy who hated him. Transferred from the family of Romero to the family of Chalmers. Placed in the arms of a mother who had learned to treasure him as her son.

Crystal entered the sanctuary next. She followed Dan, her attire showcasing beauty as a sixteen-year-old that was but a precursor of the deeper loveliness adulthood would confer. Her eyes, fixed on Jake, radiated love. The wedding, she told him last night, forever made him her dad. He snuffed back tears.

He had waited so long. To what end?

This. This girl. Orphaned at birth, hungry for love, she had been God's gift to him from the moment he met her as a scrawny eleven-year-old crybaby. Her need had met his need. Today it would be met forevermore in the gift of family.

The basket Crystal carried held more than her bouquet. Tiny hands waved from within. Coos of contentment sparked giggles from the guests. Alexis! It was all Jake could do not to guffaw.

He had waited so long. To what end?

This. This baby. She had spotlighted the power of God's sovereignty over wickedness, of His good purposes that overrode men's evil. Far from being Ric Romero's claim on Eve, this little sweetie had claimed the hearts of Eve and Crystal and Dan and him, had united them in the delight of being a family. A family of kits and kittens.

Jake swallowed as Eve joined the processional. When had he ever seen her this beautiful? She wore a knee-length sheath of pristine white—"The bride of Christ is not tainted, Jake, and in God's grace neither am I"—that featured extravagantly puffed long sleeves and a choker neck. A rhinestone tiara flung a short veil over hair styled in a French twist. Like Crystal, she carried a basket of flowers for her bridal bouquet, though, thankfully, *sans bebe.* Her face shone with a joy that was unfettered, accepting what had happened in her past, unafraid of what would happen in the future.

He had waited so long. To what end?

Love.

A plain and simple answer, but one that was deep and high and wide and broad. An answer that explained everything. It began in God's love, it extended to His beloved.

Dan and Crystal with Alexis arrived at the altar and stood beside him, then Eve. He and Eve said *I do* as husband and wife. Together, in their hearts, the family said *I do* to love.

The End

Dear Reader,

Your comment posted on Amazon tells us about your reading experience with *Targeted* and is hugely helpful to us and other readers. Long or short, positive or negative (well, maybe not that so much!), your input is valuable. Simply go to amazon.com, type in the name of our book, *Targeted: A Novel*, and scroll down to "Write a Review." Thank you!

You can CONTACT us at our website at www.donandstephanieprichard.com. Leave us a comment and we will write back!

Our author FACEBOOK page is www.facebook.com/4u2read. We'd love to hear from you!

Look for *Targeted* as Book 3 in *STRANDED the Trilogy*.
STRANDED, Book 1
FORGOTTEN, Book 2
TARGETED, Book 3

ACKNOWLEDGEMENTS

Special thanks to the following for helping us with our book:

Brenda Anderson for editing guidance that filled in gaping potholes and smoothed out ugly cracks.

Carrie Lewis for using a fine-tooth comb on our writing skills.

Norman Skinrood for keen-eyed proofreading.

Lina Nelson for great first-hand descriptions of life in a Philippine village.

Gary Shaw for excellent information about conducting a federal trial.

John Spiegel for the wonderfully accurate description of a weld repair operator.

Ken Raney for completing our trilogy with the fantastic cover design of *Targeted*.

CPSIA information can be obtained
at www.ICGtesting.com
Printed in the USA
LVHW012312220620
658752LV00019B/2286